*St. Martin's Paperbacks titles
by Laura Baker*

STARGAZER

LEGEND

Legend

Like us on
Facebook

Laura Baker

St. Martin's Paperbacks

LEGEND

ISBN: 0-312-96662-8

Printed in the United States of America

St. Martin's Paperbacks edition / October 1998

St. Martin's Paperbacks are published by St. Martin's Press, 175 Fifth Avenue, New York, NY 10010.

10 9 8 7 6 5 4 3 2

To Mom—
You told me I would . . .
You made me believe I could . . .
And the day I did . . .
You said, "I told you so."
—Christie Ann Schuetz—

With Warmest Thanks:

to Evelyn Lopez, for a drawing, a story, and a message of faith.

to Leonard Butler, Chief of Navajo Police, for taking the time to answer my questions. Any mistakes in this story with regard to Navajo police procedures are entirely my own.

to Kelley Pounds, for a day which made all the difference.

especially to my husband, Tom, who thinks nothing of driving over washboard roads or through sand pits just to photograph a run-down trading post and a herd of goats.

One

~

"This one's a real monster."

Jackson didn't reply. He had little patience for idle speculation about criminals. Today, in this place, he had none.

He stared at the unchanging landscape, the endless gritty brown desert, and aggravation chafed at him like so many bits of dirty sand.

Of anywhere he could be on earth, deep on the Navajo Reservation was the last place he would choose. He would deal with that, he told himself. He could work anywhere—even here.

"These murders are the worst anyone remembers on the Res," the agent continued. "But I suppose you've seen it all."

"I've seen my share," Jackson said and left it at that. But Agent Nez wanted to talk.

"You have to admit, these aren't your normal murders."

Jackson stared at the barren horizon. "Serials are never normal, Nez." It was his standard line to get past conversation. It was also not quite the truth. In all his years as a profiler, he'd always been able to find the logic in even the most mind-baffling crimes. In every serial case, all the numerous, disparate, seemingly unrelated details always fell together into a picture—the *only* picture of those crimes. Consistency in the chaos, that's what he called it.

Except, in these murders, the details didn't seem to fit. He couldn't find the connection, though he knew it was there, just out of his grasp, like the memory of a nightmare skating out of reach.

"Have you seen worse?"

Only in my worst dreams. The horizon closed in. Trees marched up to the side of the road, shutting out the sky; their jagged shadows ran in a dizzying rapid-fire across the windshield.

The uneasiness he'd fought returned—the niggling sensation that he should have refused this case. Except, of course, he hadn't been given that option. He refocused on the vanishing point of the two-lane highway.

Nez kept his silence for a few miles, but Jackson knew the young agent was forming his next question by the way he tapped his index finger on the steering wheel.

"You have to wonder what kind of sick person we're dealing with."

"That's what we get paid to figure out, Nez."

Jackson knew what Nez wanted—what they always wanted: a trip into the macabre mind of the murderer, a thrill ride on a nightmare, a quick lesson on how he came up with his profiles. It was always like this; his unique approach to profiling made skeptics snicker and evoked whispers from his peers about power, psychic abilities. The talk made him a loner. He kept his distance and his own counsel—he owed no one an explanation.

The car careened over several more hills, propelling them to the scene of the most recent murder, only two days old. The smell of blood would still be strong and so would, he hoped, the victim's last thoughts.

Jackson took a deep breath, closed his eyes, and tried to clear his mind. All the details he'd learned would find their own place in time. He had studied the files on the plane trip from Dallas to Window Rock, looked at everything, from the report of the first officer at each murder to the medical examiner's protocols—everything except the crime scene photos.

He never looked at the photos before he visited the scene, deliberately keeping himself ignorant, unsuspecting . . . just like the victim.

With a bump, they rocked off the blacktop onto a dirt road. The car lurched from side to side with each unmerciful pothole, scattering Jackson's concentration. The last thud jolted straight through the seat to his tailbone, evoking a grunt. Jackson glared at the agent.

Nez glanced over. "Not the smooth roads you're used to in Texas, I bet."

"Just how much longer is it to Black Mountain?"

"In miles, seven. In time? At least twenty minutes."

Jackson squinted at the relentless brown desert. He hated this place to his bones. Sharply, he pulled the files from his briefcase and opened the one on the first murder. "It says here Al Newcomb was found by his wife. Was she the one who also noticed the masks gone?"

"No. That was one of Al's employees at the trading post."

"Did this employee have any opinions about why someone stole the masks?

"No, and it's hard to figure," Nez said. "They're not marketable. These masks are too recognizable as ceremonial objects."

Jackson made a sound of disbelief. "Since when has the law stopped anyone?"

"Since the Fed case with the Santa Fe dealer. Five years and five hundred thousand buys a lot of attention. Dealers are nervous."

"Glad to hear it." Jackson smiled. He thumbed through some pages. "I see there's no interview with the wife."

"She was hard to talk to—didn't want to mention her husband's name."

"Real sentimental, huh?"

"She's traditional Navajo. You don't mention the dead's name."

"Great." *Ceremonial masks and superstitious Navajo.* Jackson cursed his luck one more time. "Newcomb have any enemies?" he asked.

Nez shrugged. "Every trader's got skeletons. Bad deals, unhappy customers, unhappy vendors. This one had his share."

"Everyone's got an alibi?"

"We're still checking. Funny thing, though, Newcomb was sponsoring an *Entah* for Billie Yazzie." Nez caught Jackson's look. "The Enemy Way. A three-day purification ceremony for someone who's sick. Newcomb was paying the singer, providing the food. Clan members come from all over."

"So trader Newcomb was everybody's friend."

"Obviously not everyone's."

The landscape opened up to an endless expanse of red earth. Not a living soul, not even a bird stirred the formidable terrain. For that matter, there wasn't a tree for a bird to light on. Barren, inhospitable, with no redeeming value. . . . Why would anyone live, and die, here? Jackson looked back at the files. "Tell me what I don't know about the second murder."

"Only similarity is the condition of the bodies. They were both . . . a mess."

"A mess? That a technical assessment?"

"Hell." Agent Nez shook his head. "What kind of sick bastard rapes a fourteen year-old girl, kills her, then tears up the body?"

"The question, Agent Nez, is what kind of sick bastard kills a man for money and worthless masks and follows that with rape and murder?"

"None of it makes any sense."

Nez slowed to let a string of scrawny horses cross the road. A young horse brought up the rear, his new body already a skeleton, his hide stretched over gaunt hips and ribs. His head hung low to the ground, as if ready to fall. The car idled past the slow procession.

"I thought the Navajo took pride in their horses," Jackson said.

"They do," Nez said.

"Just not enough to feed them?"

"To live out here you got to be tough, self-sufficient. No different for man or beast."

"Harsh land breeds harsh people," Jackson muttered. He caught the quick glance from Nez. "Nothing personal, Agent Nez."

To Jackson's surprise, Nez smiled. "What you say is true. The land *does* breed the People. She is our mother."

Jackson's gaze slid to the agent beside him. He'd been a little surprised when the Bureau car stopped at the plane and a Navajo stepped out. He wondered how many Navajo the Bureau employed. He didn't count himself.

He opened the window a crack. Dry earth shot from the tires and pelted him in the face. With a curse, he shut the window and grabbed his map of Arizona. "Where the hell is Tah Chee Wash?"

"You won't find it on that map. Tah Chee is a Navajo place name." Nez opened a map. "Here." He stabbed the paper with a lean finger. "The girl's body was found by some kids herding sheep. We didn't hear about it for two more days."

Nez looked at Jackson expectantly. Jackson bit. "They didn't want to talk about the dead."

Nez smiled. "That was part of it. Strangers are suspicious. Especially if they're dead strangers. And if that stranger's body is mutilated, some powerful evil is at work. The kids took one look at her shredded body and fled the place of witchcraft."

"Witchcraft? You're not serious."

Nez looked evenly at Jackson. "Beliefs run deep on the Res."

"How about you, Nez? You believe in witches?"

Nez smiled again, but it didn't reach his eyes. "I believe in evil."

"Yes," Jackson agreed quietly. "I believe in evil." Jackson had personal, intimate knowledge of evil. A burn spread in his gut and Jackson gritted his teeth against the pain. He let his breath out slow. "Where did the girl live?"

"Whippoorwill Springs." Nez pointed to his map. Then he slid his finger up to Tah Chee Wash. "She was found thirty miles away on the Black Mountain Plateau."

Jackson saw there were no roads, nothing but wilderness. "The middle of nowhere," Jackson said. Something clicked. "Was she restrained?"

"Hands tied behind her back."

That fit. The killer was organized. He may not have planned the murder, but he had given some thought to the dump site.

Jackson looked for Black Mountain and Dinnebito and noted that the sites of the three murders formed a rough triangle.

"She have any enemies?"

"She was boarding at the Piñon School. She'd had problems with her studies and behavior—acting out, mostly. In the classroom, with the boys. Her mother pulled her in the spring and she was helping out at home."

"Parents can just pull their kids?"

"No, but if they're in the canyons herding sheep when the authorities come . . ." Nez finished with a shrug.

"So, you let delinquents roam the hills."

"We haven't come as far as the big cities where you let them wander the shopping malls."

Jackson quirked a smile at Nez. "What about the boys at her school? Records?"

"Not in our league. Just school stuff. And their alibis check out," he added.

Jackson flipped open the third file. "The last victim. Joe Clah. There's no mention of who found him."

"We don't know. The tip came from an anonymous phone call."

Jackson looked out the window at the barren scene and frowned. "A phone out here?"

"The closest phone lines are back four miles at Cottonwood. Clah lived at the base of Black Mountain."

"A recluse?"

"A medicine man."

"Nothing in the file about a medicine man," Jackson said.

"That's what the locals in Cottonwood called him."

"Did people come way out here to see him?"

The car bottomed out on a dry arroyo. Nez rode the gas to negotiate up the other bank. "No one in Cottonwood admitted visiting him. And we don't have much information on Clah. Seems he was quite the loner."

The burn deepened. "Nothing," Jackson said. He closed the file and looked at Nez. "In a nutshell, you've got no witnesses, no suspects, and no motives for Clah, Newcomb, and—what's her name?" Jackson flipped through the file.

"Wynema Begay," Nez supplied. "Thought that's why you're here. I mean, you're the hotshot on unsolvable serials."

"Yeah." Jackson stared out the window. That he had a talent for solving serial murders was no secret. Though he was sure *talent* wasn't the word most often whispered about him. Maybe *hotshot* was. He didn't know. Whatever the description, it was never said to his face, just whispered behind his back as he went about his business delving into the darker side of humanity. He couldn't explain it—he *didn't* explain it to anyone. But something inside him *connected*—with the victim, with the murderer, with the *hunt*. And he was good at it.

These murders will be no different, he told himself. *Just clear your head, concentrate. Find a thread and pull. Get it done and get the hell out of here.*

* * *

The wide dirt road narrowed to a car's width, then to a mere track that wound through hillocks of rock and tenacious clumps of weeds. It struggled over foothills until, at the base of Black Mountain, the road gave up.

Jackson stepped from the car into a swirl of dust. He stood still, quiet—only his eyes moved, spanning the surroundings. The air cleared and still he saw nothing—no buildings, no sign of life.

"Did Clah live in the rocks?"

"Over here." Nez gestured to a red hill, a small hump of bald earth.

The illusion shifted and Jackson suddenly recognized the hogan. It melded so perfectly into the landscape that, if he glanced away, it once again became a mound.

Nez walked around the hogan to the east side. The yellow crime tape made the door obvious. "We found him inside." Nez gestured for Jackson to follow him.

"Stop." The barely audible order froze Nez in place. Jackson brushed past him and pushed open the plywood door. Warped wood creaked at the leather hinges.

In the moment it took to step inside, Jackson readied himself—pocketing his sunglasses and closing his eyes. A rush of urgency pulled at him. *Patience,* he demanded inwardly. Slowly, he opened his eyes. His gaze went immediately to the blood-soaked area. *Not yet,* he ordered.

His gut twisted, knotted. The pain doubled him. He stood there bent, panting, and cursing. He waited for it to pass, *willed* it to pass. After several deep breaths he straightened. A trickle of sweat ran down his spine. His head felt light, disconnected. *Get a grip, Walker.*

With forced concentration, Jackson let his gaze take in the room. He did an inventory—unemotional, dispassionate—just an accounting.

In the middle of the floor were the remnants of a fire. White ashes and blackened sticks splayed beyond the circle of rocks. Directly above, a hole in the hogan roof provided the only light. To his left stood a small wood table, poorly made, with two barrels for chairs. The mud wall behind held a shelf, stacked with a few dishes, a tray of utensils, and cans of food. On hooks below hung a dented pan, a couple of mugs, and a ladle.

His gaze followed the circular mud wall to the opposite side. From two hooks hung clothes and a coat. Below the hooks lay a shallow pile of rugs. Within this small dome of earth had dwelled a man—a medicine man, Jackson reminded himself. How had he lived with so little?

Jackson approached the blankets, his legs feeling simultaneously stiff and weak—like rods of steel stuck through jelly. The rugs had obviously been Clah's bed. His body weight had slightly indented them. Crime scene investigators had tried to outline the body in chalk, but given up when tracing the arm in the red earth. They had scratched in the dirt, then finished with masking tape, held down with pebbles. The result matched the surroundings: primitive, incomplete.

He knelt on one knee to study the swath of blood. His insides bunched and protested. Sweat beaded on his brow. His vision blurred and Jackson closed his eyes. After a moment, he opened them slowly. His focus shifted with dizziness, but he stared, resolute, at the evidence of the awesome violence. Blood filled out the outline and beyond—like a child's hasty coloring. Except this wasn't child's play. Jackson had never seen so much blood.

Clah had died where he lay. No struggle, no fighting for his life. "But were you surprised, old man?" He whispered. " Did you open your eyes a moment before the attack?"

Jackson took in a slow, deep breath. The coppery scent of death filled his nostrils and settled at the back of his tongue—the taste of salt and metal. Nausea burst within him, rose fast up his throat. The taste of bile kissed the scent of blood. The room spun. He tensed, every muscle fighting for control.

Concentrate on Clah, dammit. Get on with it, do your job.

He closed his eyes and imagined himself comfortable on his blankets, drifting to sleep.

"The night's quiet. The canyon still. What do you hear?" The monotone came naturally. "You hear noise outside, but think it is a breeze, or small animals. The door creaks. Your eyes fly open. What do you see?"

He drew in a breath, then another: a diver preparing to submerge. Then he placed his hand on the dried pool of life. He expected the moment of panic, knowing it would mutate, like quicksand turning to crystal-clear ice water.

Violence swept through him swift and sure, harsher than ever before. The abyss opened, blackness swallowed him. A childhood fear—consuming dread a man should never know—seized him.

Control the nightmare, he told himself. *Let it flow without censure. It will soon pass.*

But his words fell mute, defeated. The horror grew. His ears rang with screams of pain; his skin stung from a million wounds. The terror of sure agony iced his veins, pumping to his heart. Torture tore through him. *God, the agony.*

Evil, slick and deadly, slid through him with cold, heartless malice. Violence ran rampant through his veins in a rush of fury, destroying his defenses, claiming him. At his core, he felt the need, the savage *rightness* of the murder.

Enough!

He tore his hand from the blood and threw his eyes open, yet couldn't see. He stumbled backward in blindness, groping for anything real to grasp. *It didn't happen this way.* He always connected with the victim, *not* the murderer.

Something tugged at his shoulder. His arm shot out.

". . . Walker? . . . all right?"

Words, not his own, cut through Jackson's terror.

"Fine," Jackson managed.

A hand at his back guided him. His legs labored, as if sloughing through mud. Pressure at his shoulder forced him to sit and Jackson found himself on something round and wobbly.

"You're white as a ghost and sweating. I'll be right back."

The blackness dissipated to dizziness. Jackson hung his head and forced slow, deep breaths.

"Here." Nez shoved a wet cloth into Jackson's hands.

He blotted his brow, behind his neck, then held it to his throbbing temple. "Thanks. I'm fine. Must be the altitude." Jackson focused on the ground.

"Come outside for some air."

"Go ahead." Jackson lifted his head to see Nez.

Nez looked about to say something, then left.

Jackson closed his eyes. *What the hell had happened?* He had never lost control before. Always, he *owned* the moment. Not this time. His insides still trembled from the assault. With effort, he raised his arm and swiped the cloth over his face. The movement was awkward, his hands slightly shaky. He didn't even trust himself to stand.

He could hear Nez talking on the radio, though mud walls muffled his words. A hotshot, Nez had called him.

He fisted his fingers. Water from the wet cloth dripped to the dirt floor, making dark circles in the red earth. He stared at the splotches until his temples pounded. Before his eyes, the moisture dried and evaporated, consumed in the dry desert air.

What the hell had happened?

Jackson shoved off the barrel and stood. The abrupt move sent his stomach rocking. He ignored it—and the stabbing cramps, and the sickly dizziness, and the headache working its way through his whole brain.

He opened the door and the blast of heat prickled his moist skin, raising goose bumps. His stomach lurched and this time he knew he didn't have the strength. He struggled to the side of the hogan, his knees buckled. From the corner of his vision, he saw Nez leaning against the open car door, talking on the radio. With all the adrenaline compacted within, Jackson let his guts empty.

The late afternoon sun cast long shadows, turning rocks to boulders and stretching pointy yucca fronds into sabers. Ridges and ripples shaded the uneven ground. Jackson stared, regaining his equilibrium. Soon he saw the shapes, the scores of footprints marring the area. Some would be from cops, some from Feds, some from Clah himself. Were any from the murderer?

Jackson lit a cigarette. The tobacco had never tasted so good. A shot of whiskey would be even better. Exhaling smoke, he stood and looked back on his steps. Clean, sharp imprints marked his path. He stepped to the left of the hogan and found the ground nearly as trampled as the front. His gaze caught glints of blue in the sand. He bent closer to see hundreds of tiny blue grains. It reminded him of the bottles of layered sand you could buy—a cheap souvenir for the tourist.

He continued around the hogan, until the rock face of the mountain blocked him. Jackson returned to the front, where Nez met him.

"We searched the area," Nez said.

"And?"

"Nothing. Only clear prints were some isolated animal tracks."

Jackson walked around the south and west sides of the hogan. Nez kept pace with him. The landscape glowed orange from the low sun.

"Old Clah had a nice view," Nez said thoughtfully.

"Of what?" Jackson saw desert—more of it than anyone needed. He walked ahead of Nez, stopped, and looked back at the mound of red earth that was Clah's home. As he suspected, the mountain effectively protected the back of the hogan. "No way to get in from the top unless you're a mountain goat."

"No mountain goats here. Just coyotes." Nez headed back to the car. "They *like* it here," he added over his shoulder.

Jackson grabbed a handful of sand and let it fall in streams between his fingers. *They can have it.*

He reached the car and folded himself into the front seat. A shooting pain stabbed his side, forcing a groan.

"You all right?"

"Never better." The look Nez shot him told Jackson he wasn't fooling him. "How far to Tah Chee Wash?"

"Thirty miles. Fifteen of it on dirt road. It's too late. I'll take you there tomorrow."

"No problem. All I need is a Jeep. And your map," Jackson amended.

"You always work alone?"

"Always." Jackson shut off any more questions by looking out the window.

Nez turned north on Highway 191. The setting sun gleamed last on the hood of the car. To the east, probably a hundred miles away, a range of mountains stood in flat black against the dark blue sky, like a cardboard cutout. Between the highway and the mountains not one light twinkled in the dusk.

"You sure there's a motel out here?"

"Holiday Inn in Chinle. The Thunderbird Motel doesn't allow smoking."

Jackson ignored Nez's glance. "How about drinking?"

"None sold on the Res. Federal law." Agent Nez cleared his throat. "This your first time to Navajoland?"

"Yes," Jackson lied. He didn't count thirty-two years ago.

Eight hours later, Jackson circled the motel parking lot one more time. One in the morning, he was the only one prowling around. He couldn't sleep, though he'd tried everything. Even a couple hundred push-ups hadn't done the trick. He just couldn't relax. Every time he lay down and closed his eyes, his heart pumped fast and his temples pounded. So he walked it off.

With customary aggression, he forced his thoughts where they didn't want to go: back to the hogan. With little effort, he could again experience the brutal impulses. An involuntary shudder clenched his back muscles.

What if his intuition had shifted away from the victim to the murderer? It wouldn't, he told himself. This wasn't some psychic ability that could float without focus. It was him, his brain, and his powers of observation.

Tomorrow—today, he corrected himself—he'd have to go see Clah's body. He looked forward to it, he realized. As gruesome as it would be, that alone should snap him back on track.

He angled across the parking lot, his tennis shoes silent on the asphalt. A sudden shriek raised the hairs on his back. He squatted, grabbed his gun, and listened. Another shriek rose and Jackson swiveled on the balls of his feet toward the pool. He crossed the lot in a run, then stopped within a few feet of the gate to the pool courtyard. He heard a shriek and several splashes. Maybe it was kids. With practiced stealth, he approached the gate, his right arm bent, the gun barrel aimed skyward.

He peered over the wrought iron. There were no kids, but *something* was in the water. The surface undulated, not in waves, but in arrhythmic, sort of jumpy spasms. Hundreds of black things bobbed up and down.

Jackson let himself in and walked closer, his gun still cocked. One of the black things jumped straight up and landed on his shoe. Jackson almost shot his toe off. The frog croaked and hopped away. The whole pool was full of . . . frogs!

For a moment, he questioned his sanity. What were hundreds of frogs doing in a swimming pool in the middle of the desert?

The only thing he hated worse than surprises were puzzle pieces that didn't fit. And so far today, that was all he'd had.

With a last look of disbelief, Jackson holstered his gun and headed to his room. If he couldn't sleep, he'd study the files—and the pictures. He'd make the pieces fit and he'd solve these murders. Then he'd leave. This place was not where he belonged.

TWO

Today she would see home. The sheep knew it, too. They didn't stubbornly linger, grazing where and when they wanted. Instead, they trundled over rocks and scampered down arroyos, a woolly mass of one determined mind. As usual, Burnt Woman led.

Ainii wished the old, cantankerous goat would slow down. The closer they neared Fluted Rock, the greater she felt the pull of the tall pines they had left behind. It was always this way and made Ainii smile at her predictable nature to want both. She indulged the dual yearnings—to be home and yet still be camping with her sheep. The sensation placed her at the crux of *ilna hooshoolii*. For just this moment, all was in balance. When she reached Ruins Wash, and the pines were no longer trees but only a deep green on Buell Mountain, the balance would tip and she would have one desire—to be home.

Of course, the sheep had already reached that conclusion. They wished only to be done with the walking and to chomp lazily on grain. She could see Burnt Woman far ahead, the black-tipped ends of her long angora hair swishing to and fro in pace with her near trot.

Ainii would miss awakening in the chill of first light to the crisp scent of pine needles. She would also miss the afternoons in the cool mountain sun spinning and dreaming of the rug pattern. Yet it was time for her to return, too. She had the Owl's Claw and, together with the bitter-tasting plant, she could make the poultice for Irene. Then Irene would not return to Joe Clah.

Ainii's pulse quickened at the thought of the evil medicine man—charlatan, she reminded herself. Though that made him no less dangerous. To those he preyed on, it made no difference he had no heritage, nor even any training. He acted like a medicine man and he knew the words to strike fear if you *didn't* believe.

Ainii knew the power of his words firsthand—the power to make lies sound like truth, to manipulate people, using their fears to ultimately make lies and fears more powerful than reason.

Irene didn't know the wound she had opened when she had told Ainii that a medicine man named Clah had promised a cure. "He says I have been bewitched, Ainii," the young girl had confided, while rubbing the lump at her neck. "He says a witch blew a bone into my navel and it has traveled to my neck."

Only Irene's frightened youth had allowed Ainii to convince her to wait for Ainii's return with the poultice. Ainii had called the police, though she didn't believe they would investigate. Real or pretend, medicine men occupied hallowed ground on the reservation and were generally given wide berth. The police must have notified Clah, because he had tracked Ainii by phone to Bill's post.

"So, *shi yaazhi,* you think you can interfere? Come with Irene and see a *real* medicine man, not a fake like your father, *Hastiin* Henio." A shudder ran down Ainii's spine at the remembered words. She had trembled then, too, and hung up, without a word, without the courage to say anything to Clah.

She gripped her knees tight to Shoogii's belly. The horse responded with a hastened walk. "Shhh, Shoogii." Ainii forced herself to relax. Her fingers went naturally to the spindle tied before the saddle. Whatever her life had been before, weaving was her life now.

After three spinnings, the yarn was ready to dye. She

would use the root bark of the mountain mahogany she had dug just this morning. With little interruption, she could finish the rug within two months and, with hard negotiation, she could clear her account with Bill and have credit for the winter.

She already had the design in her mind. She could see the play of the pattern and, with the rich brown from the mahogany for the background, Ainii knew this would be her best rug.

Bill, too, would love the rug. He would see its beauty and then forgive her for not listening to him.

Nervous bleats broke her musings. She scanned the herd and saw curly rumps bunched together, their tiny tails twitching. Leaves shivered silver on the tamarisk trees. *Must be the wind.*

She saw Dakota race between cedars. For a second, Ainii thought Burnt Woman had wandered into the gnarly forest. Always the troublemaker, the wily old goat liked to find her own way home and she always had a following of twenty or thirty who paid no attention to *where* they went. But Ainii didn't hear Dakota's scolding barks, ordering Burnt Woman back to the herd.

Shoogii snorted. Ainii saw her horse's ears flatten in warning. She grabbed her rifle.

"Shhh, now, Shoogii. Is it a coyote?" she whispered.

Suddenly a cluster of sheep screamed. Shoogii put on a burst of speed. From the corner of her eye, Ainii saw Dakota racing to the same sheep.

"*Woshdee!*" She swung her arm to the side.

With a quick turn, Dakota aimed his run to come from the back side. Shoogii made fast cuts through the sheep, his hooves clattering on stones. Ainii could now see the coyote. It faced Daisy and, from thirty yards, Ainii saw her sweet face skewed with terror.

"Aiee!"

The coyote's fierce gaze darted to Ainii. Daisy didn't move, nor did the sheep around her. They all stood frozen, their screams and bleats as if the slaughter had begun.

Shoogii, used to roping, pulled in close. Ainii balanced the rifle on her skirt and drew out the mahogany stick. She whirled it over her head in time with Shoogii's gallop. The coyote glanced between her and Daisy, the predator realizing he was the prey. There was the chance he might attack the horse, but Shoogii didn't falter. Dakota bore down from behind, his shrill barks cutting over the pleas of the sheep.

Ainii swung the stick but missed. The coyote hunched back, its ears flat, teeth bared. Shoogii cut fast and Ainii swung again. With a yelp, the coyote spun to escape. Dakota charged and caught him by the neck. Snarls, yelps, barks, and bleats filled the arroyo.

Ainii leveled her gun but couldn't get a shot. Dakota and the coyote were one furious blur of teeth and fur. Shoogii dug at the ground and whinnied.

"Patience, Shoogii."

At her click, Shoogii backed up a few paces. Ainii aimed again.

The coyote rolled over Dakota. Ainii shot. With a scream, the coyote fell limp. Ainii slid from Shoogii, rifle in one hand, stick in the other. Dakota hadn't moved and a hard lump pounded in Ainii's throat. Shoogii advanced alongside, snorting, impatient. Ainii knew Shoogii worried as much as her about the feisty dog. She poked hard at the coyote. He rolled and, with a yelp, Dakota squirmed free.

Pinkish fur ringed his neck. Ainii checked gingerly for punctures, Dakota's hot panting breath in her face.

"You were very smart, Dakota. And brave." Ainii picked him up to her lap. Dakota whimpered. Shoogii pressed closer. "Oh, *shi yaazh,* show me where it hurts."

Gently, Ainii pressed her fingers around Dakota's side, twice having to push Shoogii's nose out of the way. When she carefully bent the front leg, Dakota made a soft, pained sound. "Ah, I see. Did *Ma'ii* bite you there?" she said softly, more worried of broken bones. All felt in place. She cradled him in her skirt. "Today you will ride with me."

Ainii stood with her bundle, but the sheep also needed comforting. They crowded her, pushing and jostling for attention. Even Burnt Woman looked at Ainii, though she stood at the edge, her black face a little higher than the rest.

"Hush, now," she said firmly. "*Ma'ii* is dead. Let's go home."

Shoogii stood still as Ainii climbed awkwardly onto the saddle. She shifted Dakota to rest across her lap. "There, now, my little hero."

Shoogii parted a path through the milling sheep. A sharp *hssss* from Ainii drew their heads and feet in the right direction. With a kick, Ainii cut Shoogii from the herd and rounded to the back. Burnt Woman took the lead.

Ainii looked over her shoulder. The coyote lay in a gray and red heap, an offering to the vultures. Ahead, in the distance, she could see Fluted Rock. Her home, her sanctuary, was just beyond.

Nez downshifted and rolled the Jeep to a stop. Holding his hand up, he gestured five minutes to the agent in the second car. That was all the time he needed, or wanted to spend, passing off the Jeep to Agent Walker. He could believe Walker was the best in the Bureau at solving serials—he certainly had enough attitude. He had actually looked forward to meeting the legendary Walker. Now he was frankly grateful Walker preferred to work alone.

Nez entered the motel restaurant and spotted Walker immediately. He sat in a corner, his back to the wall. Like a gunfighter, thought Nez. He had the look of an outlaw—loose spread of lanky legs and shadows beneath his eyes, as if he slept with both eyes open.

"The Jeep's outside," Nez said without preamble. Then he saw the crime scene photos spread across the table. An uneaten plate of eggs and bacon had been shoved to the side. "No wonder you don't have an appetite,'' he said with a gesture toward the grisly photos.

Walker looked up. Tiny, pinched lines of exhaustion ringed his bloodshot eyes. Nez recognized the haunted look of an agent pushing his limits and he found himself wondering about Walker's reputation. If the man was as good as they said, how did he survive? How did he ever get past all the horror he dealt with? With newfound respect, Nez pulled out a chair and sat down.

''Is this how it always goes? You don't eat or sleep until you catch the murderer?''

A faint smile creased Walker's lips. ''Not usually.'' Walker stacked everything except a picture of each victim, which he set out side by side.

''How do you find a connection?''

At Walker's quick glance, Nez was sure the agent wouldn't answer.

Walker looked back at the photos. ''It's a lot like finding your way through a strange house in the dark. You know there's got to be walls and furniture. You just don't know where.''

The words told Nez nothing, but Walker's tired voice said it all. Nez almost offered to help, but Walker spoke first.

''Don't worry, Nez. There's always a light switch.'' Walker stuck the photos away and took a sip of his coffee. ''And I always find it.''

Nez could say *Good luck,* but somehow he knew luck wasn't a part of Walker's agenda. He stood up and set the keys on the table, then he remembered the piece of information the chief had passed along. ''There is something more about the last murder. There was a complaint filed against Clah ten days before the murder.''

''About?''

Nez looked at his notes. ''Misrepresentation and misconduct as a medicine man.''

Walker snorted and Nez had the uneasy feeling Walker had little regard for medicine men. He wondered what this Navajo from Dallas knew of his homeland.

"And?" Walker asked impatiently.

"Tribal Headquarters sent him a letter about the complaint. Clah called and talked to an officer. According to the officer, Clah was more than a little upset."

"For being accused of conduct unbecoming a medicine man."

"Yes," Nez said, more than a little bothered himself by Walker's slightly sarcastic tone. "The officer also got the feeling Clah knew the person who had filed the complaint."

Walker set down his coffee and Nez, for the first time, felt he actually had the agent's attention. "Clah said, 'That *dol holianda* wouldn't know a real medicine man.' " Nez looked up from his notes. "Loose translation is 'crazy woman.' Can also mean 'bitch.' "

"Nice words for a medicine man."

"Yeah." Nez folded his notebook.

"And the name of our . . . informant?"

"Ainii Henio. She lives . . . Do you have the Indian Country map?"

Walker pulled out the map and unfolded it.

"Here." Nez pointed.

Walker saw only white space with some brown shading symbolizing canyons—no roads, no towns, not even any landmark names. "Where?"

"South of Fluted Rock, near Ruins Wash." After a pause he added, "Want me to take you there?"

"No." Walker stood and collected the photos into the files. "But you can tell me something."

The agent's deep voice actually asking for something caught Nez by surprise. "Sure," he said slowly.

Walker's face was serious. "Why would there be hundreds of frogs in the swimming pool?"

Nez stifled a laugh. He could tell Walker about the summer rains and that Chinle, entrance to the great De Chelly Canyon, was also the mouth of the Chinle Wash. Canyons and water equaled frogs.

The Navajo storyteller won out. "A frog's life is de-

voted to finding water. They found it where you are staying? Frogs are a good omen, Walker.'' Nez smiled.

Walker quirked an eyebrow. "An omen, Nez? Maybe
I should have cut one up and read the entrails.''

"You could just carry one in your pocket.''

Walker laughed and the transformation was so startling
Nez could only stare. Just as abruptly, Walker sobered
and the weariness returned to his eyes. "No frogs in my
pocket. No rabbit's feet, either.''

*And nothing up his sleeve or that he could pull out of
a hat.* Nothing.

All night he had tried. The photos of Clah were
smudged with the touch of his fingers, tracing the body,
the wounds, the trails of blood. A sense of the murder
sequence, the flashes of instinct—one leading to the
next—none of it ever came. Instead, the sheer violence
had torn through him, screaming through his veins like an
out-of-control train on a collision course. He could tear
his fingers from the photos and still the maelstrom would
continue, lingering for long moments.

Worse was the fear. It snapped at him, tried to overtake
him. Even now, with no effort, he could conjure the terror
at the core. He had quit, defeated and exhausted.

Still, he couldn't sleep. So he'd studied the files and
compared the photos from the other scenes. What he
didn't ask himself was whether this time he couldn't do
it. What he *did* tell himself was that he was it. He was
the best. There was always a pattern, always a connection.

The descent from Highway 191 to Nazlini matched Jackson's mood: grim. Stark, rocky hills gave way to gray
sand dunes, a frozen lunarscape that pressed against the
winding road. Nazlini amounted to no more than some
trailers with tires on the roofs.

Jackson followed Nez's directions and took the first dirt
road past the last trailer. The spread of pink sand, as wide
as two lanes, gave the illusion of maneuverability. But the
road hadn't seen a grader in years, if ever.

He stiff-armed the Jeep down the rutty middle. The tires bounced across the washboard—the resounding vibration shook through the chassis, the floorboard, up the steering column to the driving wheel, and straight up Jackson's arms. Each jounce and bounce, every one of the hundreds, fueled his irritation.

He attacked the road, his knuckles white, his elbows rigid. Ahead, halfway up the next rise, he could see a wide circle of sand in the center, churned and trampled. Wheel tracks skirted around each side.

The hell with it, he decided. He gunned the engine. The Jeep rocked and bucked like a toy dragged by a child. The tires dug at loose sand, then gripped hard ground. He shifted, accelerated, and charged through the middle.

With a lurch, the front cleared the last mound, tires spun for traction. He muscled it up and over.

Suddenly a goat appeared directly in his path—its narrow black face staring at him. Jackson honked. The goat stood stock-still. He laid on the horn, downshifted, revved the engine, and turned the wheels. The Jeep struggled, slid back, and stalled.

Jackson jumped out. "You damn goat!" After a moment, the goat turned, flicked its tail, and continued across the road, as if bored with the spectacle. With a hiss, the tires sank in the soft shoulder. Jackson kicked the side, the Jeep tilted, and the front tires sank.

With a silent curse, he started up the Jeep and slipped it into neutral. He put his shoulder to the side and pushed back down the incline. Sand swallowed each footfall. Sweat prickled his scalp, ran down his temples, dripped from his brow.

With every inch gained, he cursed the sand, the goat, and the *dol holianda* who'd brought him here. She probably *was* crazy. Got her kicks causing trouble for others. Maybe that wasn't enough. Maybe she had a real beef with Clah and would do more than file a complaint.

By the time Jackson had cleared the sand pit, he didn't

care *what* Henio's problem was with Clah. *He* was her new problem.

He jumped into the Jeep, threw it into reverse, let it coast backward to the bottom, and took it up the opposite incline about halfway. He then gave it speed down the hill and eyed the shoulder. He jammed the gas, the Jeep jerked, and, with a final lunge, made the top.

This time, a whole herd of sheep blocked his way. Jackson found solid ground, turned off the Jeep, and waited impatiently, his fingers drumming the dash. Tension grated like sand chafing his skin.

A song floated to him. At first he thought it was the wind through the trees. He scanned the forest for the source and thought he saw a horse and rider. There, then gone.

The song flowed over him with a haunting rhythm, drawing him from his seat, all his senses alive to the elusive song, like a scent or a taste he recognized but couldn't name. The sheep moved across the road quietly, continuously, the sound of their hooves on the red dirt a dusty background to the earthy melody.

The rider emerged from the trees—a woman sitting high on an Appaloosa. He first noticed her denim skirt bunched to a bundle as if she carried something precious in her lap. Below the hiked-up hem peeked a small knee hugging the horse's side. The rest of her slim leg disappeared into a high cowboy boot—scarred and dirty.

From an imperceptible nudge, the horse veered around errant sheep and guided them back to the herd. A single thick braid of long black hair swayed gently across the woman's back in time with the big horse's steps. A kerchief covered her nose and mouth, a well-worn rancher's hat shaded the rest of her face.

She glanced at him, her large brown eyes assessing and dismissing. The whole time she hummed, her singsong voice thrummed through him as she ushered her charges across the road.

Jackson watched until the cedar trees claimed the entire

procession. Dull stillness replaced her fading song. He
sank to his seat.

After a moment, he started the Jeep—its deep rumble
two octaves below her voice. As he drove past her path,
he slowed and looked into the trees. He saw the fuzzy
rumps of the herd and the speckled gray of the Appaloosa.
But the woman disappeared within the spread of cedar
and juniper boughs.

He had the memory of her eyes, though, as he drove
on the lonely road. He'd seen that look before in his cat—
the steady gaze, observing all with total detachment. The
look that said, *I see everything and I'll let you know when
it matters.*

A pickup crammed with Indians careened over the rise
and roared past him, spewing sand and rocks. Jackson
swerved to the side and spun sand before finding hard
ground again. He steadied the Jeep and cursed his distraction.

He attacked the center of the road with vengeance. The
Jeep flew over rises and bottomed out, each impact of man
and metal satisfying in a way he could predict and control.

He passed another unmarked side road. Jackson glanced
at the scrawled directions. Nez had said there would be a
small wooden sign with SAM'S ROAD hand-painted on it
and just past there was a road that descended into a canyon. Jackson calculated he should have seen it by now.
The next road was a clear shot across the plateau. The
one after narrowed and turned into the trees. Jackson took
it, but with each meandering turn his irritation grew. He
was at the point of turning back when the road curved
and dumped him right back on the main road. Three other
roads spurred off at the same place. No signs, of course.

He took a sharp right back into the maze. Soon the road
sloped down. Small stones, then rocks replaced the sand.
One side dropped off and trees marched down an em-
bankment. A canyon wall rose, narrowing the road. Jackson hugged the inside. Suddenly a vista opened of a
canyon valley below. The road straightened, dove for the

bottom—as if the builders had tired of the endless serpentine—became a one-lane wooden bridge, then died.

Jackson parked and got out. He stood in a pasture of green valley grass. Fingers of canyons reached into the valley. Down one lived the elusive Ainii Henio. She had to. He had not skidded down three hundred feet nose-first to be wrong.

He also couldn't spend all day traipsing around canyons. He wouldn't have to, he thought, noticing power lines leading the way into the closest canyon. No road paved the way and Jackson considered who would seek such isolation.

He climbed back in the Jeep. A mile in, the narrow canyon floor widened to a bowl, surrounded by cliffs. Cottonwoods flanked a large hogan. Upright logs stood over shoulder height, with red adobe chinked between. From there rose a dome of branches, woven and interwoven. The hogan was not completely round, nor the logs of even height, which made the whole structure appear rather odd, yet right at home.

Jackson knocked on the door. He didn't expect an answer. The only flickers of life were butterflies skittering through the small garden. He tested the knob. It turned. A careless nudge, then two, of his boot toe opened the door.

Warm air, scent full, spilled over him—earth, pine, and something else. His mind locked on the smell, hunting it. Not so much in the room, but within his memories. He should know it—it seemed important. The more he tried to remember, the more the smell skittered away, just out of reach.

Jackson shook his head in annoyance and walked briskly into the room in no particular direction, just *away* from the cloying memory.

His footsteps went from echoing on wood to soundless on rugs. He circled the round room, passing from kitchen to sleeping to living areas with no barriers but large rugs hanging from the beams. Dominating the most space was a huge upright loom, its parallel fibers distinct in the light pouring from several closely spaced windows. Balls of gray, white, and tan yarn filled a basket on the floor.

Boring colors chosen by a boring woman. A woman with too much time on her hands who had decided causing trouble for others might be interesting. This trip had been a waste of time.

Jackson strode from the hogan, careful to duck at the threshold of the low door. Nothing irritated him more than puzzle pieces that didn't fit. This piece not only didn't fit, it was worthless. Whoever Ainii Henio was, whatever her interest in Clah, Jackson didn't need to hear it. He knew her kind: lonely and cranky with her life in an unmapped canyon down an unmarked road.

Movement on the canyon wall drew his attention. Specks of white danced down the rocky slope. Maybe they were cattle, but probably sheep, he thought given their size in the distance. They wound out of sight, then back in, obviously on a trail. His gaze shifted to the empty corral. Perhaps the problematic Henio was returning home.

Jackson leaned against the Jeep and waited. The specks became fuzz balls, then sheep. One larger, with a black face, led the herd.

Jackson straightened. He searched the straggle of animals. Then, at the back, over a rise came the Appaloosa. As the group approached, he could see the red of the woman's kerchief. He knew, just as his eyes were on her, her gaze had fixed on him.

She didn't slow or stray, but drove straight for him. Jackson felt a pull deep in his belly.

Abruptly, the herd veered toward the corral. He saw her swinging something above her head. Some sheep fanned off from the herd.

"*Shash! Ma'ii! Shash!*" She yelled, whirling what he saw now was a stick. The stragglers scurried to the herd and the mass of curly rumps filled the corral. She slid from the horse and slipped off his bridle and the blanket from his back. She still held something bunched in her skirt. As she walked toward her hogan, all Jackson could see were the slender legs.

"Ainii Henio?"

She stopped at her door.

Jackson walked to within a few feet of her. "Jackson Walker, FBI." Normal people asked questions when he confronted them, but she just looked at him, her eyes wide and curious. The kerchief had dropped below her chin and Jackson's gaze went to her mouth. A few speckles of sand lay on one lip.

Jackson drew his gaze up, to the brim of her hat. "Are you Ainii Henio?"

After a pause, she answered, "Yes." Her voice was low, as if she had just awakened. "What do you want?"

"You filed a complaint against Joseph Clah?"

"Yes."

Jackson noticed she neither blinked nor wavered in her gaze. She should have looked away, the gesture of someone wondering what all this was about. "Why the complaint?"

"Because he is a fraud."

Still she hadn't looked away from him, moved in any way, not even a fidget. Her look didn't challenge him, merely awaited his next question. Suddenly Jackson wanted nothing more than to break her calm facade.

"You know, Clah was not happy with your complaint."

"I know."

"Oh? Did you talk to him again?"

"Yes."

"And? Maybe he told you to stop interfering in his life?"

He saw a flicker of surprise in her eyes and knew he had hit a mark. "But you couldn't, could you?"

She stared back at him with a gaze not intimidated but considering. "He is dangerous, Mr. Walker."

"*Was*, Ms. Henio. Was."

Her brow creased with confusion. Unimpressed, Jackson forged ahead. "What was it, Ms. Henio? What was your real problem with Clah?"

"He'll never change."

"That's true. You saw to that, didn't you?" Jackson circled her arm with his fingers. "You've got muscle, but not enough. Who helped you?"

"Helped?"

"*Kill* him, Ms. Henio."

Three

"Clah is dead?"

Jackson heard her surprise and a hint of relief. He tightened his grip on her arm, his fingers touching around the heavy denim. She didn't flinch or pull back but merely glanced from his hand to his face, her huge brown eyes steady. Jackson's pulse jumped. "You're glad he's dead, aren't you?" he accused, more harshly than he had intended.

"Yes," she answered without hesitation, still staring at him.

Her direct response surprised him. Her eyes held a swirl of emotion, yet she didn't look away—she stared at him, unblinking, unmoving, awaiting his next question.

It took Jackson a second to collect his thoughts. "Tell me, why would you want to see Clah dead?"

"His lies destroy people," she answered evenly.

"Like who?"

This time she hesitated. She glanced to the ground. "My father," she finally answered, then she raised her gaze to his.

Jackson stared into the depths of her eyes, their immeasurable calmness. His hand dropped from her arm. The still moment expanded within him, like a hush of all noise—clarifying, hypnotizing. He had the almost overwhelming urge to lean toward her, reach a consoling hand to her.

He caught himself just in time. Jackson took a quick step backward and narrowed his eyes on her. He'd never been taken in so fast and so sure. Jackson shook his head. "You're good," he muttered.

She blinked. He saw the brief flash of confusion. Long lashes swept her cheeks. The more vulnerable she looked, the more irritated he got. *Damn her innocent look.* He shook his head to restore his concentration. "Destroyed your father? How?" he demanded.

"With words, talk . . ." Her voice drifted off.

"Talk doesn't destroy people."

Her brow creased with surprise. "Words create thoughts and thoughts are power, Mr. Walker," she said, as if explaining a simple truth.

The bundle in her arms squirmed. A black nose poked out. She crouched and uncovered a small dog in her lap. "Shhh, Dakota," she whispered, while stroking the dog's body and legs. Her big eyes watched Jackson, waiting for a response. He could barely take his gaze from the long fingers feathering through fur.

"Thoughts didn't kill Clah, Ms. Henio. He died painfully." He heard the irritation in his voice and couldn't stop it. "The bodies were mutilated. Slashed to shreds."

"Bodies? Slashed?" She rose, her mouth slightly open. He could see surprise—and something else—on her face.

"Especially Clah's," he said with emphasis. "As if someone were particularly passionate about *his* murder."

Her eyes riveted on his. "What do you mean, 'slashed'?"

"Gored. Torn to ribbons."

This time he could put a name on the something else he saw in her eyes—fear. The kind that yelled for help, the kind that clutched your heart. His heart.

"And the others—who were they?"

"A young girl and a trader from Dinnebito."

"The thief, Newcomb," she said, her tone a final judgment. "And the girl?" The concern in her voice was echoed in her questioning eyes.

"Wynema Begay. A young girl from Whippoorwill."

"They died the same way?" Her urgency gripped him.

"The same way."

"*Yenaldlooshi.*" She whispered the word like a curse. Her voice held the shush of a silent terror. A terror he .saw in her eyes. A terror he had caused.

He could barely stand to see it there—and he couldn't look away. It was like looking at himself—what he knew was in his own eyes when the violence from the photos, and from Clah's own blood, had swept through him.

At the thought, the memory replayed with vicious speed—too fast to stop or avoid. With but a breath to prepare, he was plunged into the abyss of clawing terror. His mind clutched for reality.

He felt denim beneath his fingers. A velvet coil brushed his hand. A heart beat against his—slower than his, moderating his own. A warm hand framed his jaw. His own heat rose to the caress—to the touch so light, it stunned him.

He opened eyes he hadn't known were closed. Staring up at him, from within his arms, was Ainii, her own eyes deep, measuring.

"Your thoughts are powerful."

"My thoughts . . . ?" The words left him.

He stepped back an arm's length from Ainii, his hands on her shoulders. Her face was drawn with concern. He had pulled her into his arms, unconsciously seeking comfort. When had he lost control? *He* was the one in charge, asking questions. He was the one with the insight, the perception. He'd built a career on his intuition, his gut instinct.

But his instincts had been set on edge the moment he'd seen Ainii—simultaneously annoyed yet drawn to her. Hell, his hands still held her shoulders. He let them drop, raked one through his hair, and turned from the dark eyes watching him.

"Where were you on Wednesday, Ms. Henio?"

"Buell Mountain."

He faced her now from five feet away. "Can you prove that? Any witnesses?"

"Oh, many Dakota, Shoogii, Burnt Woman." She smiled. Her eyes sparkled, as if an inner effervescence awaited just below the surface.

"Who?" he managed.

"A dog, a horse, a goat, and about one hundred and fifty sheep."

Jackson felt a smile tug at his lips. He didn't want to smile, he didn't want to enjoy this woman. Irritability itched at his scalp. He ran a frustrated hand through his hair. "How about a witness who can speak?"

"No, Mr. Walker. No one *you* could speak to."

She studied him and Jackson felt a loss at her serious gaze. He looked away, settled his gaze on the corral. "Why were you gone?"

She didn't immediately answer. Jackson glanced back in time to see her make a decision. "To bring the sheep back from the winter camp."

"Was that the only reason?"

"Yes," she answered. She bent to her dog.

Jackson found himself staring at the crown of her head, and pondering her answer. "Who else didn't like Clah, Ms. Henio?"

She shrugged, her attention still given to the dog. "Many people, Mr. Walker."

Jackson crouched next to her, his arms resting on his thighs. The next instant, a cold dog's nose nuzzled into his palm. Ainii looked over with a tentative smile. "He believes he deserves everyone's attention today."

"Why today?"

"He is the hero today. He attacked a coyote." As she spoke, she ran a loving hand over the dog. The dog rolled onto his back, offering his stomach to her while still nudging Jackson's hand with his nose.

Jackson barely stifled a chuckle. "He *is* a hero, to kill a coyote."

"I believe the bullet did that job, but we won't tell

Dakota.'' She leaned close with the whisper.

He could see small freckles of sunlight on her nose and a dark smudge limned one high cheekbone. She smelled of earth and pine needles and Jackson again found himself without words, his thoughts tangled in her gaze as surely as the twigs of cedar caught in her hair.

Jackson stood, to gain some distance, some objectivity. ''I didn't kill Clah, Mr. Walker.'' Her voice was soft but matter-of-fact, like the steadiness in her gaze at him.

Jackson believed her. He realized he'd known it all along. Then why had he badgered her? Even now, irritation bubbled within him, but he couldn't say why.

His legs moved and he found himself walking to the Jeep. ''Stay available, Ms. Henio.'' His voice came tight.

Without a backward glance, he got into the Jeep, turned it away from the hogan, and drove out of the canyon. He stayed in first gear and let the Jeep idle slowly along the creek—his thoughts dragging behind him to the woman. She was an odd one—so quiet and pensive, yet with presence—as if she owned the word *calm*. He had the sense that nothing could ruffle her.

Except he had. He remembered the look in her eyes when he spoke of the murders. He winced at his own callousness. When had he lost his ability to interrogate objectively?

It didn't matter, he told himself. He had learned enough. Ms. Henio had not killed Clah. Her surprise and confusion were sincere. The terror he'd seen in her eyes was also real, a flicker of vulnerability that had tugged at him.

Jackson accelerated, pulling away. The valley grass pulled at the tires, slowing the Jeep, and he shifted to second, then third, ripping tender stalks from the ground, breaking free.

Ainii watched until the Jeep disappeared, the echo of its rumble fading a few moments later. She could scream now and no one would hear. But she couldn't break the silence. The air pulled taut around her, suffocating her with memories.

A starless night. A sacred canyon. The pungent scent of crushed sage. Her father, his body painted, his hair wild, dancing, singing, around and around, trampling the huge drypainting in the sand. She had watched, hidden in the sage, aware of the presence of the animals, all in awe of the lone figure who fearlessly baited *Yenaldlooshi*—the powerful witch who could transform into the magic wolf.

When the evil shapeshifter had appeared, terror had gripped her throat—the child's throat, squeezing out the air. She couldn't breathe. She couldn't scream.

Ainii shut out the rest, but not in time to dam the flood of emotions: fear braided tight with excitement and pride—the sensation of standing close to a miracle. Close, but apart—unwanted and unworthy. Ainii set her jaw against the swift rise of grief, still sharp after five years.

At least Clah, too, was now dead. But so were others—stalked by the evil *Yenaldlooshi*. A memory of the beast brought her heart pulse to her throat. No one deserved to die with such torture, not even the thief Newcomb.

She thought of the girl. What drove *Yenaldlooshi* to her? She hugged Dakota to her. He nuzzled her neck and licked her chin. She should have asked Walker more about the girl, but he'd given her no chance. He had arrived with an agenda, but now she wondered about that purpose. He'd come to question, but then didn't listen.

So arrogant, so . . . high-strung. She'd known that the moment she saw him in the canyon leaning against his Jeep, his jeans-clad legs crossed at the ankles, aviator sunglasses hiding his eyes, but not his gaze. She'd *felt* his look, assessing her, judging her—the observer, like Hawk, acutely aware.

She, too, hadn't been able to look away. He was unlike any Indian she'd known. On the one hand, he had the black hair and lean, angular features of an Apache. Yet he stared, like a Navajo would, with unabashed curiosity.

But his stance was Anglo—casual, yet disarmingly direct.

His approach at her hogan had also been direct, with no pretense, no apology—but also with no control. He'd been so easy to read: his emotions—his urgency—at the surface. She could see the battle clearly in his eyes.

She hadn't meant to touch him, but his anguish drew her hand to his jaw. She still felt the jolt at her fingertips and saw the surprise in his eyes. What barrier had she pushed? What wall within him had she touched?

His vulnerability intrigued her . . . and worried her. Did he understand the evil he pursued? Which would Walker rely on: his arrogance or his vulnerability?

He would need both to kill *Yenaldlooshi*: his weakness to attract the magic wolf and his courage to face him. But no one knew how to catch the evil shapeshifter. Her father had died without imparting the final knowledge. No one knew the dangerous ceremony.

Not Ainii, not even Arland. Though her brother at least knew more than her.

Ainii sank against the hogan. The sun's heat, captured in the mud walls, released to her on contact, seeped through her, warming her, consoling her. Father Sun and Mother Earth . . . joined. Their powers united to comfort her.

She leaned into the warm adobe and raised her face to the sky. She was not her father, the great medicine man. She was Ainii Henio, the weaver. She found her balance between the warps and wefts of a rug, not in the conflict of this world and that of witches. Whatever evil *Yenaldlooshi* wrought, he would not draw her from her canyon, from her sanctuary. She was not the one to face this battle—that was for a man like Jackson Walker.

Ainii slowed past the ruins of the Pine Springs Trading Post, the brick building no more than a roofless shell where sheep and goats wandered. A track of sand through cedars led to the Haskie homestead: a collection of trailers, hogans, corrals, small gardens, and junked cars. Ainii parked in front of a small log home. Several dogs barked her arrival. She stood beside her truck, patiently waiting.

Mrs. Haskie opened the front door and stepped out.

"*Ya'at'eeh*." Ainii smiled, but did not approach until invited.

"*Ya'at'eeh*," Mrs. Haskie didn't smile, nor did she move an inch toward Ainii.

"I'm looking for Irene, Mrs. Haskie. Is she at home?"

"No."

"Is she at the trading post?"

"No," Mrs. Haskie replied again, her face expressionless.

Ainii's concern for Irene picked up a notch. "Is she feeling worse? Did she go see a doctor?"

"No."

Ainii considered the stern woman, the head of the Haskie family. She wouldn't lie, but then maybe Ainii had not asked the right question.

"Is she inside *your* home?"

Mrs. Haskie paused; a troubled look crossed her face. Finally, "Yes." Then her lips, sorry for the forced admission, closed tight in a flat line.

"I have something for her, Mrs. Haskie. For her neck." Ainii was careful not to invite herself in.

Mrs. Haskie stared at her for a moment, then turned and went back inside, but left the front door open. Ainii grabbed her pouch from the truck seat and followed.

Children of all ages sat on the one couch in the small living room. Beyond was an equally small eating room. Mrs. Haskie, and what Ainii guessed were two of her daughters, sat at the linoleum table. A baby sat in a high chair, half an eaten cracker in his hand. Eight sets of eyes settled on Ainii and not one sound.

Ainii waited. They stared. Finally, one of the oldest approached Ainii and gestured for her to follow down the short hallway to the last door. Ainii knocked and a small voice said "*Yah'aninaah'*." Ainii entered. Irene sat at a window, so still, like a silhouette.

"It's me, Irene. Ainii."

"Oh!" Irene glanced quick, then back at the window, but Ainii saw the worry on her face.

"I have the poultice, Irene."

"Thank you. You are good to bring it so far."

Her voice was tired and Ainii's concern leaped. "How's your neck?"

"About the same."

"Here, let me see." Ainii lifted aside Irene's heavy hair. "Can you turn so your neck is in the sunlight?"

Irene shifted but didn't look at Ainii. The girl's eyes were downcast and her face solemn. Ainii prayed she wasn't too late with the poultice. She saw the soft lump hadn't changed in size and was only slightly red, probably from rubbing.

"Good, good," she said and reached for her pouch. From it she pulled a cloth bandage and the jar with the prepared plants. "This will also relieve the itch," she said, carefully applying the lotion. She held the bandage and poultice in place with gauze and tied it off.

"There, now." Ainii sat back on her ankles. "You'll notice a difference in just a day or so."

Irene nodded but wouldn't look at Ainii. Ainii gently tilted Irene's face up. "I promise you'll be better soon."

Irene sat quietly. Ainii wondered what could really be wrong. "I'm so glad you didn't go back to see Clah."

At the mention of Clah's name, Irene glanced quickly at Ainii, her eyes wide, then she slid her gaze sideways. Ainii tried to get eye contact, but Irene stared out the window. Ainii saw her jaw clench. "Clah is dead," Irene said, then looked at Ainii, her eyes shimmering with anger.

"Are you mad that I made you promise not to see him? He would not have helped, Irene."

A tear caught in Irene's lashes, but she didn't blink. Her gaze, full of emotion, reached to Ainii's core. "No, I'm not mad at you."

Her words came tight as if uttered over an obstacle.

The truth was, Irene was very mad. But at who? For the first time, Ainii wondered about Irene being at her mother's. "Is it Albert? Did you two argue?"

Tears slid down Irene's cheek. "He was very mad."

Ainii played a hunch. "He was mad at you for seeing Clah?"

"I should have known."

"Clah was good at deception, Irene. Albert will soon understand that and forgive you for seeing him."

Pain replaced the anger in Irene's eyes. "You warned me," she whispered.

Ainii took hold of Irene's shoulders. "Clah was evil and you were too innocent to know. Albert knows your heart, Irene. He loves you or he wouldn't be mad."

"You don't understand." Sobs cracked Irene's words. She stood abruptly and paced a few steps. Suddenly she turned to Ainii, a look of fierceness in her eyes. "You can't tell anyone I saw Clah."

"I haven't—" Ainii began.

"You have to promise," Irene interrupted.

Ainii embraced the shaken girl. "Shhh, now." She stroked Irene's hair. "You haven't done anything bad." Irene's shoulders shook and Ainii tightened her hug. "Clah is dead. No one has to know." Ainii stroked Irene's back and repeated the whispered words over and over.

The ascending blast of a diesel truck tore through Jackson. He swerved to his lane as a whoosh of fifteen tons rocked the Jeep. With a fast downshift, he cruised to the side of the highway and stopped. Adrenaline pricked his whole chest.

He hadn't been watching the road. He'd been with Clah, his hands on the mangled mess of remains. The dead possum he'd seen a mile back had done it, its flattened body in better shape than the savagely torn Clah's. The medical examiner was still extracting pieces of embedded clothing from what remained of Clah.

Jackson grabbed the paper bag beside him and pulled out the aspirin bottle, with a wistful look at the whiskey. He dug through the cotton, anger rising at his inept fingers. He'd known from the photograph that the body would be a mess. He'd anticipated it, planned for it, even counted on the harsh reality to snap him out of this damned purgatory of mixed images and restore his focus back to the victim: the person he empathized with, the one he *connected* with.

Instead, the murderer's need to slaughter had raced through him—just as the adrenaline did now, pumping Jackson's heart. Every scream of the helpless victim had *fed* the burning hatred. A rage of righteousness had consumed Jackson, gripping his consciousness with murderous intent. The killer's thoughts had claimed his own, tapping into the dark pit in Jackson, the place where nightmares were born. Hell within had opened up and swallowed Jackson.

He glanced again at the paper bag. Then, with a fierce grind of the key and gears, he forced the Jeep to life and back onto the road. He stopped at the first available motel and got a room, but the close quarters only added to his tension, constraining his need to pace.

He walked out of the room, across the parking lot, away from the lights, until he was alone with the dark. Still he walked, each step meant to force his thoughts on a linear track.

When his legs finally just stopped walking, he found himself in the middle of nowhere, surrounded by the night. Behind him, in the distance, he could see the faint lights of the motel. He had only to head back in that direction to his room and his Jeep. If it were only that easy to find the path through these murders. But nothing made sense.

For one, Wynema Begay and Newcomb didn't appear to have suffered like Clah, if you could call slashed and bludgeoned less savage. Their post-death beatings just didn't match the magnitude of Clah's.

For another, when he had touched Wynema, the terror he had perceived was one he knew well—heart-racing fear laced with the hope to live: a hope that didn't die until her last breath.

But in Clah, Jackson had found only pure terror, heart-*stopping* terror, as if Clah had literally died of fright. Then the murderer had pounded Clah's body to a pulp, as if Clah's murderer wanted him more than dead. Why? According to Ainii, Clah had destroyed people's lives with lies.

Ainii's face filled Jackson's mind, just as it had many times that day—arriving unbidden, with the startling clarity he sought in the murder images but couldn't attain. Her eyes haunted him, their depth and purity mesmerizing.

They were also revealing. He'd seen the gamut of emotions: unintimidated, then curious, then fearful, then consoling. All of it passionate, yet detached, as if she watched her reactions. Which made her either incredibly perceptive or a good actress. Either way, someone a lot more interesting than a boring woman lived within those dark eyes.

The mysterious Ainii Henio. He had a lot more to learn about her. That thought brought a biting laugh . . . as if he needed one more puzzle to solve.

The night went like the last: sleepless. Maybe it was the trucks or the globe of light that shone through his window. Dammit if he didn't miss the screams and croaks of the infernal frogs.

That night, Ainii went to sleep thinking of the rug pattern. She awoke on the scream of a hawk. In the night stillness, she held back her panting gulps for air to listen. Nothing. She swiped wet tendrils of hair from her forehead. Her heart pounded furiously.

She'd been dreaming. About what? All that remained were sensations—of soaring, then falling—and the scream.

What was Hawk's message to her?

Ainii slipped her hand beneath her pillow and withdrew the feather. She ran it through her fingers as she padded to the window.

She knew Hawk's power: flying high, close to Father Sun, he saw life's signals intuitively, without emotion. She already knew this lesson. She'd learned it well from her father: emotion fogged clear vision. "Hawk knows he must concentrate," he said, "without fear, without frustration, without regret—with *only* awareness, or he will fall from the sky. Be like the hawk, Ainii."

And she was. Whatever emotions she carried, she buried deep. She had been able to walk away from her father's grave, from the people who killed him, from her home and sacred canyon—and never look back—taking with her only the feather her father had given her so many years ago.

Ainii placed a palm against the window and felt the cool night beyond. She let the cold through her hand, let the fine hairs prickle on her arm, let the chill race over her skin. As the breath of night swept over her, she focused on the warmth within her. The chill evaporated. Just as her father had taught: Detachment brought clarity. "I have not forgotten, Father," she said aloud.

Four

The slap of files on Jackson's desk brought Nez's head up with a jerk. Jackson felt the agent's gaze on him and he could only hope he didn't look as wrung out as he felt.

"How about some coffee, Walker?"

Nez's tone and his raised brow were the only comments he made on Jackson's appearance. Then he lowered his gaze to the files. "What are those?"

"Reports from the M.E."

"And?"

"The lab is running PCR tests on swatches from Clah, Begay, and from both sites. We should have the autorad tapes in a week with the DNA results."

"DNA won't do us much good without a suspect."

Jackson eyed Nez and wondered if the comment was a veiled jab, but he saw only the face of a dedicated agent, listening to the facts. He hated to disappoint the agent that facts got you only so far.

"What about the weapon?" Nez asked.

"He can't narrow it down. Maybe a board with nails. That would explain the uneven ripping."

"Then why the difference in brutality between Clah and the others? Maybe it took more to kill Clah."

"Maybe."

Nez looked pensive. "You don't think so."

Jackson returned the even gaze. "No, I don't think so."

"Why?"

"For one thing, Clah died where he slept. There was no sign of struggle."

"True. But you can't tell from the pictures of Clah's body whether he put up a fight. His body's too much of a mess to find any defensive wounds. So what's your other reason?"

"It's just a sense I get . . ." Jackson let his voice trail off.

"From the victims?" Nez finished.

Jackson fiddled with the files. He did not like talking about how he worked.

"Well, that's why you're here. For your instincts."

Jackson glanced up, expecting to see a smirk. God knows, even his instincts weren't working this time. Instead, Nez was shuffling through his files, grabbed one, and pushed it across the desk.

"Looks like the masks missing from Newcomb's post were stolen property." Nez shrugged. "Not as good a guy as we thought."

Jackson slid the file closer. "Well, I'll be damned." Had Ainii been right about Newcomb being a thief? He let out a whistle. "Newcomb had quite a hoard of contraband."

"And a profitable business. The copied ledger sheet has some impressive numbers."

"Of sales. What about purchases?"

"That's the sweet thing for a corrupt trader," Nez explained. "There are Navajo thieves just like anyone else. They bring him contraband, he pays them, then sells it. Sometimes he'll even issue a fake provenance for the unsuspecting dealer in Albuquerque or Santa Fe. Most times, it's all black market.

"There was one local," he continued. "Turns out Newcomb worked a quiet deal with a medicine man over a pouch. It had been stolen from that same medicine man and sold to Newcomb."

"So, our good trader Newcomb trafficked in stolen ritual objects. Interesting." Jackson stared ahead.

"Idiot."

Jackson's gaze flashed to Nez.

Nez's face had hardened with anger. "Anyone who would buy the sacred things of a medicine man is an idiot."

"You said yourself it was a profitable business."

"Money can't buy the power of those items," Nez said harshly. "The power belongs with the medicine man. These people are dealing in things they don't understand."

For the second time that morning, Nez had surprised Jackson. He considered the man: an FBI agent, a Navajo. Jackson realized Nez might think of himself first as a Navajo, then an agent. It was a thought so foreign to Jackson, he couldn't dwell on it. He went back to the conversation. "Bottom line is that Newcomb had quite an enterprise going."

"Yeah," Nez replied flatly, "selling our ceremonial objects."

Ceremonial objects. Newcomb the thief. Clah the fraud. Ainii's words spun through Jackson's thoughts. She had told him the truth about Newcomb. Maybe she was right about Clah, too. If he was a fraud, he'd need the right items for the convincing image. And where better to get them than from a trader dealing in property stolen from medicine men?

Jackson looked at Nez. "What do you know about Ainii Henio?"

Nez let his chair rock back. "The girl who filed the Clah complaint? Nothing else. Didn't you find her?"

"I found her. Now I want to know more about her."

"You can check the files, but I'd never heard of her before. The Phoenix Tribal Region can tell you more. If that fails, try Window Rock. The Tribal Headquarters' numbers are on your phone."

Jackson found nothing in the FBI files on Ainii Henio. Which only meant she hadn't been arrested for a federal crime or applied for a government job. The regional Tribal Headquarters had nothing on her, either. Window Rock had her enrollment and that of her father's.

"But he died five years ago," the clerk said.

Jackson absently held the receiver long after the clerk had hung up. He'd assumed Ainii had filed the complaint on Clah on behalf of her father. He'd assumed wrong.

Jackson stood to leave. Nez looked up. "I'll let you know what we learn from the other traders."

"I'll handle the one near Ganado," Jackson said, maybe a bit too quickly. He glanced at Nez. "It's on my way back to Chinle," he explained. Sanders Trading was also the closest to Ainii's home and where she probably did her trading.

"Why aren't you staying here in Phoenix?"

"I did last night. I like to move around." Jackson tried to sound noncommittal.

Ainii parked her truck next to another loaded with kids in the back. "*Ya'at'eeh*," she greeted the children and grandchildren of Bitter Water Woman.

The oldest returned her greeting. The youngest looked back solemnly, her big eyes revealing nothing. The four boys paused in their chatter to acknowledge Ainii, then continued their banter with exuberance.

Ainii addressed Bitter Water Woman's daughter. "Sandra, how is your weaving coming?"

Sandra's shy smile widened. "Fine. But slow. It's folded three times already."

"*Aiee*. It will be huge!"

Sandra laughed softly. "Bill says he already has a customer for it."

"Is your mother trading?"

"Yes," Sandra said, with a smile anticipating the long wait.

Ainii nodded goodbye and crossed the dirt lot. Big Shorty and Gray Whiskers sat on their customary bench out front. Every Monday, they made their unofficial office here; in this place where Navajo came to trade, to gossip, they could also share concerns with the elders. Ainii nodded with respect to the two councilmen and stepped inside the post.

Available light came from the door, a few windows and two low-wattage bulbs in the beamed ceiling. Bill liked to keep things lean but adequate, one of the many ways he made his Navajo clientele feel at home.

A tourist studied the wall rack of folded rugs. At the base of the display, Bitter Water Woman sat on a pile of lumpy flour sacks, which were no doubt stuffed with her wool. The man had to step awkwardly around her to pull a Ganado Red from its pole. Bitter Water Woman stared ahead, her crinkled face expressionless.

At the far end, three Navajo women stood around the woodstove. Their guttural chatter drew occasional sideways glances from the tourists at the rack of postcards. Ainii heard the words and the worry. They were talking about the murders.

It would be this way all over the Res, Ainii thought. Scared *Dineh* talking, speculating, scurrying to bring order back to Navajoland.

It had been this way five years ago. Talk flying, rumors building—frightened people desperate to place blame. She took a step back, away. Then she heard Bill's voice.

He stood behind the high wood counter, his leg hiked on the rung of a stool, his arm resting on the glass top— his pose casual but for the steely focus of his eyes as he negotiated with Curly Joe. Without looking her way, he acknowledged Ainii with a quick rise of two fingers from the hand braced on the counter.

"I want the bridle back."

"You can have the bridle back, Curly," Bill said, but made no move to lift the silver-decorated leather from the hook behind him.

"I need it, *Hastiin* Sanders."

"Then that's a good reason to get it."

Curly looked beyond Bill, obviously coveting the fancy

bridle. "I will bring it back. You know I will trade here all winter."

"I know you'll want to, Curly." Bill straightened and reached for a can of tomatoes from the shelf behind him. "I'll miss you if you don't come in." He took off the lid and slid the can and a plastic spoon across the counter. "It would be a long winter."

Curly paused, then lean brown fingers circled the can. "Yes, it would." He walked to the other end of the counter with his tomatoes and started eating.

When Curly was out of earshot, Ainii quirked a questioning brow to Bill. "Why the concern?"

"Because I know Curly wants to pawn the bridle for gambling money. His wife warned me yesterday."

Ainii glanced at the elder Navajo. "A can of tomatoes won't change his mind."

"Oh, I don't know. You'd be surprised what a can of tomatoes can accomplish." Bill glanced down the counter. Curly seemed to be relishing every bite. "I bet right now he's considering whether getting his bridle is worth finding his saddle and all his belongings sitting outside Mouse's hogan."

Ainii chuckled at the real prospect of Curly's wife not hesitating to divorce him over gambling. She looked back at Bill. His warm gaze embraced her, though Ainii wondered why he looked so long, as if measuring her—or his own words.

Then all he said was, "Good to be home?"

"You know how it is. I'm always torn between the canyon and the mountain. It's so peaceful in the pines."

"No one to bother you," Bill offered, still watching her. Ainii got the distinct impression he had something else on his mind. His look, his tone, were so serious.

"It was nice to get away," she said.

"It's been busy while you were gone." He tossed the lid from the tomatoes into the trash and wiped the counter. Ainii didn't miss his quick glance at her. Suddenly she knew he was talking about the murders, about Clah, about *Yenaldlooshi*.

"We have to talk, Ainii."

"I know Clah is dead, Bill."

"And I know you talked to him." His tone was flat, unequivocal . . . and angry.

Before Ainii could respond, Bitter Water Woman appeared at the counter. With a calculated look of disinterest, she handed Bill one sack of wool.

"You will weigh it." Her matriarchal tone reached Curly Joe. Ainii saw him straighten slightly.

Bill walked to the large metal scale. As he lifted the sack, he casually bumped it against the counter. Ainii could hear the soft crunch of rocks within the wool. Bitter Water Woman looked blandly out the window. After weighing it, Bill returned the sack to her.

"Six dollars," he offered.

The creases on Bitter Water Woman's face ran deep. She gripped the sack and returned to her spot.

Bill walked around the counter and took Ainii's arm. He leaned into the vault. "Marie, I'm stepping outside a minute." He ushered Ainii to his private courtyard. Adobe walls enclosed flagstone and worn wooden benches. Hummingbirds, dizzy with excitement, danced iridescent around bougainvillea shrubs. Slender limbs, heavy with fuchsia blossoms, drooped over huge terra-cotta pots.

Normally, Ainii loved to drink in the seductive contrast of the oasis within the desert. Not today. The profusion of life, of color, heightened her anxiety; as if she were the one at odds, contrary to nature. She had disappointed her friend—the only one she could really count.

Bill walked to a bougainvillea and plucked yellow leaves. Ainii knew he used the silence to give his anger a rest.

"You know Bitter Water Woman has the best wool," she said in a light voice.

"I also know I'll buy it. So I act disinterested." He moved to the hibiscus and studied a blossom, shriveled from the attention of hungry bees. "Now she will reconsider."

Ainii looked at the friend who was so much a part of her life: slim as a strand of rawhide; brown as one, too, but only where the sun reached—like his bald head and his forearms. A white man, yet so Navajo in his thinking. "You know, you're a master manipulator, Bill."

Bill barked out a laugh. "Negotiator, Ainii. I learned from the Navajo. And the best of the Navajo—your father." He plucked the wilted flower. "Did I tell you how we met?"

"I assumed it was here." Ainii found a sunny spot on the wooden bench.

"No, we met at a council meeting. He was arguing against the BIA issuing me a license to trade. He wanted a co-op for the Navajo." Bill smiled at her. "He was very convincing."

"He always was," Ainii said thoughtfully. "I'm surprised he lost."

"He didn't."

"But this post is yours. It always has been." She leaned forward, fascinated with this new story.

"Not at first. Your father convinced the BIA to give the Navajo the post. He argued they should have a place to take their jewelry and rugs, where everyone could sell. He said the Navajo would benefit and the tourist would benefit."

"That sounds like Father; looking out for everyone." Warmth spread through her—from the story, from the sun on her back, from the contented buzz of the bees.

"Yes, it sounded good. But it didn't work. Navajo from all over brought in every scrap of anything they had ever made. The post had to buy it all. Didn't matter if the workmanship was bad or if they already had four dozen wire-twist bracelets." Bill shook his head. "Plus, it seemed every clan on the whole reservation had a member who worked the store or knew someone who worked the store. The post paid for every Blessing Way, every Enemy

Way, every Mountainway Chant from here to Mexican Hat."

"Must have been a lively place." Ainii smiled, imagining a Navajo trying to say no to a clan member's plea for help.

"In more ways than that. The worst part was that the buying policy drove a wedge between the stellar craftsmen and the rest. A bracelet made by a master silversmith is worth more than an average one, but how do you explain that to your sister, or your cousin? Made for a lot of bad feelings." Bill tossed the collection of yellow leaves over the adobe wall. He joined Ainii on the bench. "Your father wanted a place that helped everyone, protected them. What he created was trouble." His gaze, full of caring, settled on her. "Did you get the herbs for Irene?"

"How did you—?" Ainii stood from the bench.

He rose and stared at her. "Marie told me about Clah's phone call. Then, Irene worried around here for days after you left. When she asked Marie for a day off, she broke down and confided about the swelling and the poultice you promised would help. I know how Clah works, Ainii," he said, his gaze level. "You thought you could protect Irene."

"I had to stop him, Bill," she said, an apology in her voice.

"Why now, Ainii? After five years, why would you now confront Clah?"

"I understand your confusion. And I understand your worry. But why are you angry with me? You know what Clah did to Father. *I* know that he was preying on Irene. He was dangerous. And now he's dead."

"And the Feds are investigating."

"I know. An agent has been to see me."

"What did you say?"

"I told him I didn't kill Clah."

"What if he looks further, Ainii?"

"Then they will learn what happened in Chinle. Clah's

words drove a crowd to kill my father. And I ran away.'' Ainii's eyes pricked and clouded. ''This time all I did was try to help a young girl.''

He held her shoulders, his grasp warm, his gaze full of understanding. ''Yes, you chose to act.'' He pulled her close in a hug. ''Now you must let others do their job.'' He held her out to look at her, his eyes stern. ''Promise me.''

''My father is dead. Now Clah is dead. All I want is my life.'' At the words, Ainii's heart constricted with a sharp pain, as if thoughtlessly scratched. Her throat tightened around inexplicable emotions. She'd spoken the truth! Why should she feel sad?

She turned away from Bill and let her fingers find the flower blossoms. This close, she could see the crumbs of pollen, but as she gently rubbed the petal between her fingers, all she felt was a powdery nothingness.

Bill's hand settled on her own. ''That's all your father wanted for you, too, Ainii. For you to have your own life.''

Jackson pulled his truck into the space facing two elder Navajo. They sat on a bench, their white hair gleaming in the sun. He slammed the door. They didn't move.

He stepped inside the post and let his eyes adjust to the dimness. Several Navajo—their only distinct feature in the thin light being their full skirts—sat by a woodstove. Though the fire wouldn't be stoked for another month, they had the look of idle women who could wait just as long as it took. Another Navajo, thin as a rail, leaned on the counter eating something from a can. An old Navajo woman sat in a motionless hump on the floor, as if she were carved from the same old wood lining the walls.

The place was a veritable study in inactivity. Yet no one's face held a trace of guilt or apology for their leisure. In fact, their glances gave Jackson the odd sensation that *he* was the one out of sync.

He agreed. He'd felt out of place from his first step

onto the Res, as if he'd entered another time, or a place where time flowed differently. There'd been only one moment when he'd slipped comfortably into the languid pace—in the canyon with Ainii. But he'd been caught off guard. That wouldn't happen again.

He walked to the long counter, his boot heels hard on the wood floor. "Is Bill Sanders here?" he asked a Navajo woman sitting on a stool.

She nodded toward a side door. The Navajo at the counter stopped eating from the can. The old woman on the floor shifted. As Jackson left the trading room, he felt the bore of several sets of questioning eyes.

The shift from dark to bright sunlight filled with color stunned Jackson. He slid on his sunglasses. Voices came from behind a huge flowering bush.

"I promised her I wouldn't tell anybody, Bill."

Jackson knew that voice. He stepped closer and saw Ainii talking to an older man—Bill Sanders, the trader, he assumed.

"It's just that she seems so worried," Ainii said.

"I'm sure what you did will work. Irene is young. This was very scary for her." But Sanders's voice was concerned. "The talk is spreading across the Res. Everyone is getting scared."

"Just like before," Ainii said, as if recalling an awful memory.

Something stirred deep in Jackson's gut. He stepped into the open to see her.

"It won't be like before," Sanders said.

"Do you really think we can count on men with guns and badges?" Ainii said just as Jackson appeared.

He looked up to both Ainii and Bill staring at him. "Don't let me stop you, Ms. Henio." Jackson pulled out his identification and flipped it open to Sanders. "Special Agent Walker. I'd like to hear why Ms. Henio doubts she can count on me."

Sanders crossed his arms and regarded Jackson. "Where are you from, Agent Walker?"

Jackson allowed him the question. "Dallas."

"I mean what tribe. You're Indian. Possibly Athabascan. Navajo or Apache?"

"No tribe," Jackson said. The hot sun bit at his neck and stabbed his temples. "Now, what's your point?"

"You're the point, Agent Walker. Do you know anything about Navajo culture or beliefs?"

"No. Tell me, does it include hawking ceremonial objects illegally like your fellow trader Newcomb?"

"How dare you—"

"Bill doesn't steal, Mr. Walker. Why are you really here?"

Her cool voice washed over him, lifting the heat. It was instant relief . . . and irritation.

"Actually, I came to find out more about you." He faced her. This time he'd stay in charge.

This time she wore jeans, well-worn ones with creases across the middle, thin blue down the inside length of her legs from hugging a horse. He raised his gaze to her eyes—darker than the shadow cast by the brim of her rancher's hat.

"What is it you want to know?" she asked, with no hint of annoyance.

"Why did you file a complaint against Clah?"

"I told you."

"You told me he destroyed people with his lies. That he had destroyed your father. Your father died five years ago, Ms. Henio. Why did you file *this* complaint?"

"She wanted to pro—"

"I wanted to protect anybody else who could get hurt." She finished Bill's sentence without even a glance his way.

"Why?"

"Why not?"

Jackson lowered his sunglasses and conjured his best glare. "Ms. Henio, make me understand why you would wait five years after your father died to file this complaint."

"Mr. Walker, you worry about the wrong things. *When* I filed the complaint isn't important, even *why* I filed it. What matters is that I did."

"No, what matters to *me* is that Clah lived only ten days after you filed the complaint."

"Then it's too bad she didn't file it years ago."

Jackson leveled his gaze on Bill. "You're an employee of the federal government, Mr. Sanders. If you care for Ms. Henio, I recommend you advise her of the penalties for noncooperation and conspiracy."

The man stared back equally hard and long. Jackson swore inwardly. Harassing people wasn't his style, yet he'd done just that—twice in as many days. Both times, Ainii was present. She seemed to kick-start something in him he couldn't control.

"I'll tell you why I waited." Her solemn voice swept through Jackson.

On those six words, he heard a wealth of sadness and the promise of a confession. Jackson almost wanted to stop her. He didn't have a chance.

"Five years ago, people were dropping dead on Navajoland. Young people, old people, tourists. Scientists in Atlanta called it the Hanta Virus. The *Dineh* called it witchcraft." Her eyes, her voice held Jackson spellbound. "My father lived in Chinle, legendary home of witches. My father had denounced Clah as a fraud, and Clah saw his chance for revenge. He spoke powerfully, loudly, weaving lies into truths, a great net that swept up my father." She stared at Jackson, the story in her eyes. "Others killed my father, but Clah wielded the weapon. My father died alone." Her brow creased, only slightly, as if her heart questioned how this could be possible. "When I found him, I buried him in the sand, burned our hogan, and left. I did nothing about Clah, the murder, or the honor of my father." The furrow at her brow deepened with every word.

"It took me five years to say anything. Even then, it

was on paper, not to Clah's face.'' She glanced away briefly, but not before Jackson saw the pain that pierced her.

"There is your *why*, Mr. Walker."

Five

Her gaze bore through him, carrying every word on the strength in her eyes, planting each one within Jackson.

Emotions he'd buried long ago leaped to life, a tangle of weeds clenching his heart with a vengeance. On a silent curse, a scythe of sharp discipline, he severed the stranglehold. In that instant, he understood Ainii's isolation, the safety and seclusion she sought. The wonder was she had filed a complaint at all.

His question came on a breath. "But why now?"

"You're back to that?" Sanders's burst of words from behind broke the spell.

"That's the funny thing about investigation, Sanders. It means asking a lot of questions. Sometimes even the same ones over and over until you get the answer you want."

"How Navajo of you."

Her quiet words exploded in him; as unexpected as a tender finger on a trigger.

"What did you say?" Did he shout? He couldn't tell.

"A Navajo might lie three times, but when asked a fourth, he'll tell the truth. If he doesn't, his lie will come at him from all four sides, from the east and west, the north and the south, and trap him."

Her soothing voice was more startling than a yell. For a second, his mind went blank of anything but her—the calm, collected presence of her. She had the unnerving ability to simultaneously intrigue and anger him.

Ainii cocked her head and considered the hapless Walker. "Did you want to ask me again?" she asked helpfully.

He stared at her, his whole face a reflection of his thoughts: surprise, anger, wonder, then finally dismissal. The last saddened her.

"Will your answer be different?" he asked, his tone flat.

"No," Ainii replied.

He turned away from her and asked Bill about Newcomb—his business, his associates—but Ainii listened to what his eyes had said to her. When she'd spoken of her father, Walker's eyes said he understood. She'd seen her own grief and guilt reflected, but then just as quickly snuffed out; as if his understanding went only so far.

It was the same combination of vulnerability and arrogance she'd seen in the canyon—except now those qualities were more pronounced, in his face, his stance, his eyes. He battled his own demons and clearly liked the upper hand. He'd need that strength to battle *Yenaldlooshi*.

Then she remembered his reaction when Bill questioned his knowledge of Navajo beliefs. His response carried more than disinterest, more than a simple fact. His single *no* harbored disdain. It was a judgment. And it came to her he had never asked what *Yenaldlooshi* meant.

"Maybe Clah found things at Newcomb's he couldn't get in Chinle? Things he needed as a medicine man." Walker's statement cut off her thoughts.

"Clah was not a medicine man," she said.

Both Walker and Bill looked at her with surprise, as if they had forgotten she was there. They shared the wooden bench by the sculpture fountain. Ainii wondered when their conversation had changed from hostile to friendly.

"If not, he wanted to become one," Walker offered. Then he smiled at her; a half-smile, somewhat drawn. Even so, the harsh lines in his face fanned easily, a smooth fade from stern to genial—and from relentless to weary.

She noticed the dark circles beneath his eyes, a slight heaviness in his lids.

"He might do anything to maintain the deception," he continued.

"You mean steal from Newcomb?" Bill said.

Walker shrugged. "Maybe Newcomb surprised him. Clah killed Newcomb."

Ainii stopped. "That's your theory? Then who killed Clah and the girl?"

"Maybe the girl saw something and Clah found out. As for Clah . . ." Walker stared at the ground.

"Doesn't it make more sense that all three murders were committed by someone else?" she asked.

"You'd think so. But there are inconsistencies." Walker looked at Ainii. "With the bodies," he added.

"You said they were all slashed," Bill said.

"Yes. I did." Walker rose, straightening his long frame. "Thanks for your help," he said, with a glance to Bill. He looked at Ainii, for two beats longer than she expected, then started for the trading room.

Ainii and Bill exchanged looks. She saw the question in his eyes and silently agreed.

"Look for what the murderer had to gain from each victim," she said.

Walker glanced over his shoulder. "Thanks for the advice."

Ainii walked toward him. "It might have been a thing. It might have just been power."

"Power? We're not talking corporate giants here, Ms. Henio. But thanks."

"The power that comes from the soul, Mr. Walker. Maybe that's what *Yenaldlooshi* sought from the girl." There, she'd said it.

Walker stopped. "I thought that word was a curse you uttered."

"He is," Ainii said.

His face darkened, hardened. His eyes shone black as polished jet. "You knew? All this time?" He advanced on her, his countenance angrier with every step. Ainii backed up once, then again. "You've known all along who the murderer is?"

"I know *what* he is. He is *Yenaldlooshi*. A shapeshifter."

"A what?" His words came staggered.

"A witch. A man who changes to a wolf."

His steps jerked to a halt. The anger in his eyes cut to confusion—the change so swift Ainii felt the air shift. His gaze jumped from her to Bill to beyond, then back to her—suddenly—with staggering force. In the obsidian depths of his eyes she saw something greater than anger, closer to hate. She stepped back again, knowing she was defeated before he'd uttered a word.

"A wolf, Ms. Henio?" His icy tone matched the glass-black in his eyes.

"Not a wolf."

His hand shot up, staying her words. "Right. A *man* that's a wolf." His steel-sharp gaze raked over her, with precise, bloodless cruelty. His rage swept through her, gripping her heart. *Why was he so angry?*

On a deep breath, she walked to Walker, her gaze steady, probing. "Why are you angry?"

"Why?" The word came as a plea. His gaze slanted. She saw a flicker of confusion. Then he locked on her eyes—fast, hard, brutally. In that instant, she saw the fear. Unbidden, her hand laid on his jaw and pulled his head close.

"I'm afraid, too," she whispered.

A shudder ran through Walker, through her fingertips. He leaned toward her ever so slightly. She rubbed the pad of her thumb across the hollow of his cheek. His beard stubble chafed. So coarse, so vulnerable.

Ainii's heart leaped to this man who would hunt *Yenaldlooshi*. His fear would give him an advantage—like the wolf: a killer on the razor's edge.

With no warning, Walker backed away from her. Ainii shivered beneath his callous gaze.

"You're crazy," he said, his tone black. Then he left.

The air held his emotions; a devil-funnel swirl of confusion, anger and hatred. Why such strong feelings? If you didn't believe, you'd laugh it off, or scoff—simple reactions given with no thought. He had done neither.

He'd leaned to her, as if drawn—a man stepping to the precipice. Ainii could still feel the roughness of his skin on her fingertips. His scent lingered near from when she'd pulled him close. He'd leaped back from the edge, but a part of him stayed with her. Such small things that promised much more.

Walker was neither simple nor thoughtless.

Bill's hands cupped her shoulders and turned her around.

"We'll find someone else to help, Ainii. I'll talk to other medicine men."

Ainii looked at him with disbelief. "What medicine man will admit to having the power to hunt *Yenaldlooshi*?"

Bill shook his head. "One has to exist."

Ainii thought of her brother. "There is someone," she said, quietly, knowing Bill's reaction.

"Who?"

"Arland."

Bill made a noise of dismissal. "You can't rely on Arland, Ainii."

"Father did." The words evoked a clutch of emotion in Ainii's throat.

"And then he quit. He left your father, he left you, and he left the reservation. You won't get him to come back, Ainii." Bill's harsh voice carried his own judgment and tangled with the emotions Ainii struggled to control.

Bill touched her shoulder, made Ainii look up. "He'll only disappoint you again, Ainii."

Ainii nodded slightly, not trusting her voice. It wasn't Arland who had disappointed everyone, but her. Yes, Arland had left . . . and then made a life for himself as an Albuquerque detective. After Arland was gone, Ainii had still not been enough for her father—even as a last resort.

"He won't have to come back," she managed. "I just want his advice."

Ainii hugged her arms close and waited for the quarters to drop and the operator to connect the call. Bill had offered the use of his private line, but Ainii needed the wind at her ear, whispering words of inspiration, the right words to coax Arland's help.

"APD. Is this an emergency?"

"No. I'm calling for Detective Henio."

The phone clicked to hold, then a familiar voice answered. "Henio here."

"Arland, it's Ainii."

"Ainii, is something wrong?"

His assumption startled her. "No, not with me. But I need your help."

"With what?"

"Do you know about the murders?"

"Everyone knows about the murders." His voice came low and close, as if he pressed the receiver to his lips.

"What do you know?"

"Ainii, I'm at work. I really can't talk now."

"Arland, this won't take long. Please. Do you know a federal agent named Jackson Walker?"

"By reputation."

"Is he any good?"

Arland paused. "He's supposedly the best at solving serial murders. Is he there?"

"Yes. And he's not getting very far." She heard a sigh. "He's Navajo, Arland, but won't listen . . . to the stories."

"Ainii—" His tone held a warning. Ainii had heard the clicks, knew APD recorded conversations.

"I can't get him to believe, Arland."

"Ainii, I can't talk."

She rushed ahead before he could stop her. "You know what's happening, Arland."

His expletive stunned her. "Ainii, drop it. Stay away from it. You're way over your head."

"That's why I called. I need your help."

"Ainii, go back to your canyon. Weave, herd sheep, stay there and you'll be safe."

"What about *Yenaldlooshi*?" she asked.

"Goodbye, Ainii."

"No! Arland! Don't hang up." She spoke to the simultaneous click of disconnection.

Ainii rested her forehead on the receiver. How could he offer nothing?

From the place in her heart holding things precious came the pungent scent of crushed sage and spicy pine needles. Floating on sacred cedar smoke came her father's voice: *Stare at the fear, Ainii.*

An ache clenched her heart, a spike of grief so deep and true Ainii buckled. It wasn't her fear to stare at—it wasn't her dream—that had died with her father, and maybe even before that.

Arland was the chosen one. He had learned more, been trusted with more knowledge. He would have received all their father had to give. But Arland had walked away—rejecting everything Ainii had ever wanted.

If her father had let her try she would have been the best student. If only he had believed in her she could help now. Frustration twisted through her, clenching her fists. How would she make Walker understand?

She saw his face, the anger and frustration in his eyes, the hard line of his jaw. A terrible battle waged within him, just below the surface. How could she ever make him believe?

An elderly Navajo woman walking by stopped in front of Ainii. "*Ha'goshii'ya?*"

"I'm fine," Ainii said.

The matriarch cocked her head at Ainii. "It's not good to hold the anger in. You should go yell. That's why we have the canyons." She chuckled.

The merry sound lingered, floating on the air and into

Ainii's ears, and stirred memories. Ainii looked after the woman, but in her mind's eye she saw someone who might be able to help.

The Jeep's tires whined as Jackson ground the gears to high speed. Fifty yards up, a reddish brown hulk stepped onto the road. On a curse, Jackson swerved and missed the cow.

His insides screamed for speed, for escape. Jackson deliberately slowed the Jeep. He set his focus on the vanishing point, but his mind's eye was on Ainii, her words, and his damned irrational reaction.

A shapeshifter! Did she honestly expect him to believe a man could become a wolf? What kind of people told these stories?

Lies, superstitions, witches—were the Navajo all so primitive? Anger twisted through him. What the hell was he doing here?

What he wasn't doing was his job. He'd let his emotions, old baggage, take over. Where the hell was his control?

He lost it every time he was with Ainii. Here, even miles away, he couldn't escape what she evoked within him—some inward draw that tugged within and without, pulling him to her.

Had he leaned to her? He winced at his weakness. It was her hand at his jaw, her warmth as she drew him close to whisper.

I'm afraid, too. His heart jumped at the remembered words.

Fear lived in his nightmares, he told himself fiercely, not in his life. And not in his job. The day he succumbed to the terror wrought by the murderers he sought was the day he would have to quit. That would never happen.

What Ainii had mistaken for fear was anger. It snapped at him, made him edgy and irrational. He had better get it under control or he would never solve the murders and get the hell out of here.

Jackson rolled the Jeep to the shoulder and pulled out his notebook. He meticulously, dispassionately recorded the conversation, until he reached his response to Ainii: *You're crazy*. His pen hovered. Her expression filled his mind: her eyes luminous, assessing him. She had stared, unscathed by the insult—her only reaction a brief flicker of surprise—then her gaze settled calm, as if his words had unveiled a secret to her.

He knew in his gut, though, *she* was the one with secrets. Like the one she mentioned to Bill: a promise she had made to Irene not to tell. In nearly the same breath, the conversation had turned to Clah and the murders. What secret? Why was this Irene so scared? Something told Jackson he might find that information very interesting.

Jackson pulled the Jeep around to the other side of the road and drove on the shoulder until he could see the post. Ainii's truck was still there. He parked under a sprawling cottonwood, turned off the ignition, slumped down, and waited.

Three cigarettes later, he spotted Ainii. She paused at a truck full of Navajo and spoke with a girl. She looked so slight against the hulking truck frame: Her shoulders barely reached the bottom of the window. For the life of him, Jackson couldn't tear his gaze away.

Ainii raised an arm, played with the brim of her hat. She looked sideways at the girl, not straight on—not with the directness Jackson knew so well.

He sat up and looked closer. Something was wrong and he had the sudden urge to go find out.

That was absurd. If there *was* anything wrong, he would be the last one she'd want to see—after the words he'd thrown at her.

He scrunched down in his seat, watched, and waited. Finally, she waved goodbye and climbed into her own truck, one slender jeans-clad leg after the other. Jackson's gaze ran up the slim length of her, snagging on the creases of her jeans. He still had that image in his head when she pulled onto the highway.

Jackson took off his jacket, rolled up his shirtsleeves, and pocketed the sunglasses. He drove back to the post and parked next to the overcrowded truck. When he got out, he made sure to smile at the kids. The eldest girl returned a half-smile. *Good.*

He peeked into the post—not enough to be seen by Bill, just enough to serve appearances. He turned to the jeep, shaking his head.

"Must have just missed her," he said loud enough for the girl to hear. He reached for his car door and glanced at her, offering a sincere grin.

"Hi. You know, I was just here with Ainii Henio and there's something I forgot to give her. You know where she went?"

Her smile faded and she furrowed her brows, considering him. "Probably home," she said finally.

"She mentioned something about stopping in on Irene. You have any idea who that could be?"

All six kids stared at him. "You should ask *Hastiin* Sanders." She looked away, obviously hoping to end the uncomfortable questioning.

"I just hate to bother him." Jackson played a hunch. "Looks like he's trading with a woman right now."

She stared ahead. The four boys, more curious, stared at him. The collective silence effectively shut Jackson out. For just an instant, he regretted his intrusion and also wished it weren't so—that he weren't the outsider.

That sentiment wouldn't get him what he wanted. He took a step toward the post. "You're right. I should just ask Bill."

Jackson caught the girl's quick glance.

"She might be with Irene Johnny," she said quietly. "In Pine Springs."

"That's the one!" He slapped the side of her truck enthusiastically. "Thanks."

She nuzzled the baby in her lap, her expression once again disinterested.

Jackson drove until he could stop out of sight of the post and check the map. He circled the spot of Pine Springs and smiled. He couldn't have asked for better: a tiny settlement, by itself, far from any towns . . . and authorities. He'd bet Irene Johnny had never met an FBI agent.

Dust furled in plumes of canyon-red from the back of Ainii's truck. A bit more brown to it than the sand in Ruins Wash sixty miles south. A subtle difference, but enough to inspire the weavers of Two Grey Hills. Like the foothills of the Chuska Mountains, dense with infinite cedars and junipers, Two Grey Hills weavings were packed tight with color—over one hundred threads per inch. All the weavings, that is, except for those made by Margie Torreon. Margie's rugs, like everything else in her life, did not conform.

Ainii would never forget the first time she had met the infamous Margie. Ainii had been fourteen and it was the third night of the Night Way: the night she and other young girls danced away their childhood. Her father's friends—medicine men and singers, hand tremblers and stargazers—had come from every corner of the reservation.

Ainii had heard the tales of Margie: stories that she had lived in the past and could see into the future; she could talk to the animals and communicate with the stars. Ainii had expected a big woman, large enough to carry the legends surrounding her; instead, Ainii's father had introduced a plump, short thing—round and squat as an orno baking oven—her small face lined with wisdom, as if thoughtfully carved over the ages by the Holy Ones.

Margie had taken Ainii's hand and wished her well with the young men that night. And then the old woman—ancient as all knowledge—had giggled: the tinkling sound a child's delight that Ainii had heard all that night and through the next morning.

Over the years, others had not been so charmed. Instead of magic and mystery, they saw sorcery and dark secrets. Instead of being inspired by a woman excelling at a man's craft, they were suspicious. When Margie decided to weave, she didn't create the classic Two Greys of her region. No, she preserved her drypaintings in rugs and nearly every singer on the reservation denounced her. Drypaintings were created for a patient, endowed with power during their creation and so destroyed during the ceremony. No reputable healer, guardian of the power of sandpaintings, would dare challenge the rules of ceremony. No one but Margie Torreon. If anyone knew how to bait *Yenaldlooshi*, knew the secrets of the drypainting, it would be Margie.

That is, if Margie Torreon, the old rebel of Shiprock, was still alive. Ainii hadn't seen her in five years—since the day Ainii had buried her father. Even at the ceremony for her friend, Margie had stood apart from the others, her face stern and her gaze always—it had seemed to Ainii—focused on her. Afterward, Ainii had quickly left to find a new home, far away. She didn't speak to Margie that day. She couldn't face the knowing eyes of the woman who had never retreated from a confrontation.

Ainii told herself again, as she had every day since, that her father would not have wanted her to get involved. He would have approved of her choice to leave, move far away from Clah and his lies. That she was here today, asking questions about *Yenaldlooshi*, would not make her father happy, but all she needed was some advice from Margie, something to steer Walker in the right direction— then she could retreat to her sanctuary.

Ainii pulled up to the rambling homestead. At the hub sat a large stone hogan. Radiating out, in an awkward circle, were two trailers and several smaller hogans for the extended family. A few honored goats, kept secure by the sawhorse fence encircling the whole enclave, moved slowly away from Ainii's truck.

She parked and stood in the drive, waiting patiently for someone to notice her arrival. On a cool breeze came the sounds of livestock and, from the distance, a dog's bark. The children were most probably herding the sheep.

After long, silent moments, Ainii walked around the side of the hogan, through a small grove of stately cottonwoods. Filtered by the leaves came the lilting sound of a woman singing. Beyond the trees, in a clearing, stood a huge loom, and sitting on a pile of folded rugs was Margie.

"*Ya'at'eeh,*" Ainii said.

Margie looked up, her crinkled face beaming. "Ah, there you are! Did you bring the corn pollen?"

Ainii started, baffled by the question. "No," she answered.

"I'll have one of the grandchildren get mine," Margie offered, then went back to her rug, humming.

"Margie, it's Ainii Henio." Ainii walked to the front of the loom to face her.

Margie looked up, still smiling. "Why, hello, Ainii Henio."

"You knew my father—"

"Yes, yes. *Hastiin* Henio. He knew things, more than others."

Ainii stared at her. Margie's words were the ones used by those hinting at witchcraft, but her eyes twinkled playfully. Ainii wondered if the old woman had crossed forever to the in-between. Doubts played at her, but she had to try. "Margie, my father knew more than he could tell me."

Margie's eyes hardened with keen focus. "More than he could tell anyone, *shi yaazhi.*" She picked up where she'd left off on the thread and her song.

"It is sad that he died without sharing the knowledge," Ainii continued.

Margie stopped weaving and her gaze lifted to the horizon. "What is sad is that he died because of lies."

Her words tore straight to Ainii's heart. Margie looked at her, the lines in her face deepening. "What is sadder still is that he heard no one say the truth while he lived." Her eyes glistened and old emotions rose swift and biting in Ainii.

She had to look away. Her chest tightened, squeezing the pain higher, until it burned up her throat and behind her eyes. She should not have come here.

Margie shifted and, leaning on a mahogany stick, she stood with difficulty, then walked past the loom, without a glance to Ainii. Ainii rose to leave, but couldn't ignore Margie's labored steps across the yard. She came around the loom and took Margie's arm.

"Can I help you?"

Margie took Ainii's hand and squeezed, then she smiled, her gentle face full of sad understanding. Tears sprang to Ainii's eyes. She wanted to huddle in Margie's arms, release all the grief and ask forgiveness.

When she looked to Margie, the old woman's face was straight ahead, her gaze fixed on a sandy spot where children's toys rested in miniature dunes. She let go of Ainii's hand, stooped for a rake, and then smoothed out the play area, working slowly, one hand managing the rake, the other leaning on her cane. Yet her strokes were careful and methodical. She was focused on the task, so much so that Ainii wondered if Margie remembered her standing there.

Margie spoke quietly above the shush of shifting sand. "In the beginning, First Man, First Woman, and Coyote emerged and realized they had left evil. They sent Diving Heron to retrieve evil from the underworld. They gave some witchcraft to Snake, but he could not swallow it, because Snake is the guardian of all things sacred. He had to hold the poisonous powers in his mouth."

Margie set down the rake, then straightened from her mahogany cane, as if she'd gained newfound strength. Before Ainii's eyes, the old woman transformed to a wise chanter. She drew a spiral in the center of the square of sand and, with a jagged line from the spiral to each of the corners, she divided the area in fourths.

But that was wrong, Ainii thought. The solid connecting lines left no escape for the powers contained within. Had the old chanter forgotten?

Margie moved around the square, telling the story as she drew. "First Man and First Woman also saw they were in a dark world. They made a deal with Sun: Sun would bring light, but only for a certain amount of time. For this service, someone would have to die every day. But First Man and First Woman planned for everyone to live forever. There was to be no death."

Margie ran the cane through the sand, creating doodles of lazy squiggles. The rhythm of her strokes crawled into Ainii, hypnotizing her.

"Now, on this day, Changing Woman and Wolf had two daughters: White Corn Girl and Yellow Corn Girl. They were killed, but the Holy Ones revived them. This angered Sun and he kept the masks of the Made Again children, the *Alke'na ashi*. And the *Alke'na ashi* were no longer two girls, but a girl and a boy."

On the lower half of the square, Margie drew two figures, a male with a round head, the female with a rectanglular head.

"The *Alke'na ashi* warned the People of hearing whistles when no one was there, they warned of dirt falling through a smoke hole, and they warned of visions of near relatives.

"We all have evil within us," Margie continued, "placed there by Changing Woman. A little thing, small as a grain of dust, implanted in the base of our baby heads. The seed of evil stays there all our lives, causing us to have evil thoughts, bad dreams, and to make mistakes."

The tip of the cane pitted the sand and soon a pox of small dots surrounded the two figures. Spider legs of chill ran down Ainii's spine.

Margie moved around the square of sand, adding lines with her cane, filling out the picture.

"At death, our evil goes north to the dark afterworld and the ghost is released."

Suddenly Margie looked up, her knowing eyes searing through Ainii. "What do you see, child?"

Ainii stared at the completed drawing and gasped. Margie had drawn the sandpainting of her father's ceremonies. Ainii's memory filled the dry lines with color: indigo blue, cobalt black, sun yellow, blood red. She saw the Navajo world, the mountains, the sky, the rocks, the animals, those that slithered, and the ones that ran. She saw it all, at once and individually, each meaningful line, every mythical stroke. The power of the drawing pulled at her core and terrible quaking seized her insides. In that instant, she was the child crouched in terror as her father, alone, baited the beast, challenged *Yenaldlooshi*.

The feather touch of an old hand at her shoulder brought instant calm.

"What do you see, *shi yaazhi*?"

Ainii looked into Margie's gaze, then quickly away, trying to hide her fear from the medicine woman. "I see the world of the Navajo swirling within the four quadrants, Grandmother." The term of respect and endearment came naturally. "Earth and sky, dark and light, good and evil, male and female."

"Do you feel it here?" Margie laid her hand on Ainii's belly, the exact source of her inner turmoil. Her muscles lurched violently at the touch as if to push off the chanter's hand. Ainii tried to step back, but the old woman's strength held her.

"*Do tah!*" Margie's command stilled Ainii. "Do not back away. That's the hand of Changing Woman. You feel her power, yes?"

What Ainii felt was beyond words. Her stomach clenched and twisted, doubling her with horrible pain.

"Stand on the spiral now!"

Ainii's heart rebelled, pounding wildly in her chest. The

powers of the cosmos were trapped in that drawing. She wanted to yell, *I can't do this!*

Be like the hawk, Ainii. Stare at the fear. Her father's words shored her and Ainii's legs obeyed without her direction. She walked without seeing, with only his words as the focus, and found herself at the center of the drawing, standing on the spiral. She had a moment of horrible calm, a stillness born of sheer fright, an instant teetering on the edge of a nightmare.

She would have run, but she couldn't move. The essence within all things, the good and bad, tore at her with desperate fingers. She heard a song, its tones rising higher and louder. And each note fed the fury of the drawing's powers and sped the fear through her veins. She felt the spiral turn, pulling her down, sucking at her toes, then ankles, then knees. A scream died in her.

Six

⌒

Something thumped Ainii on her chest. Hard. She peeked an eye open, then shut it against the blazing sun.

"*Biyooch'iid, shi yaazhi*," Margie said harshly.

Who lies? Ainii couldn't form the question. A second thump deepened the pain, straight to her heart.

Ainii tried to brush away Margie's hands.

"Hush. *Nika'iishyeed*."

"Your *help* hurts, Grandmother." Ainii pushed up on an elbow and turned to her side, bumping against Margie's knees. She squinted up at the old chanter. "Why do you hit me here?" Ainii touched her sore chest. "And who lies?"

"I was mad," Margie said only, then stood and shook out her skirts.

The pain took Ainii's heart and squeezed until her eyes stung. She had disappointed Margie—just as she had her own father. He had been right to not want to train her.

It came to her just then how great her father had really been. He had spent hours creating the painting while, with each grain of colored sand, the powers had mounted; then he had stepped within, willingly placed himself at the vortex, and withstood the terrific battle. And he had done it all alone.

"This will have to be enough," Margie said.

"What do you mean, 'enough'?" Ainii tried to stand, but her knees buckled. Margie reached a hand and pulled

Ainii up, then held her straight at arm's length, her steady gaze kind but unwavering.

"You came to me for knowledge, Granddaughter. I gave you part of the sing. Now you will not be so harmed."

Suddenly Ainii understood. A medicine man cannot perform a sing without first having experienced it as a patient, otherwise the powers he called on could be crippling. "Don't worry, Grandmother, I won't do the ceremony. I can't."

"You can't alone, *shi yaazhi,* that is true. You need your other half. Your father carried both halves within him. He was a rare one." She smiled. "But you will do fine."

"I didn't come for the sing, Margie. I wanted only some clues, some information about *Yenaldlooshi.* Something to help the man who hunts him. Not me. It was never for me."

The old chanter's eyes flickered sharp, like a knife's blade striking stone. "You failed because you followed your mind, not your heart. What trouble the mind can talk you into! Only your heart knows the truth!" Her finger jabbed Ainii at her chest, the same sore spot. "What called to you was your heart. What carried you to the spiral was your heart. And what awakened you, with some help"—she tapped lightly this time—"was your heart."

Ainii nodded, not wanting to disappoint the chanter even more with any protests. She hadn't followed her heart, she'd been pulled by the powers and swallowed whole in fear. If only she had remembered to stare at the fear, if her mind had been stronger!

"You can do this, *shi yaazhi,* you have the passion."

A cold hollowness spread through Ainii's chest. "I'm not my father, Margie," Ainii managed. "I'm not even Arland. He had the training, not me."

Margie's eyes flashed bright—her hard stare matching her stern voice. "Arland is gone," she said sternly. Then her gaze softened. "Your father said and did things he regretted, *shi yaazhi*. He also admired you.''

"Stop it, Grandmother." The sudden emotion in her throat stunned Ainii. She swallowed painfully. "That's past."

"No, Granddaughter. You chose to act by coming here. Now you must make other choices. This time the swirl of evil is bigger."

Margie's meaning pressed full weight on Ainii. "Whatever it is you think I can do, I can't."

"You know that you can do more than crush herbs for poultices."

Margie's voice came quiet, the hiss of an arrow, swift and sure to Ainii's heart. Ainii fought the instant reaction of her body. She took a shallow breath, then another, deeper, to stabilize. Then it struck her that Margie had somehow learned of Ainii's life . . . all this time. Instead of adding to Ainii's anxiety, the thought filled her with calm assurance. She found the courage to face Margie. "I don't need to do anything. The federal police are here, Margie. They will catch *Yenaldlooshi*."

"You believe this?"

"That's why I came here. To get advice. I thought there might be something I could tell him to look for, something he's missed . . ."

"Who?" Margie looked at Ainii with interest.

"The special agent in charge." Ainii thought of Walker. She saw the hard lines of his face—so uncompromising. Yet his eyes revealed depths of emotion just within his control.

"I see."

Margie's tone drew Ainii from her thoughts. She caught the old woman looking at her with interest.

"Then you can tell him of the marks, *shi yaazhi*."

"What marks?"

"The claw marks left by *Yenaldlooshi* on his victim. The magic wolf has five claws—not four like a timber wolf."

"Five, like a man," Ainii murmured. Suddenly Ainii

had a thought. "You could do the ceremony, Margie. You know it."

The medicine woman's eyes gathered so much sadness, Ainii's heart clenched. "No, *shi yaazhi*. He does not come to my call."

"You've tried." The realization struck Ainii cold. Margie had tried and failed?

"Yes. I tried." Margie took up her cane. "But this one is not what he appears. He is more than a were-animal, more than a witch." Margie walked to her loom; with each step her back hunched more, her steps came more difficult. The old woman had replaced the chanter. Her fingers found the ball of yarn. "You will also need something of *Yenaldlooshi*," Margie said, already weaving. "Your father did not need such things." She paused, as if trying to remember where next the thread went. Ainii sensed the old woman's thoughts were with her friend— someone who understood with her the weight of power. Then her hands found the work. "But you will need something."

Then Margie chuckled and the lightness of the sound threw Ainii off balance. "So, did many young men give you gifts?"

Ainii struggled to catch her meaning, then thought of the Night Way. When the young bucks finished a dance, they showed gratitude and respect with a gift. "Yes, Margie. My favorite was a turtle carved of turquoise."

"Ah, good gift. Did that young buck win?" She winked.

Ainii approached the loom. "No, but I kept the turtle."

"Good, good. The turtle knows you can't get anywhere unless you stick out your neck." She looked up and Ainii saw a glint in her eyes. "He also teaches the importance of balance. You will learn this, I think. Like the children of Changing Woman and Wolf. They know that once something happens, it will happen again." Margie picked up where she'd left off on the thread and her song.

* * *

Ainii sat in her truck and stared at the grove of cotton-woods. She thought of Margie's last words: *Once something happens, it will happen again.* Any Navajo understood the meaning: Life was a precarious balance—once mischief struck and found a weakness, it always struck again, and again, until the imbalance was corrected and tranquillity returned.

Her life had once been tranquil—just two weeks ago—before she had talked with Irene, before she had filed the complaint on Clah, and before she had met Jackson Walker. She now saw that those isolated actions had taken over her life and controlled her.

All because of Clah. Because of him, she was reliving her father's dishonor and death. Because of him, she was reliving her own cowardice. If not for him, she would have her life as it was in the canyon. Clah was dead and his evil with him. Yet, when she could finally lay the past to rest, instead she was caught in the fabric of his evil—entangled with the past as she sought advice to catch the killer. Clah's killer! Why should she care?

Anger washed away the ache, like cold water cleaning sand from dirty wool. The answer came with ease: She didn't care and she didn't have to be involved. That task would fall to Jackson Walker.

She started the truck and pulled it slowly around and through the front gate, separating the flock of hens, their bodies a quick flutter of orange.

Ainii rounded the last corner of her canyon and saw Irene's truck sitting outside her hogan. Her heart immediately lightened, but her smile died when she saw her friend.

Irene's face was swollen with tears, her eyes red, her cheeks flushed.

"Irene, what's wrong?" Ainii walked to her, arms outstretched.

"You promised."

Irene's cold voice stopped Ainii midstep. "What?"

"You promised not to say anything."

"I didn't—"

"An FBI man. He questioned me."

"But Irene, I didn't."

"He asked about you. Our friendship." Irene's eyes filled with tears. "Maybe did I know Clah?"

Ainii's mind raced with possibilities. Had Bill told Walker? Was Walker following her? A quick sob escaped Irene. Whatever had happened, the distraught Irene needed help.

"Come in, Irene, please. You need to talk."

"Who else would tell him?" Irene's plea drew Ainii's arm around her shoulder. They walked to her door.

Suddenly Irene stiffened and stopped. "No, I can't. I have to get back."

Ainii comforted. "Just come in for a bit." Ainii guided Irene inside and settled beside her in the sunny place by the loom. "Irene, Walker is interested only in who murdered Clah and the others. Not in you or what you've done."

Irene looked out the window. "I lied to him."

"Oh, Irene."

Irene worried her hands in her lap, wrapping the fabric of her skirt around her fingers. "I know that's bad, but—"

"You have to tell him the truth, Irene." Ainii saw Walker's eyes, cold and full of purpose. He had undoubtedly scared Irene to death. "I'll go with you."

"*Do tah!*" Irene's wide eyes were full of terror.

"Lying only makes it worse."

Tears spilled from Irene's eyes. Ainii wrapped her arms around her and rocked the sobbing girl. "Ahhh, *shi yaazhi.* It's okay. You were scared. We'll go together to see Walker."

Irene pulled away. "You don't understand. I lied to you, too."

The fear in Irene's eyes stabbed Ainii. A cold swirl of foreboding unfurled in her chest. "What about, Irene?"

Irene's gaze pled for understanding. "About Clah."

The coldness spread. "What about Clah?"

"I went to him again." Her brow creased as if against some pain. "I wanted to wait for you," she hurried on.

"Irene, it's okay. There's nothing to forgive."

"I believed him."

"I know."

"I *begged* him to help." Her laugh caught on a sob. The sound sent chills through Ainii. Irene stood; her words came in a rush. "I told him I risked everything to see him. Albert's anger, his mother's anger. Even yours."

The coldness froze in Ainii. "You told him I made you promise not to see him?"

Irene faced Ainii. The sun at her back cast her face in shadow, but Ainii could feel the wealth of sorrow.

"He told me not to worry. That great medicine men are misunderstood. He told me to take off my blouse so he could heal the witchcraft." Her monotone unleashed shivers within Ainii. "I did as he asked. He watched. His gaze was cold. I closed my eyes so I wouldn't see him."

Irene wrapped her arms around herself. Ainii rose to her, dreading to hear what came next, wanting to stop Irene, knowing Irene had to, finally, say everything.

"He told me a witch had shot a bone through my navel. He would have to follow the path to get it out. His lips were cold on my belly."

Ainii pulled Irene into her arms.

"His fingers were cold on my breast."

Ainii hugged her tight.

"They were like ice. And he squeezed hard." Irene shook in Ainii's arms. She held her, rubbing her back, though her hands ached to clench with rage.

"That's when I knew," Irene said, her words muffled. "I pushed him off."

A rush of relief swept Ainii. "You got away?"

"He tried to stop me, then he just laughed." Irene looked at Ainii, her eyes full of apology. "He said, 'Tell Ainii Henio, *Ya'at'eeh.*' "

Ainii's knees gave. She stepped back, shaking. The full

horror of his words pushed her down to the ground. "Irene, I'm so sorry."

Irene sat close to Ainii. "Ainii, Albert came home after me. Angry. I know he followed me. I know—" Her voice broke. "He won't talk to me."

Ainii heard the words, but didn't understand—as if Clah's evil existed, clutching at her thoughts.

"Ainii, that's why I lied. You understand?"

Irene's plea reached Ainii. "You lied to protect Albert. I understand. But Irene, Albert didn't kill Clah."

"I don't know," Irene said, her whisper full of hope and doubt.

Ainii looked at the girl, damaged by Clah, so afraid. She couldn't tell Irene about *Yenaldlooshi*. The terror of the shapeshifter would destroy her. "Believe me, Irene. I know Albert couldn't do it."

She took Irene's hands. "Walker will know it, too." Irene's warm clasp clenched Ainii's heart.

She walked Irene outside. Dakota sprawled on his back, soaking the sun on his belly. He rolled lazily to his side and smiled at the two women arm in arm.

"I'm glad you came to me, Irene. It will be all right. I promise."

Irene hugged her. "I knew in my heart you were right. I just didn't listen. I believe in you, Ainii."

Ainii watched the truck until it disappeared from the canyon. In the wake of its rumble, silence washed in. At that moment, she never felt more alone. Because of Ainii's name, Irene had suffered at the hands of Clah. Because of Ainii, Irene's torture persisted at the hands of Walker. Contrary to Ainii's reassurance to Irene, Walker might actually think he'd proved his theory and found the missing murderer of Clah.

But he was wrong! What she needed was some evidence, some small proof that Walker couldn't ignore.

She would find something at Clah's. Search his hogan, his belongings. She would give Walker evidence, then he would have to believe in *Yenaldlooshi*.

Ainii shuddered, then willfully clamped down on her fears. She could do that. She had to. Then Walker would have to hunt the shapeshifter.

It was late. He didn't care. He knew he should stay on the highway to Chinle, call it a day, give up, go to bed.

That was a laugh. He hadn't had more than catnaps in three days.

He faced Black Mountain. Low clouds threatening rain matched his mood: dark and brooding. The Jeep's still headlights captured a fraction of the whole desolation stretching to Clah's hogan.

God, this place was relentless. Nothing about it easy or customary. Least of all the people. He'd driven here straight from Irene Johnny's, tired. Tired of badgering for information and hitting stone walls; tired of provoking wide-eyed stares of fear while lips held tight silence; more than anything, tired from within—from frustration and anger.

Oh, he'd learned Irene knew Clah. She couldn't hide the instant reaction in her eyes when he'd mentioned Clah's name. He could have broken her silence in a heartbeat at the station, except he had no reason to haul her in.

If anyone deserved the third degree it was Ainii—if only to give him the satisfaction of, for once, keeping control around her. And, he had to admit, he wanted the chance to break through her cool facade. It had to be a facade. No one with that warm touch, those eyes—that gaze that seemed to see all—could remain detached.

In fact, she wasn't detached. She had the uncanny ability to tap into his feelings, draw them to the surface, and put a name to them. Even if that name was wrong.

With a curse, he forced out his wandering musings about the mysterious Henio. The woman was a damned distraction, nothing more.

He started the Jeep and drove to the hogan with no thoughts—only determination to get the job done. The swirl of dark clouds around Black Mountain gave the place a surreal atmosphere, almost cartoonish, like a picture of doom drawn by a heavy hand.

Any moment, lightning should curl through the clouds with the threat of godly power. He could feel the electricity and his anticipation grew.

A rumble of thunder rolled down Black Mountain. Jackson could feel the growing storm's energy in the ground beneath his feet. This time, he would not fail.

The sky hung low and dark around Black Mountain. Gauzy wisps of gray reached down from the clouds but never touched the red earth—the rain defeated by rising desert heat. Yet the clouds grew, doubling, darkening, full of threat and foreboding as if building forces for the final assault. A broadside gust of wind rocked the truck. Ainii let the tires find their path down and up another arroyo. If the clouds won, a rush of water would claim the now-dry arroyos in minutes. And she'd be stuck on the solitary end of the road to Clah's hogan.

She stifled a shudder and pushed on, fighting road and wind. It was only a hogan, she told herself, and she sought only evidence—something to push Walker in the right direction. But she couldn't ignore the violent spectacle of dark clouds circling Black Mountain, as if the Holy Ones—drawn from the four sacred mountains—amassed here, angry and impatient.

Ainii prayed their impatience was with Walker and not her.

Her gaze caught sky, then earth with each bounce until, with a gasp, the truck gained the final hill. And there, before Clah's hogan, was Walker's Jeep—unmistakable and startling.

Ainii cut the engine and sat. What was he doing? How would she explain why she was here? She saw him as he was at Bill's: his keen eyes judging her, his last words trying to insult. A swell of purpose brought her hand up to open the door and pulled her from her seat.

She walked around the hogan and saw a barrel held the door open. The smells of life, death, and decay pushed beyond the threshold, flooding through her, around her, past her in a rush downhill. Ainii braved the assault and stepped into the hogan.

Scant evening light, shrouded by clouds, cast the inside of the hogan in cavelike gloom. A sudden crack of thunder raised the fine hairs on her arms. Then, to her right, the darkness moved slightly. A shadow, close to the ground, mutated to the silhouette of a man. It was Walker, hunched over, intent on something, seemingly unaware of her presence.

"Walker?"

No response.

Ainii took a few steps toward him. His hand was pressed to a pile of rugs. A strip of masking tape stretched above his hand and another came to a peak below his hand. She took a step closer and realized the tape made a crude outline of a shoulder and arm. Clah's shoulder and arm. And where his heart would be lay a swath of deep reddish brown, the color of boiled mountain mahogany—the color of dried blood.

Walker was focused totally on his hand, on the stain, his whole body curved to the task. The gravity of his focus drew her closer and she saw his eyes were closed, as if searching inward. Like a medicine man.

His long fingers splayed across the blood and suddenly it was her father's hand, laid on the chest of a patient, seeking the source of distress. The image came to her full-blown, unbidden, her as a child at the side of her father as he worked his powers, solemnly. For an instant, she smelled the burning sage, felt once more the ardent *life* in the air with such intensity her heart swelled with pride and love.

The memory dissolved and before her was only Walker. Except now she questioned her own assumptions about this man. The arrogant FBI agent was gone. In his place knelt a seeker, a man on his own quest of understanding—

doing what, at one time, long ago, she had dreamed of doing: to gather knowledge. She would be kneeling there, her fingers to the fibers, absorbing all she could . . . and knowing what to do.

That would be her. Except her father had judged her inadequate.

In her place knelt Walker, a man who had called her crazy. Who didn't believe in *Yenaldlooshi*. Ainii's throat tightened and her eyes burned with unshed tears. She swallowed hard and denied the claim of her emotions—they served no purpose. She should be relieved: Jackson Walker had the medicine man within him, however impossible that seemed.

She watched quietly, barely breathing—a witness to something powerful.

Thunder boomed. Light flashed through the hogan. And Walker was staring at her.

Ainii lost a breath at the sight of his face. Savage lines drew him taut, wild. His eyes, small and shiny, narrowed on her with such fierceness her heart jumped. Yet she stared, enthralled by what she saw in their depths—as if what he knew, what he sought, what he *feared* were all right there, coalescing to a certain knowledge.

"Are you all right?" She reached a hand to him.

His brows drew inward and his eyes widened. The cloud of fury lifted in his gaze, replaced by confusion and fear—then, just as swiftly, steel control. "What are you doing here?"

His voice, deeper than the storm's growl, more coarse than crumbling earth, pulled her to him, to kneel next to him.

"I came to help."

Her calm voice dispelled the last vestiges of violence coursing through him. For a desperate, irrational moment he wanted to cling to the images. However frightening, they seemed less dangerous than the uncontrollable calm her voice evoked: like warm rain drawing his head up in surprise, then drowning him. He forced control into his voice.

"That's interesting," he said. "Now, why would you want to help me?"

She withdrew her hand. "I thought you might need it," she said simply.

He had a nearly maniacal urge to laugh. Hell, yes, he needed help. Help restraining himself from grabbing her. He'd make her promise to leave him alone, stay out of the way, stop manipulating his damned emotions. The iron gates of his guard clanged down.

"You didn't know I'd be here, Ms. Henio. Just what are you looking for?"

"Evidence of *Yenaldlooshi*. Something to make you believe."

"That won't happen. So you've wasted your time." Jackson stood and wiped his palms on his jeans. He walked to the door, but Ainii didn't move. "You're trespassing on a crime scene, Ms. Henio."

She looked at him with that all-knowing gaze that stripped him defenseless. "How do your powers work?" Her words came on a breath, light as a whisper, and with more punch than a trained fist.

"What?" Jackson managed.

"Your powers. What you were doing here."

He looked for a hint of sarcasm or morbid curiosity. Instead, he saw sincere interest in her eyes and something more he couldn't name, and that made him uneasy. "What I was doing is my job."

She cocked her head. "No, I mean with your hand. Pressed to the blood. How does that work for you?"

"It's just a method." Jackson heard the irritation in his voice. "I . . . I was thinking."

"Do you think like the victim or the murderer?"

The question stunned him. She looked at him, forthright, attentive. He couldn't answer. He didn't even have the answer anymore. "It's not as easy as that," he finally said.

She looked at the rugs, held out a tentative finger to the bloodstain. "No, I'm sure it's not easy." She turned back to Jackson. "I saw that in your eyes."

"You saw nothing but frustration," he said.

He could tell her what he saw. Her gaze invited him, told him she would listen and understand.

That was a lie. No one could understand, even if he had the courage to explain. He held the truth close, out of the light of day, because no *good* citizen would want to hear what Jackson knew: that evil wasn't something "out there," lurking, an entity confined to godless souls.

Evil existed within, along with all of man's traits: goodness, kindness, a talent for math. We all had the capacity. Some just practiced harder than others. For others, evil came naturally.

For Jackson, evil was there to be exploited, turned against itself. That's what he did best, until now.

Thunder boomed right over the hogan. Its power reverberated down the mud walls and across the floor.

"Seems the Holy Ones are also impatient." Ainii stood. "I would not like to be the one who frustrates them."

She walked past him out the hogan door. Wind whirled her long hair in a crazy swirl, as if unseen hands drove through the mass and became entangled. He could nearly feel the cool silkiness between his fingers. Jackson clenched his fists.

"But you do it so well," he mumbled.

Seven

〜

They stood in the middle of nowhere, a storm raging around them. Behind her, in the distant sky, jagged streaks of lightning knifed the horizon. The wind buffeted her, yet she seemed to easily hold her ground—so centered and not the least bit concerned. As bolts of electricity searched the barren ground for an upright target, she stood calm, as if protected by an invisible shield.

It occurred to Jackson that Ainii was the perfect lightning rod—a conduit through which all extreme energy could pass without hindrance . . . without hurting her. Yet she was such a slight thing. He knew he could sweep her up with no effort.

Damn, she was beautiful. Jackson felt a powerful tug deep in his gut—one he would never have expected to be evoked by any woman he met in this place.

He reined himself in. "You better go now." He flicked a glance to the threatening sky.

She faced him, her eyes full brown, assessing—again. Irritation crawled under his skin. What the hell did she want from him?

Then she walked to her truck, opened the door, but didn't climb in. Instead, she grabbed something and slammed the door. Jackson saw she carried a flashlight. Without a glance his way, she continued to the side of the hogan.

"What the hell are you doing?"

"What I came to do." The flashlight's beam swept the ground ahead.

Jackson followed her around the hogan with the walk of a man helpless against a woman's will.

She stooped and pointed to a print. "There."

"A paw print."

"Look at the size, Walker."

"So, it's a very large paw print. Do you plan to show me every animal track around the hogan?"

She swiveled on the balls of her feet and looked up at him, her gaze keen, matter-of-fact. Jackson wondered what it would take to see a flash of anger in those eyes. And, once there, would she be able to control it so readily?

"You're not very observant, are you?" she asked.

"I'm adequate," he replied.

She stood and the space between them shrank. "You're better than that. I saw you in the hogan. And I've seen it in your eyes. You just don't think this matters."

"You're right. I already told you you were wasting your time."

She considered him. "How do you know this doesn't matter?"

"I deal in facts, Ms. Henio, not myths and legends. Not the primitive superstitions of—" Jackson stopped himself.

She smiled. "I see. And you get *facts* when you lay your hand on the victim's blood?"

She'd done it again. Twisted him around until he was the one on the defense. "*What* I do and *how* I do it is my business."

She took a step toward him and the gap between them disappeared. "But you can't explain it, can you? Why, Walker?"

"I don't have to, Ms. Henio."

"Let me help."

"Why, Ms. Henio?" He lowered his voice, coaxing a confession. "Why is it important to you to help me?"

She paused. Then, "You don't know what you're facing."

Her gaze betrayed the conviction of her words. In the moment it had taken her to answer, Jackson saw a great need in her eyes. He'd gotten through, cracked her armor. Now he wanted nothing more than to pull her close.

He fought the urge to reach a hand to her. "No offense, Ms. Henio, but I know more than anyone I can think of. Certainly you."

Her face sobered. "Determination and arrogance will get you only so far, Walker."

"They work fine for me," he said.

She opened her mouth as if to say something, then closed it. She started for her truck, her shoulder lightly brushing his arm. His hand shot out and stayed her. "Don't—" Don't what? He didn't know his own thoughts anymore, just that he didn't want her to leave.

She gave him a half-smile, the kind that comes from a place deep inside. "I know you can do this, Walker. You have the *ha'taalii* within you."

Her words separated them. Jackson let his arm drop. Her eyes saddened and her gaze slid from him to the horizon, taking with her something Jackson knew he would miss.

She gave him a quick glance, then turned to her truck. "Look at the prints," she said. "Then look at the marks on the victims." With that she stepped into her truck and left.

A drop of rain fell on Jackson's nose, another on his cheek, followed by more on his head. An icy trickle slid down his back as he watched Ainii pull away. He stared after the taillights even after the drops turned to slashes of rain, until the night consumed the truck and thunder drowned out the truck's rumble. All that was left was stone-cold blackness as far as he could see—as if nothing but night existed: no stars, no promise of dawn . . . no Ainii.

Jackson walked numbly to the Jeep, slid in, and started

it. Its noise echoed eerily, muffled by the suffocating darkness. He'd never felt so alone in his life.

At the bottom of the first hill, the slant of rain and curve
of the road almost tricked him. He got back on the path,
his attention fully engaged. He negotiated shallow gul-
lies—already awash with runoff—and thought ahead to
the deep arroyo he had to cross. Had Ainii made it? He
shifted with fierce purpose and gunned the engine.

The road cut through rising sand embankments to the
mouth of the arroyo . . . no sign of Ainii. Jackson stepped
into the cutting rain and walked to the edge. His boots
sank in wet sand. He could hear the ominous roar of water. Then he saw it.

A rush of water, branches, and sagebrush drove through
the arroyo. He looked hard past the rain, across the wid-
ening creek, to see Ainii's truck. Nothing. Maybe she'd
made it. Moments were all he had, or he wouldn't make
it.

He ran back to the Jeep, slipping twice. He took the
Jeep down, down, to the flooding arroyo. Arms stiff, gaze
fixed, he challenged the rising stream. The angry water
bullied the Jeep, rocking it, pushing it, slamming the sides
with fierce surges. Was he on course? Would he come out
on the path or would he be facing the steep bank? He
tried to steer slightly against the torrent to compensate.
The back tires slid, gripped, slid again. He gave more gas,
just a little, holding his breath, praying for traction.

He saw the other side. Then something slammed the
Jeep. Water splashed in and over. The world was a sheet
of water.

The engine died. The steering froze. The front of the
Jeep turned downstream. Jackson tried the ignition. Once,
twice. Grinding, sputtering, the Jeep didn't respond to him
but to the water, its hulk taken in the force.

Jackson grabbed the handle and tried to open the door.
Water seeped in, then rushed over the threshold. He
shoved with his shoulder, but the current muscled against
him. Furious at himself, at the water, Jackson punched the

side. The water slammed back at him. Suddenly the door yanked open.

He was staring at Ainii.

For a second he questioned his sanity; then he saw the rise of land behind her. The Jeep must have careened into the bank.

"Get out!" she screamed.

Already the mad rush of water was hauling the vehicle away, out of Ainii's reach. Then he saw her step into the water.

"No!" he yelled, sure that she would die.

The river swelled, pulling him from the Jeep. Or was it her hands? He felt her arms around him, clinging fiercely. Jackson grabbed her waist and pulled her to him.

"Hold on!" he yelled. He fought for a foothold, fighting the mad rush of water. They made it to the bank and scrambled up the side. Ainii sank in the sand.

"How . . ." Jackson stopped to breathe. "Where did you come from?"

"I drove farther down. Crossed where the river was wider . . . the water shallower." Her words came between breaths. Her hair clung in thick rivulets to her cheek, down her back.

"You saved my life." He knelt next to her and, with two fingers, smoothed a wet tendril from her temple. His hand found her shoulder. He rubbed his thumb across her collarbone.

Her lips parted; her eyes widened. Her breath came shallow. Her composure was slipping within his hands. He could taste the promise of sweetness on his tongue. Only inches away, he could capture those lips.

She looked at him, spiked eyelashes framing dark eyes. "One time determination and arrogance didn't work for you?"

The smile in her eyes drew him closer, toward her, to her mouth. He slid his thumb up her neck, felt the quick pulse at her throat. His own heart jumped in response.

A kiss. Just one. Then he could dismiss her—get past

this obsession with her. One kiss would break the spell. "We'll see," he said, a breath away.

His words fanned her lips. His mouth brushed hers, then pressed. Ainii's senses swirled with his smell, his taste: earth and rain, bitter tobacco and a sultry smoothness. The layers and depths pulled her in, seeking more.

She stretched toward him, a silent quest. Jackson shifted; his mouth covered hers. His response to her, immediate, welcoming, drew her hand to his head. She combed her fingers through wet hair.

On a groan, he pressed her down to the earth. His hands raked through her hair, tangling, pulling her closer. Suddenly the whirlpool had narrowed, drawing her deeper, past thought, past curiosity. His urgency drove through her, to her core, back to their lips, and through her again. Until all that existed was a cord, pulsing, connecting them.

Without warning, Jackson stopped. Ainii's lips throbbed at the sudden release. She threw her eyes open and her heart jumped at his gaze. He glared back, angry, confused, as if surprised to see her. A question ran deep in the darkness of his eyes. Ainii felt wet sand against her back.

"Why?" Her voice betrayed the emotion lodged at her throat.

He didn't answer, but pushed up from her and stood. Cold air swept Ainii, drawing a shiver through her. Jackson stretched a hand to her. Ainii took it and Jackson pulled her from the ground, as if she were weightless, something he barely noticed. When her feet were grounded, he dropped her hand.

Ainii wanted to reach to him, but instead drew her arms around herself to stave off the growing chill. He stared at the arroyo, its mad rush of water subsiding. It occurred to her he was like a flash flood: a sudden torrent, dangerous, even lethal, that just as abruptly disappeared into the ground to hidden reservoirs.

She knew better than to dare forces of nature. And Jackson was a force unto himself.

"I'll give you a ride," she offered and started up the slope to her truck.

"Thanks," he said after a moment.

She heard his reluctance, knew he still stood there. She could even feel his gaze on her back, then heard the soft smoosh of wet ground beneath his footsteps.

"Where are you staying?"

"Chinle. The Holiday Inn."

He sat far to the side, the cool maleness of him rising from his wet clothes. He had a prickly, pinched look about the bridge of his nose and eyebrows, and a dangerous, cornered cast to his eyes. His presence dominated the small cab, as if her cargo were a quiet but lethal mountain lion.

His silence clawed at her—a fierce, angry silence, coiled tight within him. With each dark mile, the silence accumulated.

Ainii took a deep breath of the weighted air and tried to bring order back to her emotions. He couldn't be angry at her for interfering, because she was only trying to help. He couldn't be angry at her for pulling him from the river—that was absurd. If he was angry about the kiss . . .

The thought drew her blood fast, just as his kiss had. She could still taste him on her lips. She could feel him against her, his mouth pressing.

Or had she pulled him to her? Had she imagined his response, the urgency in his hands through her hair?

She couldn't deny that something within her had clicked as she watched him in the hogan. Feelings she'd buried years ago had rushed to the surface—a tide of jealousy and awe, and more: a connection with Jackson, a thread of understanding and surprise. He wasn't what he appeared.

She remembered Jackson's eyes in the flash of lightning—sharp with fear and frustration, as if pushed past the brink of endurance. Not the calm gaze of a medicine man, but the tortured look of a sorcerer whose powers had run amuck.

Was it always this way for Jackson? Ainii glanced at his dark, brooding reflection in the windshield. No, she didn't think so. It suddenly occurred to her that perhaps his anger was colossal frustration—whatever it was he did, this time it wasn't working.

Maybe Bill was right and they couldn't count on Jackson. A frisson of anxiety ran through Ainii.

Ainii pulled into the motel parking lot and slowed. Jackson already had the door open before she'd come to a full stop.

"Thanks for the ride," he said as he stepped out.

The white glow of the high street lamp underlined the shadows beneath Jackson's eyes. He didn't look mad anymore, just exhausted.

"Don't give up, Jackson."

He shut the door soundly and looked in at her through the window. Wet hair curled slightly at his temples, softening the hard lines of his face. "Right," he said.

"Determination and arrogance, remember?"

He gave a half-smile. "You're a puzzle, Ms. Henio."

"Ainii," she offered.

A shriek cut through the night. Ainii turned quickly to look out the back window.

"It's the frogs," Jackson said.

Ainii let out her breath. "The frogs. Of course." She looked back at Jackson and found him staring at her. "I'd forgotten about the frogs," she said quietly.

"You get used to them."

She smiled at the memory of their croaks coaxing her to sleep as a child. "You're right."

Jackson actually smiled back.

"They're a good omen, you know," she offered.

His face sobered and the exhaustion returned. He straightened from the window, his hand still on the rim. "Thanks again for the ride," he said and walked away.

She watched his long strides eat the ground to the double-door entrance. She was the puzzle? The man was a walking mystery. What made a man like Jackson tick?

And when, she wondered, had she begun to think of him as Jackson?

Ainii pulled away from the motel and started on the lonely highway back to Ruins Wash. He'd become Jackson to her the moment his breath had touched her skin and his lips had pressed on hers.

"The paw print of the Northwest Territory wolf, also known as the timberwolf, may reach five and a half inches."

Jackson spread his hand over the drawing in the book. His fingers reached beyond the wolf track in the picture by an inch. The paw prints circling Clah's hogan exceeded the reach of his fingers by several inches. Which made the tracks at Clah's hogan nearly twice as big as a timberwolf's—the largest wolf known in North America . . . and never found in Arizona.

Jackson slammed the book shut. More puzzle pieces that didn't fit—just what he needed.

He leaned back from his desk and stretched, the creak of his chair the only sound in the deserted headquarters. From the corner of his eye he spotted the black-framed clock high on the bureau wall. Six in the morning. Breakfast time.

Jackson rose and headed for the vending machine. With a clunk, it delivered a can of orange juice. He leaned against the machine as he took a couple gulps and let his bleary gaze wander over the dark office he called home.

For two days he had lived here. They'd replaced the Jeep yesterday and he could have returned to Chinle, but he'd never considered it. If he couldn't sleep, he might as well work around the clock.

Here, he kept his focus . . . most of the time—except when his mind wandered to Ainii. Images of her stole over him, captured his thoughts, entangled them. Instantly, he was back at the arroyo, his fingers caught in her wet hair, the moment snaring him, his senses alive with the touch and taste of her. He experienced again her lips against his, felt the rush of awareness when she arched to him—the fundamental *rightness* of her in his arms.

He relived it. Over and over again, the scene replayed. Each time, his body ached toward some conclusion. She was like a drug and he was close to an addiction.

Jackson shook off the musings. She was a distraction and whatever time he spent thinking of her was time he lost on the case.

He pushed off the wall and wandered the office, rotating and loosening his neck muscles. He stopped at Nez's desk. The bright yellow corner of a file peeked from beneath some papers—the medical examiner's file. Jackson pulled it out and took it to his desk.

An hour later, as agents arrived, Jackson was only peripherally aware of the morning noises. He'd found the DNA report and another puzzle piece.

The scrape of chair legs across from his desk told Jackson Nez had arrived. "Have you read this report?" Jackson asked.

"You look awful," Nez said.

"Thanks for the editorial."

"You know there are cots in back by the washroom. When's the last time you slept?"

Jackson raked fingers through his hair. "I found this on your desk."

"Course, the nice thing about Indian blood is that you don't need to shave often."

"Are we done with the personal hygiene lesson?"

Nez laughed, walked to the coffee machine, and filled his mug. "The report must have come in while I was testifying at the Harrison trial," he said, returning to his desk. "Something interesting?"

"Yeah. The DNA." Jackson handed over the file and waited for Nez to read through it. Nez raised his eyes and Jackson knew the agent had reached the summary.

"*Canidae* DNA?"

"Canine. Includes dogs." Jackson paused before adding what he could barely believe. "Also includes wolves and coyotes."

"They found this mixed in with Clah's blood?"

Jackson nodded.

"And no human blood besides Clah?"

Jackson and Nez looked at each other. "So an animal killed Clah." Nez shook his head. "Amazing."

Jackson nodded, but his thoughts were on his hand touching the blood. His mind responded instantly to the memory with a charge of adrenaline and a powerful surge of violence. Just beyond his grasp was the mind of the killer, but he sensed a purpose, a righteousness, the presence of cognitive reasoning. His mind rebelled from the implications.

"That explains the savagery."

Jackson jerked back to the conversation. "Yeah."

Nez's look made Jackson wonder what the agent had heard in his voice. Jackson took a gulp of warm orange juice and winced.

"So, now we call the Department of Fish and Wildlife. They get to pull out their rifles." Nez closed the file. "Case closed on Clah."

"Guess you're right," Jackson said.

"You don't believe the report? You're the one who pointed out the inconsistencies in the condition of Clah's body compared to the girl's and Newcomb's."

"You're right." Jackson's mind clutched for the logic. That's why he hadn't been able to get anywhere with Clah—the murderer was an animal, not a human. It all made sense now.

Clah had been killed by a wolf. It was ironic. Ainii was right. Though this wasn't what she had meant. Jackson willed down the nagging sense he was missing something. He pulled out the files on Wynema Begay and Newcomb and stood to leave.

"You gonna tell the chief and call Window Rock, or you want me to?"

Jackson paused. "I'll call them. Go ahead and notify

Fish and Wildlife.'' He added Clah's file to the others and left.

Two hours out of Phoenix, Jackson neared the cutoff to Nazlini—the road to Ainii. A cloudless blue sky defined pink sandstone bluffs, the very picture of Southwest serenity. It bade him to follow. He felt the tug at his core. He had only to slow down, turn the steering wheel, and the Jeep would take him to her.

The urge to do just that rose swiftly within him, becoming a desperate need, and all the more forlorn because he had no reason to see her—and probably never would again.

He accelerated past the turn without a sideways glance.

The radio crackled just as he cleared the next rise. ''Agent Walker, respond.''

Jackson picked up the mouthpiece. ''Walker here.''

''It's Nez. I've got a strange message here for you from the M.E.''

''Yeah?''

''Quote, on Clah there appears to be five parallel strokes. On Newcomb and Begay, four, unquote. You know what this is about?''

Jackson swerved to the side and stopped. ''I asked him about the groupings of slashes, any patterns.''

''Any particular reason?''

Because Ainii had told me to. ''Just checking everything,'' Jackson said.

There was a pause. ''Groups of five on Clah,'' Nez said. Jackson didn't like the ominous tone.

''What's the problem?''

''Wolves have four claws, Walker. The fifth is way up on the side, like a dog's.''

Jackson pictured the paw print from the book—four toe pads, with a small dot past the end of each representing the claw marks—four.

''But the DNA . . .'' he said aloud.

''Maybe it's a mutant wolf.'' Nez laughed.

Jackson willed down the images gnawing at him.

"I haven't called Fish and Wildlife yet," Nez offered. "What do you want to do?"

Jackson checked the traffic and did a quick U-turn, back to the Nazlini road. "I'll get back to you," he said and clicked off.

The blacktop was a blur, the scenery nonexistent. Jackson's mind struggled to comprehend the incomprehensible. Five marks on Clah—five, like the number of fingers on a hand—and canine DNA. Four on Newcomb and Begay, but no trace of prejudicial DNA.

Soon, dust flew from the Jeep's tires, then small rocks, then he was on the cliff road, with no recollection of driving there. The Jeep careened in a breathless slide down the canyon road to the valley.

He charged single-mindedly back to Ainii's hogan, with only one purpose: to learn everything Ainii knew about *Yenaldlooshi*—the stories, the superstitions, the details people believed. Someone had gone to an awful lot of trouble to make it look like Clah had been killed by a myth.

Ainii heard the Jeep. It could be Bill. It could be a couple of other people. But she knew it was Jackson. Her hands stilled at the rug. Anticipation and anxiety stormed through her. She had thought of nothing but Jackson—the arrogance in his eyes, the vulnerability on his lips. The mixture potent, like the calculated dose of *datura*—too little wouldn't heal, too much could kill.

For two days she had thought of him, the primal force of him. He harbored power, strong like her father's, yet different. For all Jackson's arrogance, he was not in control. Not as much as he'd like to be, she knew. She sensed a constant struggle within him: layers of dark and light, good and evil.

He was a tapestry of conflicts, varied, complicated, with ragged edges, loose threads that threatened unraveling. And she wanted to know more: more of what made him, what held him together.

She listened to Dakota's barks and wished, just this once, that the dog would be quiet. She wanted to concentrate, hear the Jeep, gauge its approach. Maybe then she could tell what feelings Jackson bore.

Dakota challenged the Jeep all the way to the door. Jackson knocked unceremoniously, without respect. He wouldn't know the ritual, she reminded herself. Not that Jackson would stand and wait for anyone.

The hard raps reverberated through her. *Be like the Hawk, Ainii.* She took a breath to still herself and opened the door.

He filled the space, looming huge and formidable. His arms bracketed the opening, as if warding off escape. In his eyes, she saw a slight softening—quick, then gone. She knew, in that instant, he was as apprehensive as her.

"*Ya'at'eeh,*" she said.

He stared at her blankly, as if not comprehending, then ducked and entered the hogan. He walked to the middle of the room, turned, and faced her. The spacious area suddenly shrank in his presence. He stood still, staring, as if rooted to the spot—like the trunk of a massive oak tree.

She would give him time to decide why he'd come. Ainii passed him and settled at her loom. She picked up the thread of black sumac and let her fingers weave. She knew Jackson watched her; the energy from his gaze tingled in her hands. She wove the thread in and out, conscious· of every movement, of the placement, of the rhythm . . . and of Jackson. He drew closer and crouched before the loom.

"Tell me everything you know about *Yenaldlooshi.*"

Ainii stared at the man crouched just beyond her loom, his focus so intent. She had thought she would be relieved when this moment arrived and Jackson accepted the truth about the magic wolf. But now that he had finally decided to listen, Ainii's heart crested on a flood of emotions.

Would he really be the one to face *Yenaldlooshi?* Did he have the strength that eluded her?

Ainii gazed on Jackson, his eyes shining with purpose, and she sought the words to guide him.

Eight

"Charlie Tahi tells a story," she began. "One night he was driving the highway to Tuba City and saw a Navajo in his rearview mirror. The man was running right behind the tailgate, keeping pace with the truck. Charlie could see the man's torso: his naked chest strung with necklaces, and his arms pumping easily up and down. Charlie sped up—he was going seventy-five—and the man disappeared. Next thing, he heard breathing right beside him. Charlie looked and there was the man running alongside. Suddenly the man took off from the road and, as he vanished into the trees, he turned into a wolf."

Ainii watched Jackson for signs of disbelief, but his gaze was solemn and intent, as if hanging on every word. "There are many stories of the magic wolf. He is huge, three times the size of a coyote: four feet high and four feet long, not including the tail. And he is very swift. He can outrun a horse. The magic wolf's tail hangs straight down. The tail of a real wolf sticks straight out from behind."

Jackson wrote fast in a small notebook. She understood his action: The investigator side of him would need the facts.

"Horses smell were-animals and warn humans. They jump, neigh, even scream," she continued.

Jackson gave no reaction, just wrote.

"The witch goes naked at night," she said, her gaze

on Jackson. "He wears only paint—black and blue with white and yellow spiders—and many necklaces—jet, coral, maybe even turquoise."

Ainii's pulse quickened at the memory of her father's stories. She didn't see Jackson anymore. She was beside her father, listening to him, learning well. Of all the medicine men, her father knew more than any about the magic wolf. He alone had faced *Yenaldlooshi*. She would never forget what she had seen in her father's eyes: fear born of knowledge—the only true fear.

"What else can you tell me?" Jackson's voice, low and steady, pulled her back. She gazed at the man opposite her—so controlled, so intent. His eyes held no fear. He could do this, she thought. Perhaps he was even meant for this, unlike her.

"*Yenaldlooshi* gets his power from magic powder, made of ground parts of human infants, especially the skin whorls: from the fingers, toes, nose. If he doesn't kill his victim, he bewitches them, shooting the powder on the unsuspecting person at a large gathering, like a Blessing Way. Or he might sprinkle the powder through the hogan's smoke hole."

Ainii's fear for Jackson grew with every word. Yet Jackson sat quietly, writing. Did he truly understand what he faced?

"A man who can transform to *Yenaldlooshi* is the most powerful of witches." She paused, needing to see in his eyes that he understood.

Jackson glanced up. Ainii leaned forward, her gaze locked on his. "He can be killed, Jackson—by just an ordinary bullet—but few would try. If you fail, you would be bewitched; and if you succeed, his relatives, who most probably are witches, would seek vengeance—still you would be bewitched." Ainii looked at Jackson. Would he be the man to succeed? Her throat constricted at the awful evil he faced.

"What does *Yenaldlooshi* mean?" he asked.

"It means, 'he who trots along here and there on all fours.'"

He closed his notebook, stood, and paced in front of the loom. "How do you know so much about the shape-shifter?"

That she would not tell him; her father, his knowledge, belonged to another life. "I told you, there are many stories about *Yenaldlooshi*."

"Stories," he murmured, looking at her. "Stories mothers tell their children." He was so close, just the other side of the loom. Yet Ainii sensed a purposeful distance—calculated and controlled, like the stiff parallel warp threads separating them.

"Children are raised to be wary of the night," she said. "They heed the sounds of their horses and dogs. They learn caution with their bodies: to bury anything personal—hair pulled out by a brush, nail clippings, excrement. Most of all, the Navajo guard their privacy, their thoughts, their songs. Like all possessions, these things can be stolen—witches *need* to steal these things to survive. This is what mothers teach their children."

"So everyone knows about this *Yenaldlooshi*." He raked a hand through his hair.

"Yes," she said.

"Anyone would know what he supposedly does, what the pattern is."

Something about Jackson's tone made Ainii uneasy. "Except how to bait him," she offered.

His sharp glance cut her off, as if her words were meaningless. He looked back at his notes. "And the claw marks?" he asked. "You left them out of your description."

"Medicine men know *Yenaldlooshi* by his tracks. The magic wolf has five toes."

"Only medicine men know this?"

His gaze chilled her, the hard, detached look of Hawk. "Medicine men and those they might confide in," she answered, carefully.

"Why the secret?"

"Knowledge is power, Jackson."

His keen eyes stared hard. Did he see her secret? Ainii looked away. "You found the five marks, yes?"

"Yes, five," Jackson answered. "On Clah."

"What do you mean, 'on Clah?' "

"Whatever was used on the trader and the girl left four parallel lines, not five."

"*Yenaldlooshi* killed only Clah." She understood now Jackson's frustration, but not his cold stare.

"Someone knows," Jackson said, staring out the window. "Someone knows enough to plant all the right clues at Clah's hogan."

"What did you say?"

"Whoever killed Clah knew everything about the shape-shifter legend. And, according to you, that somebody would probably be a medicine man."

"Yes," she admitted. "Medicine men must know some witchcraft in order to protect and heal. They are valued . . . and distrusted." Grief rushed through Ainii, too swift for her to stifle. She felt the sting of it in her throat, behind her eyes. Her father had not deserved the distrust.

"A medicine man would know just what to do."

Jackson's voice drew her attention. He still stared out the window, his face drawn in thought. Abruptly, he turned and headed to the door. "Thanks for your help," he said over his shoulder.

Something wasn't right. Something in his easy stride pulled her from the floor. "How will you catch him?" Balls of yarn fell from her lap and rolled freely.

Jackson stopped and looked at her. "That's my job," he said.

"But how will you bait him?"

"Bait?" He shook his head. "Don't worry, Ainii. Thanks to you, I know where to look now."

"Where?"

He considered her. "You said it yourself. Clah was a fraud, pretending to be a medicine man. It makes sense he angered people, people who considered themselves the real thing. Somewhere out there is a medicine man with a grudge and enough hatred to kill.''

"A grudge?'' His words slammed her chest, loosening all the captured emotions. He hadn't come to understand *Yenaldlooshi,* he'd come to get the ammunition to hunt a medicine man—someone who would know how to *act* like the magic wolf.

Ainii stepped around the loom. "You're a fool, Jackson Walker.'' She walked to him. "No, you're worse. You're a fraud. Do you deny the power inside you? Do you deny there are things you can't explain away, things you can't list neatly in your notebook?''

She saw the fury build in his eyes and didn't care. "Why can't you believe?''

"You seriously expect me to believe in a shapeshifter?''

Ainii studied him. The hard lines of his face were even more uncompromising. "Yes,'' she said quietly.

His thunderous look darkened. Ainii let the storm pass through her. She took it in; the violence in his gaze shook her to her toes. When it passed, she saw the core of his anger. "It is good to be afraid, Jackson, if that fear comes from knowledge.''

"I'm not the one with fear in his eyes. You are. What is it you're afraid of, Ainii? That I might prove these stories are just myths?''

"I'm afraid you'll die trying, Jackson Walker,'' she whispered.

The stricken look on Ainii's face cut through Jackson and struck sparks against the thin wall guarding his emotions. She truly believed in the shapeshifter! He thought of the stories she related, the power and danger of the wolf—she'd offered them to help him, because she had actually thought *he* believed!

The notion was absurd, and yet, the power of her confidence in him sent a jolt through Jackson. From the moment Ainii had opened the door to him, he had wanted to pull her into his arms—but no more than now, as he heard the conviction in her voice that he faced mortal peril.

It took all his strength to step back. "I appreciate your concern," he said and turned to leave, but not before he saw the final bit of hope she'd had for him extinguish in her eyes.

Jackson eyed the man at Nez's desk. There was something familiar about him, though Jackson was sure he had never met him. He would remember another Navajo agent and this Indian definitely had the stance of an agent or a cop. The two men stopped talking as Jackson approached.

"How's the interrogation of medicine men coming?" A smile pulled at the corners of Nez's mouth.

Jackson smirked back. "I think you know."

Nez laughed. "That bad?"

"They could teach rocks about silence. I've never met so many tight-lipped, stone-faced people."

"What was your question?" the stranger asked.

The man's matter-of-fact, I've-been-there tone confirmed Jackson's judgment. He was a cop. It was his gaze that bothered Jackson: The man hadn't taken his eyes off him since Jackson walked up. "I asked if they knew Clah, Newcomb, or Begay, and if they knew any enemies of Clah or the others."

"You mentioned the names of the dead to medicine men?"

Jackson turned to Nez. "It's an investigation, remember? We deal in facts, not superstitions. It would seem to me these medicine men would be as interested as anyone to have the murder solved and the rumors put to rest."

"Rumors of a witch hunt, you mean?"

Jackson glanced at the stranger, ready to take offense with the interruption, but the man's face was calm and serious—a look he recognized, but from where? "Witches and werewolves," Jackson responded. "It's like Halloween out there, with whispers of goblins and ghouls."

The whole time he talked, he was trying to place where

he knew this cop. He should remember this man; that face was important, was part of an important memory he just couldn't place.

Every time Jackson looked up, the man was staring back.

"That's why I brought Detective Henio in from Albuquerque, Walker."

"Henio?" Suddenly Ainii's face filled his mind. The memory of her slipped comfortably into place, with an ease that instantly annoyed him. He focused on the brother and it occurred to him that the tribal records had mentioned only Ainii and her father. He had to be mistaken about Detective Henio.

". . . asked for his help."

Jackson saw the detective's hand extended. He looked at Nez. "Help how, Nez?"

"He's from here."

"So are you," Jackson replied.

"So are you, for that matter, Walker. And you're doing a great job relating to the locals."

Jackson shot Nez his best glare, then turned to Henio. "Thanks." This time he extended his hand. "But I work alone."

"I understand," Henio said. "So do I."

Jackson heard Ainii's voice: the same calm acceptance. They had the same oval face, the same bone structure, except Ainii's cheekbones were higher and her eyes were wider. He looked at the detective's eyes. There was something else different about them.

". . . had a similar case." Nez's words cut through Jackson's thoughts.

"What?"

"Tell Walker what you told me, Detective."

"There was a girl in Canoncito just last year and a judge in Albuquerque this spring. Both torn up pretty bad."

"Any leads?" Walker asked.

"None."

"No connections?"

"We just heard about the girl. The tribe had kept it a secret."

"Tribe?"

"The Canoncito Navajo. A small reservation in western New Mexico."

Jackson sat on the edge of his desk. "A tribe of Navajo kept a murder secret? How? Why?"

"The Navajo of Canoncito keep to themselves. They don't talk about suspicious murders of young girls."

"So how did you find out?"

"A trader in Albuquerque overheard his silversmiths talking. He called the police, but we got nowhere in the investigation."

Jackson stared, unimpressed. "No offense, Henio, but just how much help can you be?"

"I didn't ask to be here, Walker."

"Then why are you?"

"That was exactly my question to Nez." Henio paused. "He said you haven't got any leads, either." Henio stared back, with a look neither apologetic nor arrogant. It just was. Jackson liked that.

He gave a half-smile. "True. What about the judge?"

Henio's face hardened. "His name was Harold Dureem. They called him Judge Dream. As in the defendant's dream come true. If there was any loophole in the arrest, any question about a witness or the gathering of evidence, he was the answer to the defense attorney's prayers. And he was the victim's worst nightmare."

Henio's obvious contempt of the man came on each word and Jackson's gut wrenched with anger. He knew too much of the injustices inflicted by tedious robed men.

"Oh, we had suspects." Henio's face brightened with hell's flames. "Women who saw rapists walk, fathers who watched murderers go free. Plenty of people with the motive to kill the *good* judge."

He stopped and looked up. And Jackson saw the difference between Henio and Ainii. Ainii's eyes held calm purpose, as if drawn from some deep cool well within her. But Henio's eyes *burned*. He had the fire, the consuming drive to best the devil. Jackson knew that look. He saw it from the inside every day.

"So, Walker, where *are* you with the medicine men?" Nez asked.

Jackson pulled his gaze from Henio. "About done. There's one more I want to see." He flipped through his notes. "Margie Torreon in Shiprock."

"Don't bother," said Henio. "That old woman is crazy. No one talks to her anymore."

Jackson wondered at his quick dismissal. "I thought you'd been away awhile."

Henio met his gaze. "Away in New Mexico. That's where Shiprock is."

Nez picked up his case and shoved files into it. "When you decide, file your flight plan with the chief. I'm off to Window Rock."

"What about the Harrison trial in Gallup?"

Nez jammed in a legal pad. "Dismissed. Lack of evidence."

"You had a confession!"

"That's right. We also had the burned-out car and the charred remains of the old couple." He clicked his case shut. "It all got thrown out on a bad warrant. It specified weapon. Interesting that the suspect read the served warrant, then confessed."

"A con?"

"Yeah, three years in Yuma. Rape. Now he walks on the murder. We never did find the granddaughter."

"That son of a bitch shouldn't get away with murder," Henio muttered. Jackson couldn't agree more.

"What is it you hope to find at Clah's hogan?"

"It's something I want to show you." Jackson glanced at Henio, then back to the road. "What did you see at the crime scenes of the girl and the judge?"

"When we finally learned about the girl, she'd been

long buried. A tribal cop took us to the canyon where she'd been found. She wasn't killed there."

"Tracks? Prints?"

"It had been a year." Henio grunted and Jackson understood the frustration of a cold trail.

"And the judge?"

"He was at a weekend meeting of judges and legislators. Discussing judicial review." Henio's hard, clipped voice stuck to the facts. "They found him in his cabin at Ghost Ranch," Henio added.

"Did you see the body?"

"Yes. What was left of him."

Jackson thought of Clah's body, mauled beyond recognition, and felt a twinge of awe at the power needed to shred tissue, rip muscles, break bones as if the victims were dolls. "Did you notice the marks? Was there a pattern?"

"What do you mean?"

"The parallel marks. Did you see how many?"

"Why would you count the marks?"

Jackson glanced again at Henio, but the detective was looking out his window. "Actually, I wouldn't have thought to look," Jackson admitted. "It was Ainii Henio who suggested I count the marks."

"Ainii?" Henio's head jerked around. "Why were you talking to my sister?"

So Jackson's instincts had been right. "She filed a complaint against Clah. Ten days before his death."

"You suspected Ainii?" A brother's love and protection came on every word. Jackson wondered why Henio had removed his name from the tribe's enrollment.

"Your sister didn't like Clah." Jackson didn't need to look at Henio to know the detective was staring at him.

"She was not alone, Agent Walker."

"So she told me." Jackson glanced at Henio. "Why did Ainii file the complaint, Detective?"

Henio turned, his eyes a glint of fire. "She only did what many others wished they had the courage to do."

Henio's lips thinned to a flat line. "It's not important why she did it, only that she did."

"Your sister said the same thing."

"What is your theory, Walker? You can't think Ainii killed Clah."

Jackson pulled to a stop in front of Clah's hogan. "Follow me. I want to show you something," he said and stepped from the Jeep. He noticed Henio hesitate a moment before following. Jackson walked to the side of the hogan and stopped just where Ainii had crouched three nights before. The massive paw prints stared back at him, undeniable, inexplicable. He stood to the side as Henio approached. The detective followed Jackson's gaze.

"I see wolf prints." Henio faced Jackson.

"What else about the prints?"

Henio stooped and slid off his sunglasses. "They're big," he admitted.

"Bigger than a timberwolf's. You notice anything else?"

"I see five pad marks where there should be four."

"You sure you saw nothing like these where the girl was found or near the judge?"

Henio looked again, then stood. "Just what is it you think these murders are about?"

"I don't know yet, but your sister has a theory."

"What was Ainii doing here?"

Nine

The challenge in Henio's voice was unmistakable. Jackson also caught a trace of fear—an echo of what he'd heard in Ainii's voice.

"She said she came to help me." He remembered her kneeling at his side, her hand out to him even as terror drove through him. He saw her eyes, his fear reflected within them, yet she had not turned away.

"To help you," Henio repeated. "My sister doesn't need to help you, Agent Walker." Henio took a hard look at Jackson, then walked away.

"You don't want to hear her theory?"

"I know my sister's theory," he said over his shoulder.

"Then why don't you explain it to me?"

Henio faced him, his features drawn tight, as if caught in some silent struggle. "My sister is traditional. She believes in all that makes the Navajo strong—the land, its animals, the sky and its stars, and the songs and their legends." He took a few steps toward Jackson. "So I know she told you of *Yenaldlooshi,* the magic wolf, the evil witch." With each word, his tone grew more harsh, sharper. "She would tell you he is huge, powerful, a beast more evil than all the gods." He stopped directly in front of Jackson, his eyes dark with fury. "And she would tell you he must be stopped. She believes all this."

"You don't believe this?"

Henio gave a half-smile. "The Navajo believe all

things hold both good and bad; these sides are part of the whole and necessary. Except for *Yenaldlooshi*. He alone is pure evil.'' Henio looked Jackson in the eye. ''I am like you, Agent Walker. I believe in evil.''

''What I believe, Detective, is we have a very creative murderer.'' And more malevolent intelligence than Jackson had ever encountered. He looked again at the massive print. He thought of the DNA report and the marks on Clah. He thought of Wynema Begay, Al Newcomb, the Canoncito girl, and the judge. Five murders over a year; three in the last two months. And nothing to tie them together except savagery.

It was the savagery that spoke to him, as if on a conduit straight to his core. He could agree with Ainii in one regard: The murderer was pure evil.

He found Henio in the hogan, crouched over the rugs, staring at the blood.

''Was there as much blood with the judge?''

''No,'' Henio answered without turning.

''What did the DNA report say?''

''*Canidae*,'' Henio said and stood. He looked at Jackson. ''Just what is your theory, Walker?''

''I'll tell you what I think, Detective. I think your sister knows more than she's saying.''

Henio's eyes narrowed to shards of jet. ''What do you mean?''

''I don't think Ainii killed Clah,'' Jackson said. ''But the funny thing is that everywhere I look, I keep coming across her.''

''Explain yourself, Walker.''

''She filed the complaint against Clah, but she won't say why. She pointed out the prints to me and she told me to check the marks.''

''It's as you say''—Henio's voice was cold—''she thinks she can help.''

''And then there's Irene Johnny,'' Jackson continued.

Henio's brow furrowed. ''What about her?''

"I questioned her about Ainii and Clah. The girl knows something."

"She's friends with Ainii, is all." Henio's stare challenged Jackson. "Tell me something, Walker. Do you ever think like a Navajo?"

Bitterness clenched Jackson's jaw. *Never,* he wanted to say, but the words wouldn't come. He thought of Ainii and her calm certainty. He thought of the stone-faced medicine men and the stoic Irene. He could do worse than acquiring their control. "Why do you ask?" he asked tightly.

"Because if you did, you would have a much easier time understanding my sister."

That would be impossible, Jackson thought to himself. He focused on Henio. "Your sister is protecting someone. I think Irene Johnny is that person and I think Irene is scared to her toes about something."

Henio didn't blink. "That something wouldn't be a federal agent, six-foot-four, twice Irene's size, with a nasty glare, would it?"

Jackson stared back. Then he looked away from Henio to the hovel of Clah's home, the bare mud walls, the cold smoke. Ashes and sticks lay beyond the rock circle. He looked from there upward, through the small hole. When he let his gaze fall, he met Henio's.

"A small hole for such a big beast, eh, Walker?"

Jackson was thinking this could be the perfect unsolved murder.

Elderberry, prickly pear cactus fruit, sumac, blackberry. Yarn balls of the rich, dark colors heaped the basket Ainii pulled from beneath her bed. At her stove, a large enamel pan boiled and fermented the mountain mahogany. In two weeks, she'd have the deep reddish brown yarn, and natural gray would balance light to the dark.

She could see the pattern, *feel* it at her fingertips, pushing to be created. She'd begin today—the rug demanded it.

More importantly, she *needed* to weave, she needed the process. She knew what to do. And, she hoped, the weaving would take her mind off what she didn't know how to do.

With the rug, she knew where to begin and could visualize the end. From the shearing through the cleaning, spinning, dyeing, and weaving: One led to the next and all were part of the whole. Knowledge from the ages, the pattern from all she knew—the timeless rhythm circled through her, surrounding her. Ainii sat at the vortex of the past, the present, and the future.

She settled before the loom, cross-legged on the stack of old rugs. She slid the shuttle home between the warp threads. Her fingers worked the yarn across the full span. Her hands sang with the rise and fall. The design flowed from her mind to the loom.

This was what she did. She was a weaver.

You're crazy. Walker's words stilled her hands. For a second she forgot what to do next. She grabbed the comb and tamped the row even, settling her thoughts. When she reached for the yarn, her fingers trembled.

Suddenly she saw her father's hands, his fist shaking, but with purpose. He was sprinkling colored sand from the tight hole in his fist, the fast squeeze of his clenched fingers directing the particles on the ground. A huge drypainting spread from the corner he hunched over, adding the last meticulous details. Father Sky, Mother Earth, and the Monster Slayers made the four sides, with the sacred mountains at each corner. Lightning, comets, and jagged blue lizards filled the inside. All created with intricate rivulets of sand—like a rug woven of the ground, hugging the earth.

From her hiding place, Ainii had watched quietly, with awe, and with dread. If he baited the evil *Yenaldlooshi*, would he succeed in killing him?

Then he looked at her. *Stare at the fear, Ainii.*

The image vanished and she was staring at her rug. She twisted the shuttle and pushed it higher. The wefts stretched apart, an endless pattern of lines, yet joined. She ran her fingers over the few finished rows. Single threads, layer upon layer, pulled the wefts together, making the weft and warp one in the design. It was all connected.

She didn't have to look any further than this loom to find her purpose. She raised her hands again to the threads, working the yarn, an inch, two inches. Then she saw she had woven the wrong color—the blood-red prickly pear instead of black sumac. A small thing, easily fixed—yet she sat and stared.

What will Walker do? What will he look for?

She saw his eyes, the maelstrom of emotion swirling—anger, disdain, hatred, fear. How could he possibly see past all that to any connection, to see the pattern?

A slight tug unraveled the misplaced yarn.

From far away, she heard Dakota's bark, at times loud, then soft, and she could picture him on a chase. The sudden rumble of a Jeep pulling close surprised her. Dakota's bark was still far off—no matter what his quest, he had never let anyone trespass his canyon. She listened intently to the Jeep and knew it wasn't Jackson. Knowing that, she almost lost interest. Borne forward only by habit, she opened her door just as her brother stepped from his Jeep.

"Arland." The first sight of her brother in five years brought a tide of love. Her heart swelled and her arms opened to welcome him.

"Ainii. I've missed you."

His arms held her close in a hug her heart knew from so long ago. "I've missed you, too. *Ha goshi ya?*" she whispered.

"I'm fine." He held her tight. "It's so good to see you."

His hold on her said more than his words; still, Ainii was surprised to see tears in his eyes when she stepped back.

"You could have come back anytime, Brother." She laid a hand on his cheek.

"Yes," he said.

Ainii saw his eyes sadden. She thought of the phone call. "I thought you might be mad at me."

"I was, *shi yaazhi*. I still am," he added. He squeezed her shoulder. "But my heart forgets that when I see you."

Ainii laughed, even as she wondered at his annoyance with her. "So you can stay awhile?" She slipped her arm around his waist and took him inside.

Arland stopped within a few feet and she watched him take in her home. After a moment, he walked to her loom, reached a finger to the threads, then let his hand fall to his side.

"This is how I pictured you," he said. "You've made a nice home."

"Thank you," she said.

"It's far from Chinle," he added and Ainii heard the sadness in his voice.

"Not as far as you are, Brother. So have you come back?"

Arland walked from the window. "Your phone call . . . I'm sorry I hung up on you." He glanced at her. "You have to understand. I must be careful of what I talk about."

"Why?"

"I'm a detective, Ainii. I'm supposed to deal in facts, evidence, rules of procedure—"

"Not beliefs, superstitions, Navajo legends," she finished, using the same words Jackson had used.

"I would be misunderstood."

"You mean someone might think you actually believe in these things? Like *Yenaldlooshi*?"

"Ainii, I can't afford any mistakes. I am building a life in Albuquerque. The life I had here is in the past. Gone."

The sadness she had seen in Arland's eyes, Ainii now felt in her heart. Arland walked to her. "I didn't come to scold you for the call, Ainii."

"Then why are you here?" she managed to say.

"You have to stop pursuing *Yenaldlooshi*. It isn't your job and it's dangerous." He took hold of her shoulders.

"Have you forgotten what happened to Father?"

"How could I, Arland? My whole life has been dictated by him. I'm in this canyon because of what happened to him. I'm a weaver because of him. He's in my thoughts. He guides my decisions. If he were alive, we would not be having this conversation, because Father would catch *Yenaldlooshi*."

"He also knew the risks, Ainii. He knew that those with power, even the *rumor* of power, can be turned against. He lived with that choice."

"And died with it." The grief rose swift to her throat.

"Because he's not here, you think you have to bait the magic wolf?"

"No, Arland. I couldn't. But you could."

He stared back at her. "You don't know what you ask, Ainii."

That was the truth. In those few words, Arland captured the core of their relationship: She *didn't* know what she asked of him, because she didn't know why he quit the training with their father.

He had left with no explanation and her father never discussed the reasons, though he couldn't hide his unhappiness. After all these years, she saw him vividly: his sorrowful eyes, despair creasing his face. She had wanted nothing more in her life but to please her father, to prove her own abilities . . . to be the worthy heir. But the harder she had tried, her father only grew more distressed, as if her every effort pained him with disappointment. The one her father wanted was gone.

Now Arland stood here, her brother, bound to her in spirit, in blood, but his eyes carried the same pain as her father's: telling her, once again, she didn't understand. The unfairness of that beat at her heart. Every day, she had told herself that Arland's life was his choice and he owed her no explanations. But the question remained: How could he have given up a life she would have cherished?

"Why did you walk away, Arland?" The words tumbled from her lips.

He knew what she meant. She saw him almost answer, then he turned away.

"Why, Arland?" she persisted.

When he looked back, his face was stone, his gaze devoid of emotion. "I didn't walk away, Ainii, I ran."

"But why?"

His eyes softened. "Things aren't so simple, Ainii. Sometimes it's not enough to want something, to want to *be* something."

"You could have taken Father's place. He chose you."

Arland's eyes flickered with pain and, for the first time, Ainii had a glimpse of how hard the choice had been for Arland to leave.

"You don't choose to be a medicine man, Ainii. It chooses you." His gaze implored her to understand. "I couldn't do what Father did. He understood that." He looked past her out the window to the grazing sheep. "You've chosen well, Ainii," he said.

Ainii couldn't speak past the emotions in her throat. The pastoral scene Arland appreciated no longer filled her with peace but with restlessness. Once, she had been satisfied in her canyon. Not now. And the contrary feeling added anxiety to the restlessness—and anger.

It seemed that nothing in her life had been her choice—including even her canyon, her sanctuary. She had run here to hide and she was still hiding.

"*Yenaldlooshi* will not just go away, Arland," she said to his back.

Arland turned and Ainii nearly flinched at the intensity in his deep black eyes. "No, he will not just go away. But that is not your concern, Ainii."

He effectively cut her off, just as her father had.

"Let the Feds do their job, Ainii. You stay out of it, stay where you are safe, in the canyon you love."

"Yes, that would be the safe thing to do," she murmured, and moved from the window, away from Arland.

Arland caught her shoulder and stopped her.

"I'm looking out for you, Ainii. Just as Father did. He would not want you to get involved."

Ainii couldn't look at him. She couldn't let him see what his words drew from her soul. His words took the choice from her and made it his and, ultimately, her father's choice for her—once again.

Be like the Hawk, he had said. Keep your mind clear, unemotional, focused, and you won't falter. Good advice given by a father who loved her. Arland also loved her. So why did she now feel trapped by those words?

When Arland left, he said he loved her, but not whether he would ever return. And his hug, though hard and long, felt as if he were already far away.

The beast circled the pile of hot rocks, pawing the ground, impatient, eager for the hunt.

Deep in his mind, the human part, he controlled the impulse to leap into the darkness. It was not quite time. Later, when all the stars beckoned and the night's black power reigned, then he would emerge. For now, for precious little time longer, he could rest here, hidden in this remote canyon.

The beast grunted, digging long nails into the sand, ready for the chase. Long, muscular legs, packed with speed, stomped the ground.

He breathed deep of the burning sage. The steam rising off the hot rocks filled his lungs and carried the sacred herb's aroma to every part of him.

The beast needed no sacrament, no ritual, no distraction of purpose. It had one need: to survive. Every part of the beast's mind and body, muscle and sinew bristled with that goal: to stalk and kill, stay alive at all cost. Its tail twitched in anticipation—the beast already knowing the result of the hunt, already tasting satisfaction.

He envied the beast. If only his own goal were as simple as survival or his need as primitive as filling an empty stomach. What drove him would never relent nor ever be satisfied, any more than he could extract more than life itself from the victim . . . or reclaim what he had lost.

The beast snarled, its guttural growl the sound of a nightmare no living thing could escape.

Including him. The knowledge seized him simultaneously, as always, with despair and sheer power. The terror he wielded was also the terror he endured.

No, he could not escape the nightmare, but neither could his prey. He couldn't change what he was—that had been decided for him long ago. What he could control was his choice of prey—and in that choice lay his purpose, his mission, the meaning to his life.

So he chose carefully, for he was judge, jury, and executioner. Those he chose deserved what he delivered. Each of them had once been the predator, brutalizing others without conscience, as if they alone ruled with no consequence for their actions. He made their arrogance laughable, their savagery a joke by comparison . . . and their sins unredeemable.

Whether one killed for survival or killed for justice— which act was the more noble? With each slaughter, he brought the universe more into balance.

The beast snorted, angry with the wait.

The beast's pure motive drove through him, its primal force true and his own choice clear. Both together were the balance, as was the nature of all things.

He slipped beneath the surface. The warm water welcomed him, blanketed him, flowing through his hair. The frogs swam close, their tiny legs touching him, tickling his sides, a hundred points of pressure pulling him down.

He wasn't afraid. He belonged here with the frogs. The satiny water was home.

He opened his mouth and breathed in the water and it filled him with pleasure. He swam easily, his body strong.

Rays of milky light and shadows slowly curved in graceful waves. The patterns swirled, coalesced, and through the surreal depths emerged Ainii, her black hair floating free, caressing slender limbs. She had come to him. Her calm, steady eyes, full of lightness and light, shone through him. His heart opened with an ache he could barely endure.

He buried his darkness within him, far away from her touch, protecting her.

He reached a hand toward her, but she was just beyond his fingers, drifting away. Her eyes widened in a silent plea. He tried to reach again, but his arms were heavy. The water turned icy cold. His lungs suddenly demanded air.

Yet he tried again to touch her, pull her close. He pushed his body to the limit.

She looked calm, accepting his failure. Every muscle in him screamed against the growing chasm.

The frogs thrashed violently, churning the water, chasing her away.

He called to her, desperate now. Cold water rushed through him, burst his lungs. He sank, lifeless, frozen from the inside.

Jackson gasped, bolt upright on his cot. Sweat ran from his brow. He stared, disoriented, into the blackness. Then he saw the crack of light beneath the door. He was in the station. He had lain down around six, given in to the eternal exhaustion.

He swung his legs to the floor but couldn't stand. His head throbbed with dizziness. Awkwardly, he pulled out his penlight and checked his watch: six-thirty. The half hour was about average, but he couldn't call it rest.

The sense that he *needed* something still clawed at him. He remembered Ainii, the water, the frogs. He knew enough psychology to guess that his subconscience was preoccupied with her. Hell, he couldn't get her out of his waking mind. When he thought of her, the kiss was always right there—the feel of her lips, the pounding of his heart, the craving so deep within him it was like a bottomless well.

He could bury the feelings in work, but not during the

naps, no matter how infrequent—or how acute his fatigue.

This dream went beyond his obsession, beyond his weakness for Ainii. He was not only vulnerable but powerless, the flaws building like dominoes ready to fall. He could see her eyes pleading, then receding with calm acceptance. No other woman had burrowed within him so quickly, with such certainty. His nerves tensed at the thought of her, anticipating a demand he couldn't deliver. He didn't remember her asking anything of him, yet he knew she did. She made him feel at once complete and lacking, as if he could never measure up.

Damn her expectations! He was not a mystic with powers, some freak medicine man estranged at birth. Comfortable anger swept away the confused emotions. What you saw was what you got. If she saw more in him, that was her problem and not his failing.

He pushed himself off the cot. Today, he told himself—today he would make some headway. How the hell did a person survive in this land of superstitions and legends?

By charging ahead, not like a bull, but like a turtle, slow and steady. He stopped at the door, his hand on the knob, and wondered at the analogy. When had he started drawing comparisons with animals? He shook his head. He'd been hanging around Navajo too long.

In the adjoining men's restroom, Jackson hung his clothes in a locker and took a shower. The hot water washed away the last vestiges of the troubling dream.

He dried, dressed, and brushed back his hair—his movements quick and efficient. When he strode into the station room, he was ready to take on whatever was dished out.

The look on Nez's face told Jackson it was going to start early.

"Hope you're good and rested," the agent said.

"Doesn't look like that matters," Jackson said. "What have you got?"

Nez locked eyes with him. "Another murder." He paused. "Same as the others."

A rush of foreboding swept through Jackson. "Who?"

"Harrison. The defendant," he added.

"Who found him? Where?"

"Curly Joe, a Navajo gambling at the Lukachukai Chapter House. He found Harrison alongside the road."

"What was Harrison doing there?"

"It was bingo night." Nez shook his head, as if in disbelief.

"The murderer-rapist played bingo?"

"Chapter houses draw all kinds. There's plenty of money on bingo night. Maybe he was gathering resources."

"Maybe he thought he was lucky." Jackson grabbed his jacket off the rack.

"There's something else," Nez said.

Jackson's nerves fired. "What?"

"There are paw prints, like at Clah's. Huge, five-toed."

Adrenaline pricked Jackson's skin. He knew that feeling—the one that said he was close. He could already feel the rush of images; his fingers itched to touch the new blood. This time he wouldn't fail.

Ten

Ainii could not find a place to rest. She found herself at the window, gazing on her sheep and goats. They strolled the yard, satisfied, content—their need only to graze on the next blade of grass. Why couldn't she be as content here? What was it she needed?

Not long ago, she had told Bill all she wanted was her life back. Here she was, with her life, except now she felt contrary, out of sorts—*out of balance*—as incomplete as her unfinished rug.

She had tried to settle at her rug, but the pattern wouldn't stay in her mind. The design and colors brought images: In the prickly pear fruit yarn she had seen the colored sand on Margie's drypainting; the sumac brought back the anger in Arland's face.

So she had paced to her stove to check the mahogany root yarn, dipping, stirring like a nervous beginner. But the swirls of dark color reminded her of Jackson, the layers upon layers of him—one conflicting with the next. He had come to her asking questions, yet he didn't believe her answers. She had *seen* the power in his eyes, yet she had also seen the chaos and confusion. Finally, she had felt the draw between them, the intense awareness, yet he pulled away. There were so many contradictions within the man.

Ainii gazed at her sheep. They were constant, predictable. They relied on her, trusted her. They were her family and they never found her lacking.

Her sheep were enough, she told herself. Her life was her own.

But the words were empty, meaningless, like a song unshared. This life she cherished had not been her choice, but the only one remaining for her. It, too, had been an escape. Ainii's smile faded. Her throat tightened.

She left the window and wandered her home, looking for the comfort, the solitude she loved. Her gaze ran over the room, her rug, to the pot of boiling yarn. These things used to bring her pleasure, but not today. Today she could not escape this relentless restlessness. It moved with her, more like within her; a disconcerting urge toward the inevitable.

No, not the inevitable. That would mean she had no choice.

She thought of her favorite canyon—she could ride there, spend the night. Maybe there she would find peace.

Ainii turned off the fire below the pot of yarn and walked to her door. She glanced behind her to her home, then walked out. Today none of this was enough to keep her here.

On the drive to Bill's to get supplies, Ainii's mood lightened with each mile. She could smell the pine needles and the cedar of her campfire. She could taste the jerky on her tongue. This was a good decision—to get away, leave for a while.

The number of trucks at Bill's post surprised Ainii. She parked in the field and trudged through the sand, wondering if she had forgotten the date of the auction, yet she didn't see any tourists gathered, only huddles of Navajo.

Their murmurs had a ragged edge, like a serrated knife. Anxiety sliced through Ainii. Had something happened to Bill? Ainii ran the last yards to the post. She squeezed through the crush of people and wound her way to the front, where she saw Bill. Her relief vanished with the look on his face.

"Bill, what's wrong?" She had to raise her voice to make it carry over the worried chatter of several Navajo facing Bill.

"Ainii!" Bill walked to her. "Haven't you heard?"

"Heard what?"

Bill gestured for her to follow him around the counter to the courtyard. He shut the door behind them, closing out most of the noise.

"Heard what?" Ainii asked again.

He looked at her—his face older, the lines deeper—and his gaze told her she didn't *want* to hear what he had to say.

"Ainii, there's been another murder."

For a fleeting second, Ainii considered just walking away. But she couldn't, not anymore. "Who?" she heard herself ask.

"A Navajo. His name was Harrison. Curly Joe found him outside the Lukachukai Chapter House."

Ainii knew the rest without asking. She saw it in Bill's eyes. She'd heard it in the crush of whispers outside. The wolf had taken another life. And he would take another and another and another until someone stopped him.

She felt Bill's hands at her shoulders. "The Feds are probably there now, Ainii. Now they will *have* to believe."

Her heart pounded at her chest, crushing the air from her lungs. She couldn't breathe, she couldn't talk, she could barely stand. *No, he doesn't believe. He doesn't believe.*

"Ainii, look at me."

She felt his hands on her face and realized she had been shaking her head. Ainii raised her gaze to Bill's.

"Whatever it is you're thinking, don't. Go home, Ainii."

Ainii looked into her friend's eyes, the one who would always be there for her, always protect her. She would tell him what he needed to hear.

"I—" Ainii swallowed past the emotions lodged in her

throat. "I came in for supplies, Bill. I'm going camping."

"Good, good." He brought her close and hugged her, and the fear in Ainii gripped her heart.

Jackson edged the Jeep through the crowd of curious Navajo gathered along the road at the crime scene. He glanced aside at Henio. The detective had sat silent for nearly the entire drive from Phoenix. Jackson had welcomed the silence, his own thoughts preoccupied with the task ahead. It was as if Henio understood Jackson's need to concentrate. That kind of comprehension was rare. Jackson found himself thinking that Henio probably made someone a good partner.

As if sensing Jackson's gaze, Henio suddenly turned from the side window, his features stern and grim—a reflection of what Jackson supposed was in his own face. "Navajo telegraph was working overtime last night," Henio said.

"I thought the Navajo avoided the dead."

"They do," said Henio, "but fear of *Yenaldlooshi* has drawn them together. Clan chiefs, councilmen, and medicine men have come to witness what the men in suits will do."

Jackson followed Henio's gaze out the window and saw a man walking through the clusters of Navajo, straight to the government vehicle. Jackson recognized the elder Navajo from the bench outside Sanders Trading. Henio rolled down his window but stared straight ahead.

"*Ya'at'eeh, Hastiin* Henio," the man said.

"*Ya'at'eeh, Hastiin* Gray Whiskers. You have come a long way to say hello."

Gray Whiskers gestured to the yellow tape just beyond the hood of the Jeep. "This is not so far from home for any of us." Then the old man's eyes narrowed on Henio. "Perhaps it is you who is too far away."

Henio slanted him a half-smile. "Then it is good you would welcome us after such a long journey."

Gray Whiskers stared for a moment before a smile

slowly deepened the creases of his face. He stepped back from the Jeep.

Jackson grunted. "So he does move. The last time I saw him, he was planted on the bench in front of Sanders Trading."

"*Hastiin* Gray Whiskers is a councilman. I imagine he sits at the post to hear from the rural Navajo. I've known him since I was a child."

Jackson looked at Henio. The detective was watching the stately Navajo disappear in the crowd.

"Everyone knows of the murders and that no one has been arrested," Henio continued, still staring out the window. "If you sat in the middle of the reservation, I'm sure you would hear the whispers flying from the four corners." Henio turned in his seat and faced Jackson with a gaze that seemed to be measuring Jackson's understanding. "It's no coincidence that he was here when you arrived. I'm sure he's heard many stories of the men in suits questioning the medicine men. They know who's in charge of the investigation. Now they want to see you do your job."

"That won't happen," Jackson said and stepped from the Jeep.

Officers in Arizona blue and tribal navy stood in the ravine and conferred over the blanketed mound. Jackson approached the nearest state trooper.

"Special Agent Walker, FBI. Who's the on-scene officer?"

"Begay," said a lean Navajo officer, his hand outstretched to Jackson. Then he addressed the officer next to him. "Tell the M.E. he can have the body soon."

"Cancel that order, Officer." Jackson's voice stopped all conversation. "Officer Begay, I need your men and the troopers behind the tape. Along the perimeter." He gestured to the road running parallel. "Keep the crowd back."

The officer started to object.

"Officer Begay, the Bureau fully intends to cooperate

with the Navajo Nation, but as of right now, this is my crime scene.''

Begay nodded to the other officers. ''You'll get a call.''

Jackson waited for privacy. When he turned to the body, he found Henio staring at it, his face rock-hard.

''That includes you, Detective.''

Henio stared back, his gaze serious, his eyes full of determination, and Jackson had a brief sense of connection—as if Henio intuitively understood. For a moment, Jackson experienced a fleeting awareness of alliance. But it happened so quickly, and was so foreign, Jackson dismissed the perception immediately.

He watched the detective amble down the ravine and duck beneath the crime tape and Jackson was reminded of Ainii. The brother and sister moved alike: both with ease and purpose, as if any ground they walked was theirs.

He had owned that same self-assurance before coming here, but he'd felt it only briefly during his stay—each time he'd been with Ainii. A part of him wished she were here now, looking to him with certainty, her eyes full of calm faith. She believed in him . . . but for the wrong reason, he reminded himself. She didn't see what was really inside him. No one did.

He shook off the building malaise. He had no room for doubt. He looked at the silent heap at his feet. This one held answers. He could feel it in his bones, within the pulse at his fingertips.

He crouched and stared at the white mound, picturing the mangled limbs, the wealth of dried blood. He breathed deep and the noises of the crowd diminished until soon he was cocooned in silence, alone with the victim.

He closed his eyes and the day became night. He imagined himself walking down the desolate road. He was alone, with only the sounds of darkness accompanying him: skitters of small animals, the warnings of night owls—the medley of shadow creatures he moved with. This was his element and he wasn't afraid.

Then a noise, unfamiliar, menacing as a mean whisper, pricked his skin.

"What did you see?" Jackson asked.

He felt for the cloth and pulled it back. When he opened his eyes, Harrison's dead gaze stared back at him, frozen wide in terror. He placed his hands on the man's chest, his fingers pressing against the cold body, his eyes set on Harrison's face drawn in a silent scream. Jackson looked hard, his body tensed to one point, until he felt the jolt, as if something reached in and grabbed him, turning him inside out, pulling him within Harrison. Fluid as warm blood, he flowed into the dead man.

Instantly, his heart pounded, his breath caught in his throat. All of him seized within Harrison's terror—that crystal moment when Harrison's last thoughts replayed the legacy of his brutality.

Images pummeled Jackson. He saw a man's fist raised in anger and he felt each harsh blow; a woman crouching in fear and his stomach clenched in disgust. And the rage within him grew, Harrison's rage—the child's torment desperate for release.

Then Jackson saw how the grown man took his revenge: His mind filled with the faces of victims—a collage of the brutalized and wounded. Each one was worse than the one before: a pyramid of pain, a dogged quest for fulfillment until only the ultimate rite remained—murder.

The last images of Harrison's sick mind filled Jackson. He saw the old couple, fighting to save their grandchild, their faces contorted in love and fear; and he saw the child, huddled in terror—the last victims of Harrison's rage, the innocents who had been betrayed by the legal system, lost in the paperwork . . . and a useless search warrant.

Jackson's own rage rose at the injustice. A part of him wanted to tear his hands from Harrison, from this despicable excuse for a human.

He forced himself to press his palms even harder to

Harrison's chest. He would know—*now*—Harrison's violent end.

"Who is it?" Jackson asked. "Who is after you?"

He relinquished the last of his control and gave in completely to the mind and senses of Harrison.

His heart raced, his chest pounding with tightness. His ears strained for any sound, any warning. But there was nothing. His skin pricked with the cold breath of death. Fear flooded him. He couldn't breathe, couldn't scream. He thought his heart would burst.

All night sounds ceased and, in the deadly silence, he could hear the quiet, stealthy approach of the stalker.

He whirled in panic, sure to see something, but the night, always his ally, now cloaked the enemy. Sheer terror blinded him.

He heard the crunch of great weight on dead branches. He heard a snarl, the sound so deep it shook the ground as if sent from the underworld.

He smelled fire, something burning. The pungent aroma filled him, seeping through every pore, turning his stomach, smothering him. At the moment he fell to his knees, he felt the breath of the predator at his neck. His mind, accustomed to evil, couldn't face this horror.

Claimed by the nightmare, Jackson's body rebelled, all his senses receding to darkness. He fought unconsciousness. He had to *see*, dammit! He had to watch!

But his own nightmare emerged full-blown and deadly—a madness with no images, only black terror. His felt his limbs mauled, his lifeblood draining.

Suddenly he was the attacker, the taste of triumph on his lips, the one most powerful, the wielder of fate, evil unleashed.

He was not the predator! He clawed his way out of the nightmare, his mind screaming against the insanity.

The image shattered.

Jackson breathed deep of warm air, felt the sun's heat on his back. He opened his eyes to daylight, to Harrison stretched beneath him, his hands dug into Harrison's dead body, his own body curved tense, rock-hard, so that it hurt to ease back on his heels.

He sat motionless, save for his ragged gulps of air and his heart pounding against his chest. He raised a shaky hand to his throbbing temple and stared at the ground, unseeing, stricken with the truth. He'd failed. He couldn't get past his own nightmares, couldn't function. And a part of him questioned his sanity.

He was aware of people far behind him. He could feel their curious stares on his back, could hear their nervous talk. If they doubted him, they were right. He'd stood alone for so long, been so sure of himself—but now he couldn't remember that time when he could walk past harsh whispers.

"Will you sit there all day and stare at the ground?"

He didn't know the woman's voice and didn't care, but long-borne instincts of decorum guided his hand to the cloth. He pulled it over Harrison.

"You, Mr. FBI. I speak to you."

He looked up, expecting to see a large woman to match her commanding tone. Instead, a small, roundish form stood above him on the edge of the ravine. She had the look of a plump, sturdy bush: A dark green skirt reached nearly to her toes, and her face, wrinkled as the bark on the nearby cedar, matched the deep red of the earth.

She stared back at him, surprised, as if she didn't expect to see him.

"What do you want?" His voice rumbled in his chest as it snagged past his exhaustion.

She came closer, negotiating the rocky bank with ease despite her age. She stopped only a few feet from Jackson, bent, and stared more, her furrowed brow reminding him for all the world of an inquisitive badger.

"What are you called, Mr. FBI?" she finally asked.

"Walker. Jackson Walker."

She shook her head as if he were wrong. "No, it wasn't Jackson," she said to herself and looked at him, her head slightly cocked. "But it was so long ago." She rubbed her chin with slender brown fingers. "Where are you from?"

"Dallas."

She frowned, even more unhappy with that answer. Jackson finally got the energy to move. He pushed up from the ground, ignoring the dizziness swirling through him down to his toes. "You'll have to move behind the tape, ma'am."

Though he towered over her, her eyes grew stern, the look of a mother intent on a lesson. "No, I don't think so. Then we couldn't talk. You had trouble here, yes?" She glanced at the blanketed body.

"Yes." *Obviously,* he thought to himself. He took a few steps toward the police barricade, but, looking behind, he saw she hadn't moved. "You'll have to come on, now." He held a hand out to her.

With a stern glance she dismissed his offer. She straightened and locked eyes with him. "Mr. Walker, why didn't you come to ask me questions?"

Jackson let his hand drop to his side. "What?"

"You questioned all the other medicine men, but not Margie Torreon. Why is that?"

"You're Margie Torreon?"

"Obviously." Her eyes twinkled in the sunlight. "Now tell me what the trouble is."

Arland was right—this old Navajo was crazy. Jackson raked a hand through his hair. "Listen, Ms. Torreon—"

"Margie," she interrupted.

"You have to come with me. This is a crime scene."

"I saw you at the body." Her voice lowered. "You want to give up."

Jackson stared at her in disbelief.

"Because your power is not working."

"That does it," he said aloud. He took hold of her elbow, gently but firmly.

She shook off his hand. "I am not an old, crazy woman, and you—" she poked a finger at his chest, "you are not what you appear, either. Don't pretend with me, Jackson

Walker.'' Her eyes lit with anger. ''You can't walk away.''

''Walker, what's going on?''

Jackson turned to see Henio walking up. The detective looked past Jackson to Margie. His eyes narrowed on her. ''What are you doing here?''

''Your father would wonder the same thing, Arland.''

Jackson heard the concern in her voice and looked between the two of them. Margie gazed at Henio thoughtfully, but the detective's face was hard.

''I had no choice,'' Henio said. ''And you?''

Margie shook her head. ''So you told this nice man not to talk with me?''

Henio didn't even look surprised at her accusation. ''I told him the truth, Margie. That you're crazy.''

Her eyes sparked. ''Yes, some people say that. But not your sister, Arland. She does not say I am crazy.''

''Ainii's not a part of this, Margie.''

Even Jackson couldn't miss the threat in Arland's voice. Instead of answering Henio, Margie faced Jackson. Her gaze fixed him to the ground. ''Listen to me. You cannot do this alone and neither can she.'' She nodded to the horizon and Jackson's heart leaped at the sight. A horse and rider with a dog alongside took the ground slowly. There was no mistaking Ainii, her slim figure silhouetted in the sun, bent to the side as if studying the ground.

He scrambled to the top of the ravine. ''What is she—''

''She tracks *Yenaldlooshi*.'' Henio was at his side, his voice a harsh murmur.

Jackson clenched his fists. *What the hell was she doing?* He flexed his fingers and felt his palms unstick—evidence of Harrison's torturous death lay in the creases. His mind leaped instantly to the horrible images and his heart pounded, as if facing an immediate threat.

''Will you let her go alone, Jackson Walker?'' Margie asked calmly.

''You're an old fool, Margie,'' Henio hissed. ''And

she's worse.'' He nodded to the disappearing horse and rider. ''She's forgotten who she is.''

Jackson had the nearly overwhelming urge to flatten Henio. The irrational impulse ricocheted through him, racing ahead of his logic, stirring his emotions. He faced the detective head-on, charged with some need he couldn't name. Henio's eyes, focused on his sister, full of love, sobered Jackson. ''Go get your sister, Henio,'' he said.

Henio's jaw clenched. ''She won't listen to me.'' He gazed at Jackson, the emotion in his eyes unmasked, there for Jackson to witness and envy—the intense bond between brother and sister. The look vanished in a veil of dispassion—so rapidly, Jackson wondered at the will compressed within Henio. ''You will have to stop her,'' Henio said, then turned his back and slid down the ravine gracefully. He scrambled up the other side and slipped into the crowd of Navajo.

Margie whistled—the sound like that of a small bird— and an old mare jingled up to Margie's waiting hand. Silver beads decorated the horse's mane and small bundles with stalks of plants sticking out hung from the horn and saddle.

Margie gently stroked the horse's neck, but when she faced Jackson, her eyes were fierce. ''And you, Jackson Walker? What will you do?''

Jackson stared after Ainii. *Damn her stubbornness*. She had no business being out there. He couldn't take his eyes off her gradually diminishing form.

''You can do this, Jackson Walker.''

For a second he thought it was Ainii speaking. Those were her words. He felt a hand on his arm and jumped. The old medicine woman looked up at him, her eyes glistening with understanding.

Suddenly his choice was clear: He had to stop Ainii. He would catch her, bring her back, put her in a straitjacket if that's what it took—anything to keep her safe.

He took the reins from Margie. ''Detective Henio will give you a ride home.''

"Gray Whiskers has already offered." She smiled knowingly and Jackson stared down at the improbable woman. "You knew I would go?"

She gazed to the now-empty mesa, then back to him. "How could you not?" she said simply, then walked to the ravine. "You *must* go after Ainii," she said over her shoulder.

Jackson stared at the improbable woman as she easily negotiated the ditch. *Of course he was going after Ainii.* That thought hit him with the double edge of need and annoyance—the two emotions he would forever associate with this interminable place.

He turned the horse to the mesa. Maybe he'd just ride like hell out of here. That alternative pounded through him with each drum of the horse's hooves on the hard earth. *What difference would it make?* He'd been nothing but aggravated since he got here: by the Navajo, by his own ineptness . . . and by Ainii. Yet, here he was again—going to her, chasing down the one person who frustrated him the most.

He saw her in the distance. She was so small in the vast landscape—the little band of horse, rider, and dog passing through. Something grabbed him deep in his gut, like the knot of a cord pulled taut to her, drawing all his senses to a bead on her.

He knew just when she would turn to him and shade her eyes. That she didn't look a bit surprised to see who followed her fired through him like a well-aimed shot.

The dog ran toward him barking, then suddenly stopped and returned to Ainii, as if on some command. Jackson yanked his horse up to her with a spray of dust and sand. "What the hell do you think you're doing?"

She looked at him so calmly, Jackson felt doubly out of sorts. "Tracking *Yenaldlooshi*," she said finally. "And you're trampling the prints."

"Who said you were needed in this investigation?"

She tilted her head as if his question were absurd. "No one, of course. You wouldn't ask me, would you?" She looked back to the ground and, with a soft click, picked up her horse's pace.

"Dammit, Ainii. Stop. You can't do this." He grabbed the bridle and her horse snorted against the abrupt hindrance.

Ainii's gaze shot up. "Who will?" she demanded.

The dog moved between the two horses, oblivious to stamping feet, and snarled at Jackson. He glared at the dog, then at Ainii. "It's *my* job, Ainii. Not yours."

"And when will you start doing your job? How many more have to die?" She flicked a glance behind to the distant place where Harrison lay. "Tell me, did he die in the same way as Clah?"

She looked at him calmly and Jackson couldn't lie. "Yes."

"I thought so," she said quietly. "What did my brother say about that?"

The mention of her brother surprised Jackson. "Why do you ask?"

"Why shouldn't I ask?"

She cocked her head at him and, in the way only Ainii could, made Jackson feel absurd. "He's an advisor. He's got his own cases in New Mexico."

Her eyes widened. "What do you mean? Other murders?"

Her alarm shot through Jackson and he suddenly felt protective. She didn't need to hear of more murders. At the same time, he wondered why the loving brother hadn't talked to his sister. And he remembered Arland's pronouncement that Ainii wouldn't listen to him. He leaned toward her. "He's a detective, Ainii. He investigates murders." He softened his tone. "He doesn't want you out here, either."

Her eyes flashed with anger. "That's too bad," was all she said, but Jackson swallowed hard at the wealth of emotion on her face.

"Go on back, Jackson. Do whatever it is you and Arland do." She stared at him, her eyes dismissing him, and

Jackson had the acute sense of something slipping through his hands.

Jackson's temper snapped. "You're coming back with me, Ainii," he said through clenched teeth.

"No, I'm not." With an imperceptible signal, she side-stepped her horse from Jackson's grasp. The dog stood his ground, facing Jackson.

"Ainii, you don't have any choice."

He swore he saw red in her eyes.

"Yes. I do." She backed her horse up a few paces. "And I guarantee you'll never catch me on Margie's horse." That was true and Ainii's horse looked ready to prove it.

"Here are the prints, Jackson. Call it a wolf. Call it what you want. But I intend to find out where these prints lead. It's time for you to make a choice." Her words settled over Jackson with the power of an inner voice, as if she had whispered in his ear. He knew she had won.

He had his gun. He had his radio and he'd seen the rifle on the side of Margie's horse. If he took the time to go back for men, Ainii could be deep in trouble before he could find her.

He glanced at Ainii's rolled camp blanket and made a decision. "Do you have enough provisions for two?"

Eleven

The barren desert gradually gave way to scrub cedar and gnarly juniper until the landscape, as far as Jackson could see, was an immense scraggly forest, admittedly only five feet high. He could be Gulliver, looking over the treetops in a faraway land—a stranger in an even stranger place.

He watched Ainii duck easily around a branch. Her tucked shirt creased across her slender back. Then she slid easily back to place on her horse. She didn't watch the ground for tracks on this narrow path, but Jackson heard her dog's barks up ahead. Though he couldn't swear to it, he would bet Ainii understood every yip and yap.

She looked as much at home here as behind her loom—a woman at ease with herself, comfortable in any surroundings. It occurred to him he'd really *never* felt that way—never totally relaxed. He'd always felt one step removed from the people around him. In truth, the sense of estrangement he'd experienced since he got here was only an extension of his normal life; this place just heightened the perception.

Except when he was with Ainii. Odd that just her presence should have an influence. She made him feel right with the world, yet simultaneously at odds with himself—like a jigsaw puzzle piece that fits the place but not the picture. What was it about her?

Her quiet song floated back to him; a melody perfectly

suited to the rise and fall of the land. The notes, long and sustained, then lilting, were so true to the journey, he could almost anticipate the song's direction. He had the nearly overwhelming urge to join in. He shook off that thought before it could take hold.

He didn't sing. He didn't hum. What the hell was he thinking of?

He looked away—but he couldn't ignore the song. He couldn't stop listening. Each note linked to the next, seeping into him, through his pores, as naturally as air . . . and just as essential.

The song wasn't enough. With no strength of will, his gaze settled on Ainii's small waist, swaying in time with the horse's step. Her braid swung to and fro, brushing her back, in a slow counterbeat. Her tight hips hugged the Appaloosa.

His mouth went dry. Why, of all the women he'd known, the ones he had escaped, the ones he had ignored in favor of work, should *this* one leave him as powerless as a schoolboy?

He wanted to hold her, feel her heart beating, see her eyes looking at him, wanting him.

He wanted what he'd started at the arroyo.

His mind took him right to that moment. He smelled rainwater and earth, felt Ainii's wet hair in his hands. He saw the fear and relief in her eyes. The need to kiss her pumped through him, hard, furious, through his body until it pulsated at his lips. The taste of her, he would never forget, he couldn't forget. He wanted more.

If she were within arms' reach now . . .

She would be tonight.

Margie's horse suddenly stopped and backed up a few paces, and Jackson realized he had pulled the reins in tight. Every muscle in his body was tense. Even his thighs ached from pressing too hard around the poor old horse. He loosened his grip and gave her a gentle kick forward. She shook her head as if confused, and a hundred little beads tinkled. He gave her another, harder kick and she lurched forward just in time for Jackson to catch a branch in the face. He yanked on the reins. Beads jangled, herb bags swung, and Jackson cussed.

Ainii didn't look back. In truth, she was afraid to look at him, afraid to face whatever thoughts claimed his hard features. She could feel his stare on her back, as she had for most the trip; sometimes warmth curled through her stomach; other times her skin pricked with uneasiness, as if Jackson were a predator stalking her. The most disconcerting were moments like now, when the two sensations mixed in a swirl of danger and desire.

It was the same way she'd felt when they'd kissed— the provocative feeling of dancing too close to a fire. More to the point, as if she were *handling* fire.

She forced down her wishful thoughts, the thoughts of Jackson that made her tremble, and focused on the path ahead, the mission ahead. As long as she stayed on the trail of the wolf, she would find the proof she needed, because eventually the wolf's tracks would change to human prints. Then Jackson would have to believe.

She knew, even without Dakota's barks of discovery, that the magic wolf had passed this way. She knew it like she would know where to dig for a particular plant, her instincts dragging her forward. Her skin pricked with the certain knowledge of his lingering presence and, with each step forward, she had to swallow her panic, ignore the voice inside that screamed, *Get away!* Even Shoogii's ears swiveled in tense arcs.

A very big part of her could quit this instant, turn around right now and run.

Jackson had no idea how much hope she placed in him.

She laid her head on Shoogii's strong neck and breathed deep. "We will be fine, my brave Shoogii," she whispered.

When she straightened, Ainii again felt Jackson's gaze on her back—with such a force unreckoning, such intensity, she had to look. She had to see his eyes. What could he be thinking with such emotion?

She turned fast and there—before the surprise—she saw a need so hungry, so *stark,* it shot through her almost like a jab of pain. Then the veil fell, shrouding his thoughts, and his familiar gaze—hard, uncompromising—returned. In that split second, she saw the place beyond his control. She saw to the heart of him and suddenly her fear evaporated. Here, on the narrow trail, with the wolf ahead and Jackson behind, she didn't feel trapped, but, instead, strong.

"Did you want something?" Jackson's voice, gruff and demanding, made her smile inwardly.

"No, but I think Peaches needs a rest." Ainii looked at Margie's horse. "She's more used to short treks gathering herbs."

"Peaches!" Jackson barked a laugh. "Yeah, she's a peach, all right. I think she's been asleep for the last half hour."

Margie's horse stomped and hundreds of beads clinked and chimed. Jackson grimaced. Ainii didn't know who looked more unhappy: the scowling Jackson or the hapless horse. They both appeared ready to bite the first thing that moved.

Ainii cut Shoogii onto a side path, then paused to give a whistle to Dakota so he would know they had stopped. At Dakota's answering yips, Shoogii continued. The ground jutted higher with slabs of red rock gradually pushing back the trees, until they finally gave way to a bare knoll of boulders. Ainii slid from Shoogii. "We can stop here for the night."

Jackson muttered something, but it was lost in the mix of tinkling beads.

A slight breeze cooled Ainii, drying the perspiration at her neck and making her suddenly aware of the places where her shirt stuck to her back. She pinched the denim at her neck and pulled the shirt away from her skin to let the air circulate. She reached across the saddle and untied the canvas water horn. "There's a water bag tied to this side of Peaches," she offered, looking over at Jackson.

He was staring at her with a look that drove straight to her stomach.

Ainii pulled her gaze away, took the water horn to Shoogii, and, with one hand cupped, poured her a drink. Shoogii's soft muzzle and rough tongue sent tickles and shivers through Ainii. She couldn't contain a small noise of pure satisfaction.

Jackson mumbled under his breath.

Ainii looked up, but Jackson quickly glanced away, his face carved into an expressionless mask. She'd never been with anyone who ran so hot and cold. Would he ever let his guard down enough for her to get to know him, understand him? She realized a part of her had hoped for just that opportunity tonight, alone, under the stars.

Ainii watched Jackson try to unbuckle the cinch on Peaches's saddle. Every small shift of Peaches's weight sent the bags of Margie's herbs swinging, poking into Jackson. His low curses rumbled over the bare rocks and skated over her skin, like the annoyed growl of a mountain lion. She backed off from the brooding man—knowing enough to give nature's wild ones their space—and set herself to the task of building a fire.

But as she gathered gnarled limbs of dry cedar, Ainii couldn't help but wonder about Jackson's easy frustration with things unfamiliar. Was he so bounded by the limits of what he knew, what he could understand?

She stole a glance at him over her armload of branches and found Jackson staring quietly into the distance. He stood on a slanted boulder, his tall, lean frame silhouetted in the setting sun, his hands at his sides in fists—the picture of cool authority: arrogant, determined, an edgy predator surveying the land from his vantage point. Ainii took a deep, shuddering breath of the pungent cedar.

Ainii wiped up the last of the soup with a rolled tortilla and set the bowl on the ground. Obviously convinced there was more, Dakota went to work with his tongue, rolling the bowl in every direction. Ainii looked over at

Jackson. She could see a glisten of perspiration on his face and the quick swipe of his hand across his forehead.

"The green chili stew too hot?"

"Not at all." His voice came out choked. He took a swig, one of the many, from his canteen. "Just never knew my eyebrows could sweat." He looked at her across the fire and a tendril of heat curled in Ainii.

"What you need is something sweet—"

"Do I?" He stared at her.

Ainii stood, aware of his gaze running over the length of her. She walked to Shoogii's saddle, conscious of her every movement, as she had been all through eating, when Jackson was either staring at her or looking abruptly away. His look made her whole body tingle with desire . . . closely followed by a rush of adrenaline, as if she couldn't decide whether to go to him or run from him.

The conflict of emotions jumbled her thoughts so she couldn't concentrate, either. Nobody had ever turned her so inside out.

Ainii fumbled with the bag of fruit, her fingers simply unable to follow any message from her brain.

"Here, let me."

Jackson's low voice at her side sent Ainii's pulse through the top of her head. He easily untied the bag and pulled out two peaches, handing her one.

Ainii watched him take a bite and use the back of his hand to wipe the juice from his chin, but he missed some. The trail of peach juice and fuzz sticking to his jaw only enhanced his untamed features.

Ainii pulled her gaze away and looked across the familiar landscape, trying to calm her inner turmoil. The sunset lay in a band of colors, like a horizontal rainbow. So many times she had stood in the same spot, staring at the same view—a well-known terrain of memories: riding with her father and brother, camping here, listening to stories.

"It's a nice view." Jackson's voice stirred through her and Ainii swallowed past the sudden spring of emotions.

"Yes," she confessed quietly.

Jackson heard the catch in her voice. He glanced back to Ainii and saw her eyes were soft, as if warmed by memories.

"You've been here before," he said on instinct.

"Yes." She walked back to the fire.

"This is pretty far away from your canyon." He heard his tone move naturally into the one he used to gather information. He couldn't help it. He wanted to know more about Ainii, what went through her head, what went through her *veins*. How did she always stay so calm and collected?

Jackson followed her. "Do you come here often?"

"I grew up in Canyon de Chelly," she said over her shoulder. "About five miles southwest of here."

"But you moved away."

"Yes," she said simply.

"Why?"

She was quiet. Then, "I left after my father died." She eyed her peach, then handed it to Shoogii as if she suddenly had no interest in it. Once again, Jackson felt estranged, at a distance from what mattered to her.

"We used to camp here," she continued, but she was looking at Shoogii.

Her quiet voice, and the fact that she was telling him *anything* about herself, drew Jackson closer.

"We would spend the days exploring the canyons. All three of us—my father, Arland, and me. Then, at night, Father would tell us stories as we sat at the campfire."

Her hand caressed the length of Shoogii's neck, evoking a soft blow of air from the horse—and a shudder through Jackson. He could reach out to her, he thought. There was nothing to stop him.

At that moment, Ainii turned, looked up at him, and her eyes widened. Did she see the desire in his eyes—or the doubt?

"And you?" she asked, taking a small step forward. "When did you leave, Jackson?"

"When I was a kid," he answered, without thinking. Once again, she had caught him off guard.

"Your parents moved from here to Dallas?" Her tone made it sound inconceivable.

"Not exactly."

Her brows furrowed with a question.

Hell, Jackson thought. Why not just tell her? The truth didn't matter. "My parents already lived in Dallas. They adopted me."

"They adopted you from the tribe?"

"Yes." Jackson shrugged, giving the information all the importance it deserved.

"I see," she said.

He didn't like her tone one bit. "You see what?"

She tilted her head, her gaze steady, her lips curled slightly upward. "Well, right now I see an FBI agent not so happy about being the one *asked* the questions."

"You're right," he allowed.

Ainii settled at the fire. She looked at Jackson, her face contemplative. "Is this your first time back to the Res?"

"Yes," Jackson said, joining her.

"You've hardly lived on the Res," she said, then turned her gaze to the fire. "I've never left the Res."

She sat quietly, pondering the fire. Jackson studied the woman, so much a part of this place. "But Arland left," he ventured.

"Arland decided he belonged somewhere else," she said.

"You've never wanted to leave?"

She looked at him, her gaze considering him. "No," she said finally, but her tone held more—her love for this place, but also a yearning. . . .

She suddenly rose and went to Shoogii's saddle. She came back holding a bag, a rod poking out of the opening. What she pulled from the bag looked something like an elongated top: a thin round stick with a wooden dowel near the bottom and a ball of spindly yarn bulging from the middle like a woolly nest. From the bag, she took out a handful of cream-colored wool, a formless mass of hair. Dakota nestled his head in Ainii's lap and Jackson felt a pang of jealousy at the dog's easy comfort.

Ainii's fingers gently pulled on fibers, twisting, stretching, until, before Jackson's eyes, she'd created a strand, then deftly attached it to the loose end of yarn dangling from the stick. She set the pointed end of the stick in the ground and turned the stick, one hand still pulling, stretching, and twisting the hairs to a thread that wound around the ball.

Jackson watched, mesmerized, his attention snagged as surely as the wool within the tender touch of Ainii's slender fingers. He pulled his gaze away to look at her face, expecting to see a woman completely engrossed, but her eyes were set to the distance, past the fire—her work with the wool a memory of her hands.

"That's amazing," he said, at a loss for better words.

She glanced to him, as if surprised he was there. Then she looked to her lap and gave a small laugh. "My hands missed the work."

"I never thought about all it takes to make a rug," Jackson said.

She smiled at him, her face serene. "This is not the difficult part. My fingers do this work for me and I can think of other things. The hard work is capturing the pattern."

"What do you mean?"

She looked off again. The fire's glow danced in shadows across her face. "The design forms in my head. All the colors, the intricate weave. I find the pattern there. Then I have to translate it, capture it in the wool, make it come to life." She glanced back at him and shrugged, as if embarrassed by the explanation.

Jackson was thinking he did the same thing when profiling. He would let the images form, mutate, and re-form, all the while his mind analyzing, untangling, looking for the connection, the thread, the *pattern*.

He looked at Ainii, her eyes soft brown, like deep velvet. For a moment, he couldn't speak, his mind snared on the thought that she would understand, intuitively, what he did. The notion to confide in her swept through Jackson as if carried on a warm wind caressing his soul.

Just as swiftly, cold reality pricked his chest. He was a fool. No one could comprehend. Even if he could find the exact words to explain, to convey the process, he would still sound like a freak of nature, a psychic or some other weirdo who tapped into the thoughts of dead people.

He gave life to the victim's last thoughts. Ainii gave life to the colors in her head.

Jackson's blood chilled. He couldn't be further away from what Ainii would ever understand or accept.

He clenched his jaw against the urge.

"You know, just now you reminded me of Arland."

His gaze refocused on Ainii. Her knowing eyes studied him, threatening to see past the barrier he'd barely erected. "What?" he managed.

"Something in your eyes," she said, still staring. "More than determination. More like a will to conquer. Arland has that look, too. As if he would not fear anything. . . ."

Her voice trailed off, yet she still looked at him, as if fear were something she lived with every day and now she was afraid for *him*.

Ainii afraid? This woman who seemed to gather every moment around her and make it hers? What could she fear?

Then Jackson remembered the one time he *had* seen fear in her eyes—when he had first mentioned the murders and she had whispered the name of the shapeshifter. Anger—irrational and jagged—ripped through him. He *would not* be drawn into another conversation about some mythical beast.

"That is something else you and Arland have in common."

"What?"

His gaze flashed on Ainii and she caught a breath at

his dark, brooding eyes. "You're both in law enforcement," she said. "And you're both Navajo, but live somewhere else."

Jackson broke the stare, but Ainii continued. "And, of course, there are the murders."

Jackson strode to Peaches's saddle and pulled out the rolled blanket. With a flick of his wrists, he unfurled it on the ground. His sharp movements sliced the air, severing the quiet mood. Ainii stared, baffled at his reaction. Why was he angry at the comparison with Arland?

She rose and walked over to him. "Why are you angry?"

"No reason." He lay down, clasped his hands behind his head, and stared straight up at the stars.

Ainii wanted to lean down, put her hand on his tight jaw, but then he closed his eyes, as if to shut her out. She backed away, confused, torn apart inside by his abrupt withdrawal.

She undid her own blanket roll and spread it out alongside the fire. She stared at the man so near, yet so far away in his thoughts, and wished she had the words to bridge the distance. When she finally spoke, Ainii simply uttered the words coming from her heart. "Jackson, I'm glad you're here."

Her voice settled over him, embraced him. In self-defense, Jackson gritted his teeth, but it was no use. He couldn't stop the stirrings in his gut, the instant response of his heart. He wouldn't let these urges, these senseless needs take over. For a while there, he'd been nearly overtaken by his attraction to Ainii, his enchantment with her. Christ, he'd almost confided in her! Of all people, she'd be the first to leap to the conclusion that his instincts were actually something paranormal. He'd forgotten who she was, what she believed: a woman raised on the reservation who believed all the superstitions and tall tales.

He itched to get up, pace . . . walk to her.

God, he couldn't think straight.

He wouldn't be able to as long as she was around. If

they *should* encounter some rampant wolf, he would need all his wits about him. Jackson made a decision.

"Tomorrow morning, you'll go back."

"What about *Yenaldlooshi*?"

Jackson's curse echoed off the bare rocks. "We're not on a wild-man chase, Ainii. If anything, it's a wolf."

"So is *Yenaldlooshi*, Jackson."

"I'm not going to argue with you, Ainii." His eyes flashed with his own inner wildness. Ainii stared, captivated by the power she saw there. If he would only use that energy against *Yenaldlooshi*.

"Why do you want to give up?" she asked.

"I'm not giving up, Ainii. I'm just not taking you along." His tired voice drifted on the fire's plumes.

"I was taking *you*, remember?"

He propped himself on an elbow. He looked frustrated and ready to yell at her. When he spoke, his voice was quiet. "Arland was right, Ainii. You have no business getting involved."

"I see. And the two of you have decided this," she said quietly. "For my own good," she added.

"Yes." He looked relieved that she understood.

"Then, of course, it would be foolish for me to disagree."

He leaned forward, the fire's sparks lighting his eyes. "I'm concerned for your safety, Ainii."

He was telling the truth and a part of her warmed, came alive with his look, like dry earth sparkling beneath a light rain. She could use more of that particular look.

The moment lengthened and his gaze on her softened even more, until Ainii was sure he was about to say something, change his mind.

"I'm going on alone, Ainii. That's it." With that, he lay back down and closed his eyes.

It was so like Jackson to think he controlled the outcome.

Dakota curled up next to Ainii and she pulled him

close. Stroking the feather-soft fur behind his ears, Ainii made a decision. One she knew Jackson wouldn't like.

Ainii rolled her blanket and crept over the rocks in her bare feet. At Ainii's barely audible trill, Shoogii walked over, his brown eyes blinking with sleepiness. On a deep breath, Ainii hauled up Shoogii's saddle and slipped it on his back, but left it uncinched for now. She couldn't afford any more noise.

She heard movement behind her and froze, holding her breath. She steeled herself to see Jackson standing behind her, furious. Instead, he had only rolled to one side, his head resting on an outstretched arm. The moonlight accentuated the hard planes of his face—uncompromising, even in sleep.

He wouldn't change his mind, she knew. In the morning he would send her back, but she couldn't quit now. She only hoped, more than anything she had ever hoped for, that her plan would work.

Silently, she led Shoogii down the path to the main trail. Dakota followed.

Ainii bent to her loyal mascot. She took the small dog's head in her hands. "*Chinle hwiini'i.*" She leaned in close to his ear and whispered. "*Dakota, Bika' anilyeed. Shidoona'a'.*"

Dakota gave her face a warm lick, then turned back up the path to Jackson. Now, if Jackson would just follow Dakota . . .

She thought about Jackson as the path rose and fell and turned corners, and she realized that, even when out of his sight, the place inside her that tightened at his look still remained clenched around the thought of him. It felt like a cord stretched taut to him, that she could always follow.

Odd that this man, so different, arriving in her life so suddenly, should claim her thoughts so thoroughly. Her heart knew him, as if he were the road to home.

Ainii had no question about her own feelings for Jackson. They had been born when she saw him in Clah's hogan, crouched on the ground, his hand to the blood on the rugs. When he looked at her, in that moment of surprise, she'd seen clear to his soul, to the part of him he kept vulnerable in order to help others, the part he hid away beneath his inscrutable stare.

He had a Navajo heart. A medicine man's heart. But would he ever admit it? Would he ever allow her in to the place he guarded?

For all she felt for him, what *did* he feel for her? The cord inside her tied in knots with a pain she'd never known.

Ainii closed her eyes, breathed deep, and searched for the source, trying to calm herself as she had always been able to do. But the tension wouldn't lessen; she couldn't relax.

For the first time in her life, she didn't have control, and she knew why: She had forgotten to remain detached.

Twelve

~~

Jackson woke up cold, stiff, and irritated, in that order. His outlook didn't improve when he looked over and saw barren rock where Ainii should be.

"Goddammit!"

He threw off the blanket and stood, sure that he was wrong. She couldn't have left.

"Ainii!"

His yell carried over the bare knoll, over the forest of cedars. The cheery predawn chirps of birds stopped instantly.

Jackson's chest tightened, his blood running colder now than when he had awakened. "Goddamn," he muttered. He turned in a circle and there, sitting on a flat boulder, watching him, was Dakota.

In three strides, Jackson stood over the small dog. "Where the hell is she?" He had the absurd urge to yank the mutt up from the ground and shake out the answer. Dakota sat, staring up at Jackson.

Jackson glared back. "I don't suppose she did the *smart* thing, the reasonable thing, and went back."

The dog looked at him.

Jackson pushed a hand through his hair. *Now what the hell do I do?* He put two fingers to his mouth and whistled. Peaches walked over, amiably enough with beads jangling, which only annoyed Jackson more. "How the hell did I end up out here with the two of you?"

He hauled up the saddle and shoved it unceremoniously onto Peaches's back. The horse was so trussed up with bags of plants, Jackson had to crouch to reach the saddle belt. A cloud of scent from stuffed herb-bags swirled around Jackson, enveloping him in a harvest of unfamiliar smells—a dry sweetness that clenched his stomach.

He should never have let Ainii come along, he thought, his numb fingers fumbling in the dark with the cinch. When he caught up to her on the mesa, he should have made her go back then. Not that she had given him a choice, he remembered with irritation. He yanked on the cinch. Peaches blew out a breath and Jackson tightened the belt.

Jackson swung up onto her back. Peaches snorted and stomped, then gave up her protest when Dakota jumped up and took the lead. Where the path met the main trail, Dakota took off to the right, continuing in the direction Ainii and Jackson had been taking yesterday. Without any signal from Jackson, Peaches also started down the trail after Dakota.

"Where the hell are you going?"

The dog stood his ground, barking at Jackson, as if he were ordering Jackson to follow.

"You're a couple of miserable conspirators," Jackson muttered.

Within an hour, they had left the trees and the trail. Behind him, to the east, a thin band of gray outlined distant mountains, but ahead, the night still claimed the land. Jackson had only Dakota's intermittent barks to follow as they echoed across wind-blown arroyos.

Apart from the barks, there were Peaches's unshod hooves scraping across the smooth sandstone, and the hoots of a nearby owl, and the faraway screech of a nighthawk. It seemed to Jackson he could hear everything, including the smallest mouse scurrying for cover, rustling through dry grass. His ears missed nothing, except for the soothing sound of Ainii's song.

That absence drummed louder in his head than all the

noise of the surrounding desert, like an echo in an empty place deep inside him. He could picture her here, just ahead of him, her slim figure rocking easily on the Appaloosa, her melody curling through him—then the image dissolved in the chilly air, leaving Jackson all the more frustrated.

If he had gone to her last night, held her close as he had wanted to, his arms around her, she would be here now.

God, how he had wanted to. The urge had grown in him, taking hold of every muscle within him, until he had strained with the effort to keep his hands clenched behind his head. He had won that battle, only to find himself outmaneuvered again.

He had to stop underestimating that woman.

Dakota's bark pulled Peaches forward. Jackson didn't think for a second it was any mistake that Ainii had conveniently left Dakota behind. He had the uneasy sense he was only along for the ride, guided by a horse, a dog, and the machinations of a wily woman.

It didn't matter, he told himself. He didn't need her here distracting him, complicating his thoughts, her song burrowing through him, her laugh tilting his emotions, her deep, dark eyes challenging him. No, he was better off alone.

Except his sixth sense told him he wasn't alone. He slowly wrapped Peaches's mane into a knot, grimacing at each tinkling bead, no matter how muffled. He kept her to a steady gait, his own ears tuned for the slightest untoward sound. Was something pacing them? Alongside? Ahead? It wasn't anything he could hear, anything he could name, just the certainty in his bones that something wasn't right.

Then he noticed Dakota's barks had stopped. He reined in Peaches and sat in the dark silence, his memory focused on the place he'd last heard Dakota. The predawn air settled on him with cold apprehension, chilling his skin. A fissure of warning skated down his spine.

He heard small, shallow pants—not Peaches. The horse snorted and suddenly stepped sideways, as if stumbling—from a dead standstill. Jackson had the gun from his holster in the next instant.

There stood Dakota, staring up at Jackson. Peaches's mane and the silver beads fell free and tiny chimes echoed merrily in an absurd contrast to the rush of icy adrenaline in Jackson's veins.

"What is it, boy?"

The dog cocked his head to one side.

"What's wrong? Do you hear something?"

Dakota growled, low and quiet.

"Yeah, me, too. Show me the way, boy." Jackson clicked his tongue to get Peaches moving. "Stick close, Dakota," he added.

Peaches swung her head down to the small dog, her massive nose dwarfing the mutt. She pulled her lip back and nudged Dakota, a warning not to sneak up—or maybe not to stray?

Dakota scooted around Peaches and took the lead. They scrambled over bald rock and hard earth as Dakota led them down a shallow wash.

The band walked quietly, accompanied by the scrape of Peaches's hooves, the arrhythmic ring of beads, and Dakota's shallow panting. The trill of some night bird echoed through the canyon and Dakota answered with a measured *boof*.

"Quiet, Dakota," Jackson whispered.

The dog grumbled. He ran ahead and was immediately swallowed in darkness.

"Dammit!" Jackson hissed under his breath.

From ahead came the thudding noise of small rocks scattering down a slope. Jackson lightly slapped the reins against Peaches and the horse responded with a quick step. She negotiated the uneven ground agilely—up and over boulders she couldn't see, each step with the potential to throw her off balance, sprain an aged ankle—all without hesitation.

The arroyo deepened, rising on either side, higher and higher, as the small troop descended into a chasm carved by a millennium of seasonal flooding. Canyon walls rose sharply several hundred feet, towering cliffs of black.

Shadows turned grottos into caves and made the deep, angular gouges in the rock wall look like narrow paths to an adjoining canyon. From the canyon floor to the looming cliffs, a predator had his choice of dozens of hiding places. Jackson kept the gun ready across his thigh.

Peaches rounded a huge boulder and there, no more than thirty feet ahead, Jackson could see a crude shelter. It was only a circle of sticks and branches that came to an uneven point maybe five feet tall. Someone had picked the spot carefully, sheltered beneath a rock ledge in a copse of tamarisk trees.

Jackson edged Peaches forward, then stopped, his gaze on Ainii's horse. Shoogii stood silent—and alone.

Jackson's gaze slanted to the shelter. It sat cold, empty. Adrenaline swept Jackson's skin in a painful rush.

He slid noiseless from Peaches, dropped her reins, and crept closer, each muscle tensed and ready.

He now saw the hovel of sticks was a sweat lodge, the branches piled tight. It had the grayish, unused look of an abandoned nest.

The trace of something pungent drifted to him, carried on the latent smell of a fire. He couldn't name it, but he knew that smell from somewhere. His mind latched on it, dragging him nearer. The scent touched memories, prodding them—like God's finger nudging monsters to life.

He stopped dead-still. His chest tightened, his temples throbbed. He felt his heart race, pumping blood too fast, too much.

Get a grip, Walker. Don't lose it.

But he was already losing it. Anxiety squeezed his muscles, constricting his throat, ran through him on a rampage.

Focus!

He forced his mind past the anxiety, past the threat he

felt to his toes, and he walked to the sweat lodge, ignoring the leaden drag of his legs. He circled it but didn't see an entrance. Ainii couldn't be in there. He looked hard at the outlying area, the ground, through the trees, but couldn't see any sign of her.

Then he heard Dakota's whimper. He rounded the lodge and found the dog scratching desperately in the dirt and yanking on the sticks. Branches fell to the side, uncovering an opening. Dakota's growls rumbled through Jackson.

He crouched, flicked on his lighter, and peered inside. Warm, stale air, heavy with a myriad of smells, took his breath away, pushed at him, enveloped him, then rushed past as if escaping its entrapment. The flame on his lighter flickered, but held.

On hands and knees he hauled himself in, twice unsnagging branches from his jacket. Once inside, he couldn't straighten, but had to stand half-bent and try to avoid sharp sticks poking from every angle. A pile of smooth rocks took the center and there was no smoke hole at the top. The enclosure provided just enough room for one person. Ainii wasn't here.

A wave of the hot air sank to his stomach and swirled through his head. He willed back the dizziness, held the lighter higher. His shadow danced across the rocks and drew his gaze to the ground. Imprints pocked the earth circling the pile of stones. A niggling uneasiness coursed through him.

He drew a breath, but couldn't fill his lungs. The walls seemed to close in, pushing out the air. This place was so small! How did a man stand it?

He snapped closed the lighter and turned to leave. Branches grabbed his jacket. He yanked, stumbled, his boot slid on a smooth rock. He grabbed out to stop his fall. The lighter flew from his grasp. Sticks, like thorns, stabbed his hand.

"Dammit!" His curse arced around him as if charged

by some unnatural energy. His uneasiness expanded in a wave of foreboding.

He groped the ground for his lighter, his palm sliding over soft dirt—not packed earth or bedrock like the canyon floor, but loose, as if dug through.

Strange that it should be so different. How had the builder reduced the hard ground to granules? And why?

The thoughts came on top of each other, within a fraction of a second, each question crackling in rapid misfires, not connecting with answers.

His hand tore through the dirt and he skinned his palm on the underlying rock. Then he skimmed something hard, smooth. He closed his fingers on what he thought was his lighter, but when he pulled it from the sand, he gripped more than the lighter. A clump of bristly softness filled his palm—like a mass of dirty hair. He itched to drop it and an irrational shudder of revulsion swept up his arm.

He opened his hand and looked closer. It was hair: black and spiky, coarse like a swatch of fur. His guts twisted and his head went light. Air slammed out of his lungs as if he had been punched in the chest.

He had to get out!

The urge rushed through him in a panic, setting fire to his nerves. His brain screamed he had minutes, now seconds, to leave—escape!

But, as if he were caught in a nightmare, every step seemed to only increase the distance to the door. His legs and arms weighed heavy, useless. His heart raced. He dropped hard to the ground, to all fours, dragging himself with pitiful, weak, inhuman pleas squeezing from his throat.

You're insane, Walker.

The thought fired his strength. He pushed himself up on his fists, then to his feet.

Branches cracked. But he hadn't touched the stick walls. He faced the opening, his gun a dead-aim on whatever moved. The air shifted. A shadow crossed the entrance. His mind leaped to the old nightmare: a doorway in a home, filled with the blackness of something evil. His heart pounded against the approaching terror. In the night-mare, he had hidden. He didn't see himself, but he knew he had huddled, like a coward, watching in horror.

This time would be different.

He took a steadying breath and braced the gun. Adren-aline pulsed at his finger, pressed flesh to the trigger.

"Walker?"

He fired. The shadow jerked, made a noise. A scream? But it didn't stop, kept coming at him. It had a form, something he knew. His mind fought for logic, yelling at him to stop.

That would be defeat. He wouldn't give up. Not this time.

The shadow reached out, touched him—a slight brush with the jolt of electricity put to water, paralyzing him. The gun dropped from useless hands.

He couldn't breathe. He couldn't see. He would lose.

He staggered back, even as he recognized, somewhere deep inside, the particular gentleness of that touch. It was Ainii. Relief broke over him in a rush of deliverance in the same moment a maelstrom of blackness stole across him in a dizzying swirl. His last thought was that he had hurt the one person who would rescue him. He had shot Ainii.

The shot had missed Ainii, though her heart had stopped, then raced wildly with a surge of energy riding on the instinct to flee. He'd shot at her. What had possessed Jack-son to try to kill her?

She had seen the gun. She had seen Jackson holding the gun, his arms aiming, in the way only a man trained and ready to kill could hold a gun. But what had taken her breath was not fear of the man; what had grabbed her heart was his voice, the desperation she'd heard in its depths . . . right before he had fired.

She crawled to him, her heart still thudding in her chest.

"Jackson?" She ran a hand across his forehead, down

his temple. He lay motionless, silent. She dragged herself beneath him and cradled his head in her lap.

Her nerves still pricked with adrenaline and the air felt charged as if each particle held the violence. Why? she asked herself again.

Her mind replayed the scene. She saw his last look. His eyes, glistening with naked emotion. He had stared past her, through her, with the crazed look of a man battling *chindi*—ghosts of the darkness. When he fell to the ground, his gaze was wide, startled, then lost—the look of defeat swallowed in sorrow. And suddenly she knew fear—fear for him, fear for the vulnerability she saw there.

Her fingers touched the chiseled face of a fallen warrior and her heart reached to him. His pain was hers, his terror hers to quell.

Ainii held him close, murmuring to him. She kissed his forehead, let her lips caress his eyelids, his brows, the furrowed crease between them. Such a deep line, even as he lay unconscious.

Her mouth traced his temples and across the high plane of his cheekbones, then to the corner of his lips. She meant only to comfort him, she told herself. She couldn't help it if her senses swam with the taste and smell of him—swirling, mingling, like a pot of her dye mixing with yarn.

From the dark depths rose Jackson's essence: first deep reddish brown—a strong color, the one all other colors came alive against; then she saw soft reddish tan, then light brown, and finally a creamy tan—all the possibilities of her beloved mountain mahogany.

The layers of colors mixed, then drifted, forming the most achingly beautiful pattern.

Her fingers ran through his hair, its thick texture rough against her palm, sending shivers through her. Her lips found his, and she savored, wanting more, an artist desperate to capture the vision.

Jackson moaned, the sound like a large animal waking.

The deep resonance curled through her, pulling her closer, into his tapestry. Then he moved his mouth, slanted against hers, responding to her, deepening the kisses. Ainii felt as if all the color she had ever seen, and more that she could never imagine, flooded through her.

Large, warm hands framed her face, then slid through her hair, his fingers kneading their way back, moving slow, like the motions in a dream. And she knew, without looking, his eyes were closed, perhaps not even fully conscious.

That thought stopped her. Did he even know what he was doing? Ainii eased away, the pressure of his hands allowing only a fraction of an inch. In the darkness, she sought his eyes and found them open, looking at her, his gaze clear, calm, focused on her as if she alone were all he wanted to see.

"Don't pull away," he said, his voice a coarse whisper that rubbed across her like a blanket on naked skin.

"No," she said simply, unwilling to move even a breath from him.

His hands loosened at her head and Ainii thought he'd misunderstood, that he would now retreat, draw back within his fortress, as he had before at the arroyo.

Not this time. Every fiber in her demanded more. She'd never felt such a tangible *want* as the one that pulsed through her.

He cocked his head slightly, his eyes filled with concern, then with shame.

"Jackson—" she started, hearing the plea in her voice.

"God, I shot at you," he said, as if not hearing her. "Are you all right?"

"Yes. You missed."

He took a deep, shaky breath. She felt his chest expand beneath her. "I'm sorry," he said.

His words held more than an apology. Ainii heard the withdrawal in his voice and her heart quickened. She wouldn't let him stop now.

She reached a finger to the deepened crease at his brow

and traced it, gently pressing, smoothing. "It's all right. I'm okay." She planted a kiss on his forehead, then the bridge of his nose. A part of her rebelled at her shame-lessness, and another part of her at her selfishness. She didn't ask how he was, what had driven him to shoot. Right now, in his arms, she didn't care.

She met his gaze, hoping he wouldn't see her need, fearful herself of what she would see in his. But his eyes held the unmistakable smoky look of passion. In their fathomless depths she saw a need that matched her own. For a suspended moment they only stared, their eyes full of silent anticipation. Their lips hovered a breath apart, and deep within Ainii a pulse beat in sweet torture.

A strong arm braced her back, lowered her down to the ground. His leg bent across her, holding her beneath him. Everywhere he touched her, her blood rose to the heat, seeking more, until every part of her tingled with need. A delicious shudder ran through her.

Jackson's mouth caught her gasp, his tongue slid over her lips, and the heat Ainii had felt turned molten, un-stoppable. Her hands ran over every inch of him she could reach: across his broad shoulders, down his back; her fin-gers discovering every taut muscle. She reveled in the strength she felt in him as she let her hands glide lower, down his sides, to his waist.

His hand cradled her face, the pad of his thumb tracing her lips, brushing her sensitive tongue, evoking a wave of pleasure. She couldn't help a moan.

He drew a sharp breath. His lips pressed against hers, his mouth captured hers, took her own breath, her thoughts. Her whole world swirled in the whirlpool where their lips met. She didn't need air, sight, or sound. Only this.

His own motions turned urgent. His arm slid down her back and hugged her hips to him. His body pressed hard and his tongue sought hers. She tasted his need, his wild-ness. It drove through her like the pounding of a cere-monial drum—a beat she felt deep in her core, one her

body knew and responded to without heed—one as old
as the rhythm of Mother Earth beneath her.

Ainii pulled his shirt from his pants and ran her hands
up his back. His muscles tensed beneath her touch. Her
fingers skidded over him, to his sides, to the front, yanking cloth out of their path. His skin moved with her, alive
at her touch. Desperate for more, she ran a hand up his
chest, stopping at the taut nub of his nipple. He groaned
into a kiss. And the pulse in her thrummed tight.

He shifted. She felt his hand moving at his waist, heard
the clink of metal. Her own buckle loosened. His hand
slid beneath her jeans. She arched to him, her movement
deliberate, taking his long fingers to the place now aching
for his touch. Every inch along his path brought wanton
torment, the steel bliss of muscles tensed and helpless.

He lifted her slightly, one hand slipping her jeans off
her hips. The other hand now moved freely, farther down,
to the spot. Ainii thought she might cry with pure pleasure. All her senses pooled there, straining, drawing to a
peak—a pinnacle always just beyond.

It wasn't enough. She found his buckle open. She
shoved down on his jeans over slim, tense hips. She felt
his hand alongside hers, tugging, both impatient. He
pressed a knee to the inside of her leg and slipped within
her. His low groan rumbled through him, through her—
both one and the same.

For a moment he arched above her, his arms locked,
his body not moving. Ainii looked up to see his face
drawn tight, his jaws clenched as if caught before a
scream. Her own body strained to take him in more. She
pressed her hips to his, pushing him in. Jackson threw his
head back; the veins in his neck stood in thick cords.

Ainii bent up to him, her hands braced on the ground,
the movement bringing them even closer. But it still
wasn't enough. Her body craved the promise of more. She
fisted the ground, straining closer to Jackson. Her fingers
closed on dirt, and something else. A chill ran through
her veins, like the breath of ancient, cold wind.

In that moment, her gaze locked with Jackson's. His eyes were fierce, intent—the look of a warrior primed for battle. Then his body moved, a measured rhythm, filling her, pushing her, taking her to the edge. All the time he looked at her, hypnotizing her with his gaze, holding her closer than an embrace.

She wrapped her arms across his shoulders and held on, never to let go.

Thirteen

He hadn't meant for it to go this far. As soon as that thought was formed, he knew it was a lie. He had wanted Ainii from the first moment he had seen her on the road, before he even knew who she was. What was it about her?

He tried to find the right word, the very one that would catch her essence, the description that would name her, categorize her. If he could find the label, then he would know her, he could predict her behavior—and he would understand his own reactions.

Problem was, he couldn't define Ainii with only one word. Even as she lay here now, exposed to him, seemingly hiding nothing, she remained a mystery, beyond his grasp.

Jackson gazed down at her. He brushed back tendrils of black hair and followed the oval of her face with his knuckle. He meandered to her mouth and traced the curve of her lips with his fingertip, rubbing back and forth, barely touching. He let his pad linger in the soft middle. God, her lips were meant to be kissed.

She opened them ever so more slightly. Jackson bent to her and kissed the corner of her mouth, then the tiny dip at the top, then the other corner. She turned and caught his lips directly on hers and held him fast. The low smolder deep within him leaped to a burn.

It took only a touch of her lips, pliant against his, and his body was again ready, energized yet relaxed—that satisfied place where he felt anything was possible. He could barely remember his eternal exhaustion, the frustration that had dogged him—even the terror that had brought him to his knees now seemed but a bad dream.

He leaned back and met her eyes—their perfect almond shape, dark and full. She gazed back with only the smallest smile at the corner of her mouth.

"You are so beautiful." The words fell from his lips before he could think.

"Thank you," she said.

She didn't blink, just looked at him, her eyes calm, not measuring him, without even a hint of expectation, with that inscrutable look he'd never been able to interpret—the one that made him feel left out of a secret. Jackson felt a clench in his chest as if someone pinched his heart.

"Do you ever stop worrying?" She rubbed her fingers across his forehead, making Jackson acutely aware of his furrowed brow. He tried to relax, but his effort must have been in vain because he heard Ainii sigh.

"I think the lines are permanent." He tried to make his tone light, but Ainii's gaze had turned pensive.

"It's your thoughts that are serious," she said.

"No more than usual," Jackson said. He kissed her nose, her cheek. Then let his lips trail to her temple.

Ainii lay quiet beneath him. Jackson tilted back slightly. Her eyes locked on his. "Tell me what happened, Jackson," she said quietly.

A shadow of the old terror chilled him, but Ainii's formidable gaze, unflinching, undeterred, made him *want* to talk. "The truth is, I don't know. One minute I was fine. Claustrophobic, maybe, but fine." He shook his head. "Then I stumbled, the lighter fell from my hand. I picked it up, but . . ."

The rest stalled in his throat. He felt his chest tighten, constricting his breath. He recognized the panic building. *Damn my weakness!* His fist hit the ground and his legs coiled to rise.

Ainii's hands framed his face, turning him to look at her. "But what, Jackson?"

He saw it all again: the doorway, the shadow—something evil, murderous, too big for him to stop. Nervous energy made him stand, slipping past Ainii's hands. She stared at him and in her eyes he saw her concern.

This is crazy. It was nothing. There was nothing here. Nothing but stones, dirt, sticks.

"What was it, Jackson?"

"Nothing," he said, forcing calmness. "Nothing but my imagination."

"What did you imagine, Jackson?"

"It's not worth talking about."

Ainii stared up at Jackson, his shoulders hunched, his head bent beneath the small dome of sticks. If he stood upright, he would push straight through the top—he had the strength in him. But his gaze didn't claim that self-assurance. Instead, his eyes held denial and doubt, and Ainii knew whatever Jackson had seen or imagined was more than nothing.

"And this nothing was worth shooting at?"

"I already apologized."

Ainii heard the distance in his voice—as if he spoke from a place he wouldn't let her reach—and she realized he not only meant to close the door on the whole subject, he was locking down his emotions in a safe place where even he wouldn't have to deal with them.

That was so Navajo.

Ainii looked at the man towering above her—tall, lean, strong . . . and so vulnerable. Warmth spread through her like an inner smile.

"Yes, you apologized." Ainii gave her attention to calmly buttoning her shirt. "And, of course, that's all that matters."

"That's right," he said, with a slight hesitation.

Ainii stood and efficiently brushed off the earth from her jeans. "That I might wonder why you would shoot at me isn't important." She stood and looked him in the eye.

"Ainii, I told you the truth. It was my imagination. I shot at you because I thought you were someone else."

"Who?" Ainii could see the struggle within him.

"I don't know who," he said with finality.

"But why now? What brought it on?"

Jackson shook his head, tried to turn away from her, but he succeeded only in catching his shirt on sticks. With a yank, he freed himself. "Just leave it, Ainii. It's not important." He took her elbow and bent her toward the opening. "Let's go."

She shook off his grasp and turned to him. "Jackson, talk to me." She laid her hands on his chest.

An abrupt wave of anxiety swept through her. Her heart leaped as if responding to an immediate threat. With sudden clarity, Ainii realized that these emotions belonged to Jackson. It was *his* panic, his *terror* pounding in her chest.

She recognized the sensations as the same ones she had experienced when she found Jackson at Clah's hogan. He'd been bent over the rugs, his hand on the dried blood, his whole body arched, tense with purpose. He had looked like a medicine man trying to make a connection with the patient. Except the patient was dead. And Jackson wasn't a medicine man, he was an FBI agent.

"Jackson, do you remember when I found you at Clah's hogan?"

"Yes."

"You were concentrating on the spot where Clah was killed. Your hand was on his blood—"

"Ainii, this isn't the time." He tried to step aside, but there was no room. Ainii pressed closer.

"I surprised you, Jackson. And the look on your face then matches what I feel within you now. Please, Jackson, talk to me."

Jackson looked into Ainii's eyes and the last of his stonewall resolve crumbled like sand. From the moment they had met, she had been eroding his fortress little by little, like warm rain cutting gulleys through hard-packed desert. He hadn't known how parched he was, how lonely he was, until he met Ainii.

No matter his frustration, his exhaustion, a look from her drew his focus to a bead. Her unwavering gaze, her unfailing calmness, held the certainty that whatever happened was for the best. Looking at her now, her gaze saying she would understand anything, her hands laid to his chest as if she would never let him move—she gave him the feeling he was the best he could be, the best there was.

He realized he had waited all his life for someone exactly like her. All his years of silence expanded within his chest, beneath her fingers, pressing to be spoken. All he could hope for was that Ainii would be the one to understand.

"The simplest explanation," he said, "is that the crime scene lays out for me like a puzzle . . . a puzzle of thoughts," he added, trying to put words to something he had never wanted to talk about.

She looked at him unblinking, awaiting the rest.

"Through the victim," he continued, "I try to put together a picture of the criminal. Every profiler begins the same way. We're taught to pay attention to every detail of the crime: the preliminary police report, the M.E.'s protocol, the crime scene photos—all of this for every crime suspected of being related."

Ainii nodded for him to continue.

"All these things together tell a story: how the crime was committed, whether it was planned. You begin to get a sense of what kind of person would commit this particular crime."

Jackson took a few steps around the pile of rocks. "But any detective can tell you that the most important piece of evidence is the body of the victim. The question is," he said, "why was this victim selected over all other potential victims?"

The image of every victim he'd encountered flipped through his mind—a ghastly collage of their dead faces juxtaposed with pictures of them as healthy, vital human beings. He knew each one by name, knew their habits, their lives, their secrets.

What he knew most intimately, what threatened to flood him now, was the knowledge of their last moments, their screams, their unspeakable horror. With each one, he had felt the fear, the pain, the terror of knowing that no one would *hear* the victim's screams.

He took another few steps. He needed to pace, but this place was so small! He looked at Ainii and drew strength from her steady gaze.

"When you found me at Clah's, I was using my own method of learning more about the victim."

"By placing your hand on his blood."

There was no horror in her voice, no telltale flinch indicating she thought she was in the presence of a bizarre individual.

"Yes," he said simply. "It helps me draw together all the threads of the crime."

"You see things?"

"No. I think things." He shook his head in exasperation. "It's not some paranormal, psychic ability, Ainii. It's just a connection with the victim, a thread that leads through the crime, makes sense of it all."

Her brow furrowed. Jackson waited for the derisive comment—that he was one sick bastard, only a step away from a freak show at the carnival.

Instead, she said, "You *think* things," in a thoughtful tone, as if she were considering this information.

"Yes."

"From the mind of the victim," she said.

"Yes . . ." he faltered. *Until now.* With Clah, and then Harrison, he'd connected with the perpetrator. He'd gone beyond the victim's pain and terror, slipping easily within the sick mind of the criminal.

As if bidden, deadly intent coursed through him, icing his veins with an evil chill. He was the murderer, killing, torturing. The rapid descent, beyond his control, scared him more than the consuming malevolence.

"And what did you learn from the victims, from Clah?"

"I . . . it didn't . . . this time was different."

With extreme effort, he cut off the memories.

"Different? How?" Her voice was close.

Jackson wanted to walk away from the questions, from the closeness. He had the overwhelming sense of being cornered, manuevered, forced to face something . . . what?

He felt a warm hand on his jaw. "What is it, Jackson? What's wrong?"

At her touch, the desperation evaporated, as if banished. Her hand held him steadfast. His panic lifted.

Suddenly, clearly, he recalled the most recent image—what had happened here in the sweat lodge: the huddled child, the monster at the door. And he remembered, he remembered the nightmare—the one from his childhood—where he was at once the cowardly child and the murderous shadow, righteous, fearless, all-powerful.

There was more he should see, more he should know. He clenched his eyes shut, forcing the rest, but the memory escaped through his grasp like a ghost.

He opened his eyes to see Ainii staring at him, her gaze troubled, concerned—and imploring him to tell the truth.

"What's wrong, Ainii, is that my method isn't working here."

Ainii saw the confusion in his eyes, the look of a man desperate for a reasonable answer.

"But you are seeing something."

"Yes, I'm seeing something," he admitted. He raked a hand through his hair. "But it doesn't make any sense."

A haunting uneasiness crept through Ainii. "Why, Jackson? What's different?"

He stared at her, his gaze tortured. "I'm not connecting with the victim anymore," he said.

His eyes were like windows to the horror he voluntarily relived for the victims. Except he wasn't connecting with the victims. Which left the murderer. What Jackson had imagined had come straight from the black heart of *Yenaldlooshi*.

The realization raced through Ainii: Jackson connected with the magic wolf! She'd known he had great power in him—she'd seen it in his eyes. Her heart swelled with awe, but when she looked to him, Ainii caught a breath at the utter desolation she saw there, as if he were lost.

It came to Ainii that Jackson had never mentioned his power, only his instincts.

The truth sent a sudden chill through Ainii's veins. Jackson's heart, even his thoughts, connected with *Yenaldlooshi,* but his mind rebelled. His very disbelief put him in even greater danger.

"Ainii, what's wrong?"

Jackson's voice startled Ainii from her thoughts. She looked up at him, his black eyes full of concern, needing an answer. With those eyes he looked into men's souls; he searched their thoughts; he sought the face of evil. He had found it here . . . in the horror of the magic wolf's mind.

And Jackson, his instincts alive, his senses always open, had been brought to his knees, defeated, overcome by the evil. Something in Jackson made him vulnerable to the magic wolf.

The shivers within Ainii turned to quakes. She hugged her arms close.

"Ainii?"

She tried to cover her emotions before she looked at Jackson. "It's nothing." She tried a small smile. "I'm sorry I badgered you, Jackson. You're right. We should go."

She had to think this through. If Jackson was vulnerable to *Yenaldlooshi,* what danger was she putting him in?

Ainii bent down for her hat, then remembered she had clutched something in her hand when they were on the ground. Quickly, she swept her fingers over the dirt. Jackson nudged her to go. She pretended to lose her balance, crouched and stretched her hand farther over the ground. Her fingers brushed a mass of something bristly.

An inexplicable shudder ran up her arm. Ainii willed her instincts to calm. She grabbed the clump, rose, and stuffed it in her pocket, then bent to the doorway.

Dakota roused from his sandy spot next to Shoogii and loped over.

"*Ya'at'eeh, shi,*" she said, but her voice came hoarse, strained.

Dakota licked her nose, then sniffed her over as she crawled from the lodge. He stopped at her pocket, snuffing hard, leaving wet spots with his nose, persisting until she had to push him aside. Ainii stood and looked back to see Dakota giving the same attention to Jackson, exploring the entire length of him. A soft whine rose from Dakota's throat.

"Hush, you pesky mutt," murmured Jackson. Then, to Ainii's surprise, he gave a brusque scratch to Dakota's head. Dakota's whine only increased and he ran nervously between Ainii and Jackson.

"Yes, Dakota, I know. *Ha'goshi'i'.*" Dakota quieted and promptly sat at Ainii's feet, though he wasn't still. His small body twitched as if charged with energy to hunt the wolf Ainii knew he smelled.

"*Do tah.*" *No,* she told him, though she had to smile at her little hero. Now was not the time to track *Yenaldlooshi.*

Neither she nor Jackson was ready. How could she have been so stupid, so arrogant? She'd been of one mind: to force Jackson to believe in *Yenaldlooshi,* then he would deal with the magic wolf . . . because she couldn't.

Because she was a coward.

And because of her own fears, she had manipulated Jackson to the very brink of his sanity. Shame seeped into Ainii, leeching away every remnant of the joy she'd had in his arms, leaving her empty, hollow.

She had used him—it was as simple as that—not only for the sake of confronting *Yenaldlooshi,* but for her own needs. She had been content before she met Jackson. But that changed the moment she had seen him on the road, rising from his Jeep, staring at her intently. He evoked a deep *want* within her, an organic need, as if her body discovered the very thing necessary. He completed her, fit to her like the tight weave of her rug.

She would do almost anything to have that feeling with her always.

She glanced at Jackson, who was readying Peaches. He slipped off her blanket, shook it, then smoothed it over her back. He looked up and his gaze—distant, protected—sent a pang through Ainii.

She walked to Shoogii and jumped on. "Are you ready?" she asked.

His gaze focused on her. "For what?"

"To ride out. Chinle is only about seven miles."

"Just like that, you're ready to leave."

"There's nothing more to do here."

His eyes turned keen. "What about the wolf, Ainii, the one you insisted on tracking?"

"The prints are gone," she said, maybe a bit too quickly. "I've lost the trail."

Jackson angled Peaches in front of Shoogii. "What's the matter, didn't your plan work out?"

"My plan . . ." Ainii's voice broke under his hardened gaze. He looked as if the one person he had counted on had let him down. "This wasn't what I planned," she said.

"Which part wasn't planned, Ainii?" He leaned to her, his eyes fierce. "The part where we made love? The part when I confided how I work? Or was it when I told you that I can't make the puzzle pieces fit this time?"

"It's my fault, Jackson. I shouldn't have forced you—"

"Forced!" Every angle in his face had an edge—so sharp it hurt her to look at him.

She took in his anger, let it pound through her until every part of her ached with his vehemence. She refused the impulse to calm the rage and ease the pain. Instead, she suffered it as the punishment she deserved. "I shouldn't have brought you here," she said quietly.

"I should never have come here to begin with." His voice was flat, empty, squeezed of all emotion. With a click, he turned Peaches into the canyon.

Early morning shrouded the canyon, flattening its life and colors to a dull gray. Father Sky owned the canyons longest, holding the sun's warmth at bay. Ainii breathed deep of the chilly air. She took the coldness within, to every part of her. The crisp air was strangely comforting.

It belonged with her, was at home within her, just like the loneliness opening up inside. She watched Jackson's back, his hips rocking with Peaches's steps. Everything about him seemed contrary to Peaches: His frame was too large for the stocky mare; his approach too cautious for the jingling beads; his countenance too harsh, too manly, for the female bundles of herbs swinging on Peaches.

Yet he rode easily, his legs loose around Peaches's belly, with the confidence of knowing the terrain. He made every place his own, as if he belonged there—even here, in this canyon familiar to Ainii, where she'd explored, camped with her father and brother.

They would come here to gather the special plants for her father's ceremonies: the spindly bitterball and the dainty larkspur with delicate purple petals. The days and evenings were spent in a solemn search within the crevices of the labyrinthine canyons. When they were successful, they paid homage to Mother Earth for protecting the sacred medicine plants within the folds of her skirts.

Among the Navajo, her father was a revered medicine man. But to Ainii and Arland, he was even more: a storyteller, the weaver of legend into their lives, the man whose love for them was as sure as the power bestowed on him by the Holy Ones.

Those days were safe, their life good, filled with purpose and love. She missed that time with the acute ache for something long gone.

Jackson's presence only amplified the grief. A lump formed in her throat and her eyes misted. Brutally, she quashed the sudden rush of pity and breathed deep through her nose. The cold air bit off her tears.

Think like Hawk, she told herself. *See yourself in the air, weightless, fearless . . . detached.*

She let the image settle over her, sweep away her fears.

She stuck her hand in her pocket and reached tentatively for the clump of fur. She closed her fingers on the spiky mass, ignoring the immediate wrack of shivers, the prickly sensation of fear crawling up her arm.

Margie had said Ainii would need something of *Yen-aldlooshi*. Witches collected the hair of their intended victims. Ainii had his fur. Now she needed only to find the courage to use it and bait the magic wolf. When *Yenald-looshi* died, his power over Jackson would end—and so would Jackson's reason for being here.

She stared hard at the man before her, starting now to memorize every bit of him.

Dakota took the lead down through the canyon, though Jackson had the distinct impression the dog had other pursuits on his mind. He followed his nose up and over rocks, sometimes meandering well away from the dry wash path they traveled. A hiss or a whistle from Ainii would bring Dakota up short as if tethered to the troop by an invisible leash. He'd stand frozen in place, but poised, his body tensed with his own inexplicable purpose. Another whistle from Ainii and Dakota would finally lope back on track.

The scene replayed countless times and Jackson empathized with the frustrated dog. He, too, was pulled in two different directions and, like Dakota, Jackson couldn't escape Ainii's magnetism. Even now, angry with himself for confiding in Ainii—angrier still that he'd allowed himself to hope for her understanding—what his thoughts turned to over and over again was how she made him feel. She affected him in a way no one ever had. She was one moment his nemesis, challenging him, provoking him; then, the next, or even simultaneously, she was breaking down his defenses, reaching deep within him to a sensitive place, touching him gently, flooding him with desire.

What was she doing to him? How had he gotten lost in her calm gaze?

He stared out over the so-southwestern landscape: to the west, an endless row of canyons, their arms open to take you or leave you; ahead, in the distance, huge tabletop mesas supporting a relentless, piercing blue sky. Someplace so immense bordered on oblivion. No, this wasn't the place for the feeble-minded or the weak-hearted. It was the home of hawks, coyotes, and mountain lions.

And Ainii.

Like Nez had said, the land made the people.

A time long ago, in a life he didn't claim, this had been his home. The thought gripped his heart and squeezed.

Suddenly he had the acute sense of being a stranger in his own life—estranged, walking blindly, ignorant of all the ancient accumulated history. From somewhere deep inside sprang a need he didn't want to name.

He slapped the reins on Peaches's rump and welcomed the brief pounding of hard ground, jarring loose his uncomfortable thoughts.

He had to get out of here. He knew he could take himself out of Navajoland, but could he excise this place, and Ainii, from himself?

They left the last of the canyon, its walls rounding down to the ground, like the pudgy arms of a demanding child, stretching fat fingers across the desert before disappearing into a handful of sand. They rode from upper canyon, through high desert, across lower plateau. All of it downhill, but so gradual that they were on level ground for half an hour before Jackson recognized the open space leading to Chinle and the back of his motel.

Jackson slipped off Peaches and walked her clip-clopping across the asphalt. Ainii rode up alongside and reached a hand out. He stared for a stupid moment before he realized she wanted Peaches's reins.

He looked up at Ainii—her eyes dark, full, mesmerizing. The way she gazed at him made Jackson feel as if he had never really looked someone in the eye. At that moment, he couldn't escape the feeling that he had let her down.

"I'm sorry," she said.

She had stolen the words right out of his mouth and he watched, speechless, as she turned the horses and disappeared.

Fourteen

From his second-story room, Jackson stared across the scrubby desert. He didn't remember walking to the window and he didn't know how long he had stood there. Maybe it had been a while, because he now recognized an ache in his leg. He thought about the ache, half-wondering why his shin hurt, but his thoughts meandered off, lost in a fog.

A splatter of taps at the window dimly startled him. Late afternoon wind churned sand and tumbleweeds, sent them flying, as if hurled by unseen hands. Jackson smiled at the stupid assault of the elements, railing against brick and mortar, against immovable objects . . . like him.

"Go ahead! Throw everything you've got at me." His thick tongue struggled around the words.

Like a child unimpressed with meaningless threats, the wind bounced tumbleweeds around and sent a dust devil spinning like a whirling dervish. Out of the sandy haze wandered some white, fuzzy blobs, pulling his attention in their direction. Sheep, his mind labeled. He could barely follow their weaving . . . or was it him? He planted his feet more squarely.

He couldn't take his eyes off the woolly blurs, pressing his shoulder, then his cheek to the cold glass as the sheep drifted around the far corner of the motel like a slow-moving, unstoppable river of white.

Then he saw the shepherdess, walking at the back,

slowing swinging something side to side and over her head. The wind moved with her, teasing her skirt.

He had to call to her, had to get her attention!

He tried to pull the window up. He felt for the latches, all the time watching the woman move inexorably away, until the whole procession disappeared, the wind dying in her wake.

A dull melancholy settled on Jackson. How laughable he was, standing here in some vain effort at control. He had no power here, no strength over this place or its people. He was only an object to be avoided, stepped around—nothing more than a minor obstacle in the timeless flow in this place of inexhaustible persistence.

He pressed his forehead to the window. The flat chill stopped his head from spinning. He pulled back. The sudden motion made his head wobble like a bobble-headed toy. *That's better,* he thought. It wouldn't do to let the stupor weaken.

He reached behind him to where a table should be, and the bottle. His hand grabbed dead air, he stumbled, hit his shin again. *The damn chair!* Nothing was where it should be.

Ainii wasn't where she should be—here, with him. *No, that's not right.* He shook his head dully. She didn't belong with him—he was the last person she should be with. He sank into the chair.

He had nothing to offer her. There was nothing left in him—nothing but exhaustion and a hollowness he'd been trying to fill ever since she rode away. He looked for the bottle, his bleary vision dragging behind the turn of his head. When he spotted the table sitting almost four feet away, the effort to lean for the whiskey seemed too much. So he just sat and stared.

Images of the last two days and nights floated in the orange liquid: the canyon, the night under the stars . . . the sweat lodge. As with every time before, his mind stalled at the last image, skating over all the memories to the dominant one: the distant look in Ainii's eyes.

He searched for clues in her eyes of her thoughts: a flicker of pity, the cool look of recrimination, a flash of horror—anything! But her gaze revealed nothing more than she allowed.

He'd never known a woman who had so completely mastered the emotionless stare.

But then he'd never met a woman like Ainii. He'd always been able to read what a woman was thinking, what she wanted. Maybe that was because the women he'd known had all wanted the same thing—a commitment from him, a lasting relationship, predicated by one small change: his job.

Oh, they'd never said as much, but inevitably the looks would come and the message was clear: What kind of man put his hand to the blood of victims? Eventually they wondered how they could let those same hands touch them.

Ainii had let him. Even though she had actually seen him at Clah's hogan, his hands pressed to the blood, she had let him kiss her. And in the sweat lodge, he had awakened to her kiss. She'd drawn him from a cold nightmare straight into hot passion. Unlike the others, Ainii hadn't distanced herself out of revulsion.

The thought settled through Jackson with more sobering power than a pot of coffee.

Then why? Why had she suddenly withdrawn? He couldn't read her. She held her emotions in check with such effortless control, gliding easily from passion to dispassion. He knew men who would kill for that talent. He was one of them.

Jackson rested his face in his hands. How had he had the luck to run into the one-in-a-million woman who had the uncanny ability to twist the natural order of things?

He heard movement at his door a second before the pounding started.

"Walker! Open up!"

The voice wasn't Nez or Arland . . . or Ainii. So they could just go to hell.

But the pounding deepened and accelerated. From the sound of it, the guy had gone from hitting with the butt of his palm to the side of his fist. Jackson could picture it . . . and he did just that as he slouched back into his chair.

But whoever it was, he wasn't buying into Jackson's silence.

"Walker, I know you're in there."

Jackson heard the desperation and in the next instant, the face of Bill Sanders came to Jackson and matched up with the voice.

"What the hell do you want, Sanders?"

The pounding stopped. "Where's Ainii?"

"She's not here." Jackson heard the weariness in his own voice.

There was silence. Then, "Let me in, Walker."

Jackson dragged himself out of the chair, stood for a few unsteady beats, then walked to the door, managing not to walk into anything. He opened the door and the bright hallway light blinded him, sent him staggering back a few steps. Sanders brushed past him. He paused at the dresser to turn on the light, then scanned the room.

"She's not here," he said.

"I told you that already." Jackson reached for the lamp and, with a flick, returned the room to blessed darkness. He settled back in his chair and considered the obviously troubled Sanders.

Sanders walked to the window, back to the middle of the room, started for the door, then returned to stand in front of Jackson. The trader had desperation written in every line of his face. Concern wound its way through Jackson, tightening his chest.

"What's—" he began.

"I don't know what I was thinking," Sanders said. "She wouldn't be here." He looked pointedly at the near-empty bottle and the full ashtray. "Feeling sorry for yourself, Walker?"

"Get the hell out of here, Sanders." A keen need for

the bite of whiskey drew Jackson's hand to the bottle. He raised it slowly, deliberately to his lips. He caught Sanders's stare through the thick glass—it warped the trader's features like that of a freak at a carnival show. But Sanders wasn't the freak. Jackson was.

Jackson set the bottle down. "You're right, Sanders. Ainii wouldn't be here and you don't want to be here. So go."

Sanders sat on the edge of the bed. "Do you know where Ainii went after she left here?"

"It's a big country, Sanders."

The trader looked away from Jackson, as if disgusted by the sight of the drunk agent.

Jackson leaned close, forced his breath toward Sanders. "And Ainii's a grown woman."

Sanders turned and looked Jackson in the eye. "What's the matter, Walker? Was she too much for you?"

The truth stabbed sharply to home, tore at the last of his facade. *Hell, yes, she's too much for me. This place is too much for me.* He gave up the game. "I just don't understand her, Sanders." He leaned back. "Why are you looking for Ainii?"

Sanders looked away again. "I need to talk to her."

"Why?"

Sanders locked, then unlocked his fingers, rubbed his hands across the top of his legs. Sanders was worried—damn worried—about Ainii, and he had a wealth of reasons that he didn't want to talk about. If this were an interrogation, Jackson would be closing in on the stress factor.

"Just what's bothering you, Sanders?"

The trader walked to the window. "What happened up there in the canyons?"

"None of your business."

"Two days and a night you both were gone."

"What's your interest, Sanders? You want all the details?"

Almost before Jackson finished the sentence, Sanders

was in front of him, his arms braced on each side of the chair. "Why the hell couldn't you leave her alone? Why did you ever have to come here?"

Jackson stared up at the trader's tortured features. "Does Ainii know you feel this way?"

Sanders's eyes widened. "You think . . . I would never . . ." Then his gaze narrowed. "You bastard! You made love to her, too!"

"What do you mean, '*too*'?"

Sanders straightened, stepped back, and shook his head. Then he started walking to the door.

Jackson pushed up, ignored the instant weightlessness of his head, and in four strides placed himself between Sanders and the door. "What the hell did you mean, '*too*'?"

Sanders raised a hand as if to ward off an annoying insect. "Never mind. That's not important."

"Listen to me, you son of a bitch, what's going on here?" He grabbed Sanders's shoulders. "You came all the way over here just to tell me that making love to Ainii wasn't important?"

Sanders locked eyes with Jackson. "No, I came to save her from a different monster."

Jackson stumbled back a step. "What?"

"You still don't get it, do you? Tell me something, Walker, how did someone so blind to the truth get to be the best profiler?"

Jackson's gut wrenched. "What are you talking about?"

"You think that because you don't believe in the magic wolf, it doesn't exist?"

The knot tightened and Jackson's legs suddenly felt as weak as his head. "This is about the shapeshifter?"

"Isn't that what you were tracking with Ainii?"

"We were tracking a wolf."

"You mean *you* were tracking a wolf. And what did you find?"

"Nothing. Just a sweat lodge." Jackson strode past

Sanders. He glanced at the bottle, but kept walking to the window.

"And what was in the sweat lodge?" Sanders walked up behind him.

"Nothing." Jackson clenched his jaw against the memory.

"You saw nothing? Found nothing?" Sanders was right behind him, his voice calm but pointed, like an interrogator.

Suddenly Jackson knew how a criminal felt, maneuvered into a corner, trapped, and too exhausted to care.

"I found some fur."

Sanders turned Jackson to face him and Jackson recognized the look in Sanders's eyes—the certain gaze of a man who already knew the answers. Jackson had known that look from the inside—but right now it seemed like an eternity ago. He had to look away.

"What did Ainii do?" asked Sanders.

"She left," He stared into the blackness. "We left."

"Did Ainii see the fur?"

Jackson thought back to them on the ground, making love. Maybe she laid her hands on the fur; he wouldn't have known. "I don't know," he said. "I didn't notice."

"Aren't you paid to notice?"

Jackson stared back into the memory. "I was preoccupied," he said finally.

"I see."

Jackson heard Sanders move away and he turned to see the trader heading for the door. "Why are you so worried about Ainii, Sanders? What are you afraid of?"

"You should ask yourself that, Walker."

He had, but he didn't have an answer—at least, not one he sought, not one he wanted to think about, because the answer might put him too close to the truth about himself. "What brought you here, Sanders?"

The trader stopped, his hand on the door. "Ainii came to the post when I wasn't there and took the box I had of her father's things."

"So?"

"So, I know she intends to use it."

Jackson shook his head. This didn't make any sense. "What the hell are you talking about?"

"Ainii gave me the box on the day we buried her father. Arland didn't want it and Ainii said her father wouldn't want the ceremonial objects with her. She asked me to keep them safe."

"Safe from what, from who?"

"Just safe, Walker." Sanders shook his head. "The sacred objects of a great medicine man carry their own power."

"Ainii is a medicine man?" Jackson's hand sought the rock-solid wall.

"Not Ainii. Her father."

"Her father was a medicine man? All this time . . ." His voice trailed off and he just stared at Sanders. He pushed through the last fog of the liquor. "Why didn't she tell me?"

"And what difference would that have made, Walker? Would you have believed Ainii? Would you have done your job?" Sanders's eyes were dark.

Jackson couldn't understand the anger arcing to him from Sanders. "What I have to wonder, Sanders, is why everyone has kept this a secret."

"Ainii wanted her own life." Sanders walked toward Jackson. "She had it until you showed up."

"I didn't send her to Joe Clah, Sanders. Ainii did that all on her own," Jackson said absently. His thoughts were on when Ainii had found him at Clah's hogan and she had asked how Jackson's powers worked, as if she needed to understand. "Why *isn't* Ainii a medicine man, Sanders?"

Sanders didn't answer for a moment. Then, "She decided not to."

Jackson knew the answer wasn't complete. He thought of the times he'd been with Ainii—the calmness in her touch, her patience . . . the knowing look in her eyes. *You have it in you,* she had said to him at Clah's hogan. The tone of her voice took on new meaning now. He faced Sanders. "You're telling me she just gave it up? This child of a medicine man simply changed her mind?"

"Yes," Sanders said.

"And Arland?"

Sanders turned from Jackson. "I guess he had other plans."

"Neither child chose to follow in their father's footsteps?"

"They were not easy steps to fill," Sanders replied quietly.

"Why?" Jackson pursued Sanders across the room.

"You don't just choose to be a medicine man," Sanders replied.

"Cut the crap, Sanders. They not only didn't *choose* to be medicine men, they never talked about it, they kept it a secret about their father. Why?"

Sanders faced him. "Wouldn't you, if your father was killed for being a medicine man?" He walked to the door. "It doesn't matter, Walker."

Jackson grabbed his arm. "If it doesn't matter, then why are you so worried? Why does it matter that Ainii took her father's ceremonial box?"

"She has no business getting involved in this."

Those were the exact words Arland had used. An eerie foreboding settled over Jackson. "What are you afraid of, Sanders?" he asked again.

"I'm afraid for Ainii," he said. "She doesn't know how to use her father's things."

"Use them for what?"

"To bait *Yenaldlooshi.*"

Jackson saw fear and concern in Sanders's eyes. "She can't bait something that doesn't exist, Sanders."

"That's true, Walker." Sanders stared back, his eyes challenging. "What have you caught lately?"

"Unless that box of Ainii's father's has steel traps,

Ainii won't catch anything, either. A wolf killed Clah, Sanders. Not a shapeshifter.''

''Believe what you want, Walker.'' Sanders's gaze dismissed Jackson.

Jackson recognized that look—he'd seen it in Ainii's eyes back in the canyon, at the sweat lodge, right before Ainii insisted on leaving the canyon. ''Tell me this, Sanders: Why would Ainii think there was anything in that box to catch the wolf?''

''Because that's what her father did for a living, Walker. He baited and killed shapeshifters.''

''He what?''

''You heard me, but do you understand?''

''Are you saying he killed wolves?''

Sanders stared at him, unblinking. ''Have it your way, Walker.''

Jackson's thoughts raced back to the first time he had met Ainii. He saw the hatred for Clah in her eyes. He heard the cold judgment in her voice: that Clah's lies had killed her father. He remembered all of Ainii's questions about how the other victims were killed; her obsession with the details, even the number of nail marks.

His thoughts stopped on one image: Ainii's face—the fear, the curiosity . . . and the calm determination.

Cold, dispassionate logic delivered the answer, the one he had lost in a tangle of emotions: If Ainii could prove the existence of a shapeshifter, prove it to an FBI agent, she could redeem her father's honor.

Maybe Joe Clah was right. Maybe Ainii was a *dol holianda*—a crazy woman, meddling, manipulating.

Jackson pushed off the window and turned to see Sanders staring at him. ''Thanks for the insights, Sanders.'' He strode past him and grabbed his jacket from the closet.

Sanders watched him, his brow drawn in a query. ''I have to admit, you surprise me. I didn't expect you to believe.''

''I don't.'' Jackson opened the door and waited for Sanders to follow.

"Then where are you going?"

"I have business to do. Like I said, thanks."

Sanders stopped in the doorway. "What about Ainii? What about finding her and stopping her?"

"I'm not stopping you. Go on. Talk to her."

Sanders shoved Jackson against the wall. "Talk to her! She is not some child, sulking. She intends to face *Yenaldlooshi* alone!"

The surprise movement jammed the closet doorframe between Jackson's shoulder blades, took his breath for a second. He broke Sanders's grasp with a sweep of his arm, grabbed the man's wrist, and whipped him around, face to the wall. "Take a deep breath, Sanders, and think about this. You *don't* want to assault me."

Sanders stood silent. Gradually, Jackson eased his grip, then let the trader turn around. Sanders glared at him, hatred hardening his eyes. For the life of him, Jackson couldn't understand why. "It's a free country, Sanders. Ainii can make her own choices."

"Something happened in that sweat lodge that you're not telling me," Sanders said evenly. "I don't know what, but because of you, Ainii feels like she *has* no choice. If anything happens to her—"

"Because she uses her father's things in a ceremony? You said yourself that she doesn't have the training for whatever you think she's going to do."

"That *ceremony* calls on all the evil to join powers. The medicine man stands as a lightning rod, willing every source of evil to gather within him. The last medicine man to survive the assault was Ainii's father."

"She won't have to face the shapeshifter, Sanders, because he doesn't exist."

"Are you willing to bet Ainii's life on that?"

Fifteen

⌒

The meager lights of Chinle receded in Jackson's rearview mirror until they disappeared and total darkness spread in every direction for as far as he could see. Only the high beam of the Jeep's headlights interrupted the blanket of black. The night leveled the landscape, held all Navajoland close, unreachable, except within the imagination.

He could envision the mountains and mesas, the endless vistas brushed in subtle colors. And he could see one particular canyon, embedded deep, protecting a single hogan, a corral of sheep, and a lone woman . . . with her own vivid imagination.

His first impression had been correct: Ainii Henio was a person with too much time on her hands—time to interfere, make plans, concoct stories . . . maybe even tamper?

What lengths would she go to to prove the existence of a shapeshifter? Could she have planted the wolf prints at Clah's? What about the prints near Harrison's body?

A jagged ache opened in Jackson.

Ahead was the turnoff to Nazlini, the road to Ainii's. Despite all his thoughts, he felt the pull to turn from the highway, to leave the straight and narrow asphalt and descend into the maze of rutted sandy roads—to go to her. If for no other reason than to make her confess all her damned secrets. He would see her, face her, hold her.

Damn him! He couldn't even control his thoughts!

He gunned the Jeep to an impossible speed and passed Nazlini, his gaze trained ahead. Jackson grabbed the radio and punched in the private number.

"Nez here," answered a groggy voice.

"Do you know where I can reach Detective Henio?"

"Walker. Don't you ever sleep?"

"Not lately."

An exasperated moan traveled across the Res to Jackson's ears. "I haven't seen Detective Henio since the Harrison crime scene, two days ago," Nez said. "How did your wild wolf chase go?"

Jackson forced his thoughts to only the facts. "No wolf, but I did find fur."

"Where?"

"In a sweat lodge in a canyon north of Chinle."

"Strange place for a wolf to hide out. And what about tracks?"

Jackson stared into the infinite black just beyond his headlights. "Lost the tracks. Maybe Fish and Wildlife will have more luck."

"Their guys are in the canyons." He paused. "You got other problems, Walker."

"What are you talking about?"

"Word got out about the wolf. The press picked it up and now we've got reporters wandering around the Res asking questions."

"Because of a wolf?"

"Because there are no wolves in the Southwest and now we've got a killer wolf, taking down men."

"So, maybe we'll get lucky and he'll take care of a few reporters."

"Yeah, well, one reporter already got a story in the *Indian News* about this wolf. It also included quotes from Navajo medicine men about the legendary shapeshifter."

"The third estate at work." Jackson chuckled. "Thanks, Nez. I needed a laugh."

"They're not laughing at Window Rock. The People

are demanding the President do something, set things back to order. The Tribal Police have been deluged with calls, tips from Navajo all over the Res. Accusations about other Navajo who were acting weird. It's turning into a witch hunt. Just like in '93.''

"What happened in 1993?"

"The Hanta Virus. People falling down dead—young people, for no reason. Many Navajo were sure there had to be some awesome evil power at work to cause so much death. The rumors flew and it wasn't long before they found people to blame."

"What are you talking about?"

"Witches, Walker. The most common suspects are medicine men. People capable of manipulating evil." Nez sighed hard. "People will die if we don't catch this wolf soon."

Jackson thought about Ainii's father, killed in 1993—a medicine man who claimed he could catch shapeshifters. She couldn't have been much more than seventeen when she buried him and left, isolating herself in her solitary canyon.

"Walker? There's more."

Jackson pulled his thoughts from Ainii. "What?"

"Word about the wolf hunt also reached the Dallas Bureau. You got a call from there yesterday."

"Let me guess. They're not amused, either."

"Actually, the question was whether you're now into profiling animals."

Jackson grunted. "I'll call them in the morning."

"It is morning, Walker. Look, they want you to hand over whatever files you have and return."

"Hand them over to who?"

"To me." Nez paused. "Walker, I didn't ask for this."

It was an apology, but Jackson heard the sympathy. A dozen retorts leaped to mind and Jackson clamped his mouth shut.

"I need the files this morning, Walker."

"You'll have them," Jackson replied.

"I'm supposed to send copies to Albuquerque," Nez continued. "For Henio's investigations."

Jackson let the Jeep drift to the side of the road and he stopped. He could see a prick of light in the distance. It could be a car or it could be a star. Sky and earth—it was all the same out here . . . and it was all more different than anywhere he'd ever been. "Did you know Henio's father was a medicine man?" he asked Nez.

"No."

"Bill Sanders told me that he baited shapeshifters."

"Interesting," Nez said. "I didn't know there *were* medicine men who went after shapeshifters."

"According to Ainii, there aren't. Her father was the last."

For a moment, Nez didn't say anything. Then, "Did Detective Henio train with his father?"

"I don't know," Jackson answered. He stared at the light, trying to decide what it was. But the harder he looked, the more it wavered from his focus—here, then gone. "Call Albuquerque, Nez. And ask for everything they've got on the murders of the judge and the girl. I'll be in touch."

"Where are you going?"

"I'm going to see Ainii." Jackson pulled the Jeep onto the highway and headed back to the Nazlini road.

His first thought on hearing that Dallas wanted him back wasn't about the crimes—his first thought had been of Ainii.

With only a penetrating gaze and quiet words she had broken down his barriers. No one had ever gotten so close to him . . . and then pulled back. He should be grateful. Intimacy would only get in the way of what he had to do.

If he couldn't question Arland about his sister, Jackson would go to the source. Why had she been so interested since the beginning? And what did she know about her brother's investigations? Where the hell *was* her brother?

As if by some inner radar, Jackson found the road to Ainii's with no trouble. He snaked down the mountain to her canyon, gliding the last fifty feet to the grassy valley. He followed the creek—his headlights off—the still surface of the water a silvery mirror winding alongside. He glanced to the moon. Tomorrow it would be full.

Before the last turn of the canyon, he could see the glow of man-made lights. Ainii was home. He let out the breath he hadn't known he was holding. He pulled up to her hogan and turned off the Jeep. Stepping out, he registered the utter silence and didn't know why that should bother him . . . until he realized . . . no welcoming barks, no Dakota. He checked his watch and winced—it was one o'clock in the morning. Even Dakota was asleep. Someone was awake inside, though—he saw a shadow moving past one of the long windows.

Jackson knocked, but when the door opened, it was Irene Johnny, not Ainii. She stepped back from the door, her eyes wide with more than surprise.

"What do you want?"

Jackson's instinctive suspicious nature clicked in. "Hello, Irene," he said casually. "I came to see Ainii." He walked through the open door and glanced around. They were alone.

"She's not here." Irene kept her hand on the door.

She might hope he would turn around and walk back out, but Jackson kept going into the hogan.

"I don't know where she is," Irene said, still standing at the open door as she watched Jackson.

Jackson strolled through the kitchen area, where he caught the lingering smell of a cooked meal. He held aside a hanging rug and entered the living area to see a cozy scene of candles, a mug of something still steaming, and a book bent against its spine laying on the floor. A quiet evening at home, though it was someone else's home. Yet Jackson didn't detect anything amiss, except Irene's nervousness.

"She asked me to stay here and take care of the animals," she said. Jackson glanced at her. She'd turned to face him while still standing at the open door.

"When did she ask you this?"

"Two days ago."

Just before he saw Ainii at the Harrison crime scene, Jackson calculated. "How long did she say she'd be gone?"

"Just a couple days. It's already been that and I need to get back to Albert."

"Your husband?"

Irene nodded, her gaze always on Jackson.

Jackson stopped in front of the loom. Ainii had only completed another inch since he was last here, but he could see the hint of an intricate pattern emerging. Seven rolls of yarn, each a different rich color, sat at the base of the loom, a single thread from each roll reaching to the same row of the unfinished rug. He wondered how she kept the design straight in her head.

"I'm leaving in the morning," Irene said. "I didn't say I could stay here forever."

"And the animals?" Jackson asked absently, his fingers on the smooth woven yarns.

"They have plenty to graze. I have sheep and goats, too." Her voice came so quiet, Jackson swiveled on his feet to see her. She was staring at the floor, the look of an apology on her face, and Jackson suddenly got a sense of the friendship between the young girl and Ainii.

"I'm sure Ainii would understand." Jackson rose to leave. "By the way, do you know of a canyon she might go to, to be alone?"

"No." Her tone held a hint of curiosity.

Jackson looked at the young girl. "Thanks," he said as he walked out the door.

The door closed fast behind him just after he saw a look of relief on Irene's face. Jackson sat in his Jeep without starting it. His instincts told him that Irene's reactions had everything to do with him being there. She had been cautious, almost defensive. He didn't doubt her story about caring for the animals, which meant she was nervous about something else.

Jackson started his Jeep, turned it around, and headed back out the canyon, driving slowly to let his thoughts organize. Irene and Ainii might be friends, but Ainii held her secrets close—from Irene, from Bill . . . and from him. Was there anyone Ainii confided in? The rounded face of the crazy old woman came to him.

Jackson stopped and pulled out his map. He found Two Grey Hills on the other side of the Chuska Mountains, then groaned at the dearth of roads between here and there. He could take dirt roads—his finger followed their empty parallel lines leading across blank white space on the map. Some even had state road numbers.

Jackson already knew from experience that for each mapped dirt road, another half a dozen meandered in every direction. He discarded the absurd hope he would find *any* signs. Trying to find his way to Two Grey Hills in the dark on the back roads, he would likely end up where he began.

He chose to go back to the highway, down to Window Rock and up the backside of the Chuskas—an added fifty miles, but he was in no hurry. The only thing waiting for him today would be Nez, his hand ready to take Jackson's files.

He started up the cliff road, though he had the uneasy feeling he had forgotten something. Then he saw a flicker at the periphery of his vision, the fast movement of a shadow. But the only thing on the road was him, hemmed in by the towering canyon wall on one side and the sheer drop on the other.

It was only his infernal exhaustion, and he revved the Jeep up the incline.

Irene breathed easier as the Jeep's rumble gradually faded. She paced the hogan in an endless circle, walking through the conversation with the agent over and over. He had seemed to believe her. Most of what she'd said was true; the only lie was about Albert.

She held her arms close, rubbing her forearms. She'd

thought it was him when she had first heard the sound of a car. Then, to find the FBI agent on the other side of the door . . . for a second she thought he must know everything and had tracked her down. She nearly confessed on the spot.

She shook her head and walked faster. Only Mama knew . . . and Ainii. Mama wouldn't tell and Ainii was nowhere to be found. Irene took another deep breath. She would be safe here and maybe Albert would calm down while she was gone.

She picked up the mug of tea and set it in the sink, then walked back to the living area, blowing out candles on her way. She made a pile of rugs, saving the Pendleton for a blanket, and curled up next to a shaft of moonlight on the floor.

She didn't want to close her eyes, because every time, the nightmare would start. She would see Clah and his cold eyes, she felt his cold hands, the icy terror, then her own shame. It always ended with Albert's hot anger. One mistake and she had caused so much trouble.

Irene pulled the blanket higher, closed her eyes tighter, and pictured her sleeping babies, their tiny mouths like perfect fruit blossoms. But her mind heard the wind, the blessed air from the lips of the Holy Ones. The wind carried their disappointment; their scoldings creaked the timbers of the hogan and beat against the door. Her skin raised with a chill.

Then all was quiet. The wind died to an immediate, unnatural calm. A bloodcurdling cry brought her straight up. Her heart pounded against her chest with the hard thump of a man's hand on a leather drum.

She held her breath to hold in her own scream and the thunder of her lifeblood beat in her ears, drowning out all other sounds. Irene threw off the blanket and padded to the door, avoiding the windows. She pressed her ear to the door and forced herself to listen.

From the corral came the bleats of the sheep and goats. They whined and cried and, even from this distance, Irene could hear their frantic trampling of the ground. *Coyotes on the hunt.*

Desperately, she scanned the room for a rifle, a weapon, all the time knowing she couldn't move from the spot. Albert took care of predators, not her. Tears pricked at her eyes and slid down her cheek as she stood there frozen.

Finally, Irene stood back from the door, her every muscle cramped from holding the one position. The corral was quiet.

She shoved her feet in her boots and grabbed the Pendleton off the floor and, with all the courage she could muster, opened the hogan door. The animals bunched at the fence nearest the hogan, a mass of curly faces staring at her. Irene walked around the side of the corral. There, at the back, was the bloody heap of a sheep, and Irene knew immediately this wasn't a coyote kill for food. The scream she'd held erupted in terror.

Ainii's knees tensed around Shoogii and the horse grunted, already struggling up the talus slope.

"Shhh, Shoogii. I'm sorry." Ainii breathed deep, trying to quiet the erratic beat of her heart. The last time she'd come to this canyon she'd been a spy, sneaking behind her father to watch the ceremony. Now the scene of him facing *Yenaldlooshi,* the beast's teeth bared within inches of her father's flesh, replayed again and again in her mind. The childhood dread swept through her.

Shoogii snorted and, once again, Ainii loosened her grip. Her hand went to the satchel swinging at Shoogii's side. Ainii's fingers touched the canvas, felt the box within. All her father's tools rode with her. She should have had them blessed by Margie, but that would have taken precious time. As it was, it would take her at least a day to create the huge drypainting.

She would offer her own prayers. Whether the ritual tools would abide her touch and answer to her command—or rebel, turn her words around, and leave her at the mercy of the magic wolf—she wouldn't know until she tried.

She wondered at her newfound determination. She had Jackson to thank, though he had no idea the part he had played. And if he learned what she was doing, he wouldn't approve anyway, because he didn't believe. Yet Jackson himself had kindled the notion in her of following her instincts. She knew the very moment the spark of wonder had been struck: when she had seen the power in Jackson's eyes at Clah's hogan.

She had caught him at his most vulnerable, his thoughts naked, unmasked, and the stark truth in his eyes had plumbed to her very core. In that instant, she had recognized the same undiluted purpose within herself.

She wished he were here beside her. Just this morning, only two canyons away, he had held her in his arms and, for the first time in Ainii's life, she had known what it meant to feel like she was part of a whole—a part of something larger than herself. She wrapped herself in that feeling now—and discovered the strength Jackson had given her.

Ainii saw the place ahead. She knew it by the curve of the sandstone cliff. And she could see, as if it were happening right now, the silhouette on the rock wall of her father dancing—a lone figure cast black on the golden stone, the fire's flames leaping with the same wild rhythm.

Her whole body responded to the memory; her heart leaped and her breath came shallow. She slid from Shoogii and stood at the same bush where she had hidden so many years ago. The image dissolved and before her was only an empty canyon, the barren ground radiating a cold bluish light from the clouded moon.

This place wasn't hers, these tools weren't hers; the best she could hope for was to pretend her way through.

For a moment, Ainii thought of giving up. How helpless she must look to the Holy Ones, standing here without a clue of how to proceed. She wasn't her father. She wasn't even her father's apprentice. Damn him for not believing in her!

The angry thought startled her and she immediately tensed against the wave of guilt she knew would be forthcoming. Instead, the anger grew, built within her—the wind forced ahead of a threatening storm. Her fists clenched at her sides. She could do this. She knew the basics and she would follow her instincts for the rest. *This* time, there was no one here to stop her.

Sixteen

Jackson idled the Jeep up to the gate outside Margie's hogan, parked, and turned off the headlights. The gray light of dawn outlined the mountains to the east, but here in the valley, Margie's homestead was still dark and quiet. Though some animals milled in the yard—their faint shapes like shadows—it appeared the other residents were still asleep.

What Jackson could see of the compound surprised him. Considering Margie's eccentric behavior, he had expected a more disorganized yard. Instead, the area was tidy, clear of the usual stockpile of junked cars, scrap wood, and tires accumulated at so many other homes.

He reminded himself not to make any assumptions about the old medicine woman—it had been Arland who called her crazy. So far, she just seemed peculiar. Besides, he should know enough now not to underestimate the women of Navajoland.

He unlocked the latch, drove in, then walked back to close the gate. Something nuzzled his leg, but before Jackson could even look, he heard a small *baaa*. The lamb pushed against him again, catching Jackson's pants in its lips and tugging.

"I'm not food," he said, walking to his Jeep, dragging the still-attached sheep. "Tell you what. You let me go and I won't arrest you for assault."

The baby sheep studied him with huge brown eyes, but

didn't loosen its hold. Jackson leaned over and, with one hand, scratched the lamb behind its ears. With his other hand, he massaged the sheep's neck, gently pulling with each outward stroke. The sheep let go of Jackson's pants but, in the same motion, found his thumb and sucked hard. Jackson got the most amazing feeling deep in his gut.

"I have a grandson who will do that for you, if you like."

Jackson looked sideways from his bent position to see Margie walking across the yard. He pulled his thumb from the sheep's mouth and the lamb gave a loud sound of protest.

"Come along, Sweet Pea," Margie said.

The baby sheep stayed close to Jackson and he saw where the expression 'sheepish grin' came from. He wiped his thumb against his pants then extended his hand to Margie.

"Agent Walker. We met at—"

"Yes, you are the one helping Ainii." Margie took his hand and covered it with her other hand. She had a strong, warm grip. She looked to the Jeep, then back to him. "Where is she?"

Margie's assumption that Ainii would be with him picked at a place inside Jackson he hadn't known was raw. He opened his mouth to reply, but Margie spoke first.

"Finally, you're here. You have questions, yes? You want to know more about Ainii," she stated. She cocked her head and studied him.

Jackson shook his head, trying to regain control. "Margie, what can you tell me about Ainii's father's death?"

"Ainii did not tell you?"

"I would like to hear what you know."

"And what does Arland say, Mr. FBI man?"

"I'm asking *you*, Margie."

Her cheerful face still held a smile, but her eyes were keen and trained on Jackson. "You have a talent for not answering questions, Jackson Walker, FBI. So, I will. You do not know where Ainii is and you have not talked to Arland about his father, have you?''

Jackson found Margie's insight more than annoying. God, these Navajo women baffled him. ''Does that matter to you?''

''You did it again!'' She giggled. Her twinkling eyes lit with merriment.

Jackson cleared his throat. The lamb nudged his leg, nibbled a little, then nudged some more. Jackson stepped to the side, pulling on his pants leg, and the sheep followed. He finally caved in, knelt, and handed the baby sheep his thumb. Jackson considered his own tactics with Margie and decided to change strategy. ''When we met, Margie, you said I couldn't do this alone. I'm here, asking for your help.''

Margie's gaze turned serious. ''Yes, you are here asking me questions, but you are still alone, Jackson Walker.'' She shook her head, turned, and headed back to the hogan.

Jackson extracted his thumb from the lamb's lips, picked the lamb up under his arm, and strode to Margie. ''You're Ainii's friend, Margie. I thought you would want to help.''

Margie turned, gave Jackson—and the squiggling lamb—a look he could only describe as tolerant, then started on her way again. Jackson followed her around the side of the house, through a small grove of cottonwoods, into an open area at the back, where more than twenty sheep grazed freely.

''You can put her down.''

Jackson set down the lamb and, without a glance back, it scampered off to the other sheep, soon disappearing in the mass of curly rumps. Jackson looked up to see Margie at the corner of the house, struggling with a large trash bag and a bucket. His irritation with her racheted up another notch. He strode over, intent on making the old woman pay attention.

''I will answer your questions, Jackson Walker,'' Margie said, effectively taking the air out of his anger.

He held the bag open for her, his eyes watering at the sweet fumes of food trash. "At the Harrison crime scene, you were surprised to see Arland. Why?"

"Arland has not been back since his father was buried."

"But you sounded concerned."

"You misunderstood. I was not concerned, I was angry." Margie walked into the corral and deftly spread the contents from the bucket into a low trough. Jackson followed, annoyed that he should have to pursue her around the yard. "Why—" But his words were swallowed in a flurry of chickens and roosters swarming between Margie's and Jackson's legs—their cackles, crows, and pecks a cacophony of noise.

Margie moved on from the trough. Jackson caught up and grabbed her arm. "Margie, why—"

"We all have our responsibilities and our burdens," she interrupted. "If we forget, then there are consequences." She pulled away and walked to the stable.

"Margie, simple question, simple answer," Jackson called after her. "Why were you angry at Arland?"

Margie stopped and faced him. "We all have our place. Arland's is in Albuquerque. Ainii's is here. Where is yours, Mr. FBI man?"

Jackson felt a growl growing in his chest. The woman made him nuts. Arland was right: Margie was crazy. He admitted defeat and turned to leave.

"You are a disappointment, Jackson Walker. Do you always give up so easily?" she said behind him.

"You're the one who keeps walking away, evading the questions, Margie."

"And where is Ainii? Did she also walk away from you?"

"If she did, Margie, it was her own choice."

Margie smiled. "I see." She dropped the bucket and headed out of the corral, gesturing for Jackson to follow. They walked to the cottonwoods, where Margie settled herself before a loom. She held a hand out to the ground beside her and Jackson sat, facing her.

Margie picked up the thread and began weaving. "There once was a child," she began.

Jackson groaned inwardly.

"This child's mother was murdered," she continued, "and the child, only five, saw the murder. *Hastiin* Henio said it was a horrible sight." Margie stopped weaving, her gaze to the distance, as if recalling something.

"*Hastiin* Henio? Ainii and Arland's father?" Jackson asked.

"Yes. Arland was a baby. Ainii was not born yet." She picked up the thread once more. "He had performed a ceremony that very night, but *Yenaldlooshi* did not come." Margie paused. "*Hastiin* Henio was a powerful medicine man, a great *Ha'taalii*." She looked at Jackson, her gaze certain and proud. "He exhausted himself, dancing furiously through the night to draw *Yenaldlooshi* to him. All the evil gathered at his command, I know this. But that night, *Yenaldlooshi* had already tasted blood and he had his own mission: to take the child and make him his own." Margie set down the yarn and stared past the threads of the loom.

"*Hastiin* Henio also knew this. He told me he smelled the blood, he heard the screams of terror. He felt the torture of teeth thrashing through skin and sinking into his bones."

Helpless to stop himself, Jackson's mind leaped to every victim he'd known; their agony ripped through him; their cries for mercy cut to his soul. He lived through their last moments, their horror pumping through his veins. They died alone at the hands of a monster.

A firm grip at Jackson's shoulder made his heart jump.

"No human being should suffer such brutality," Margie said, voicing Jackson's thoughts.

Incredulous, Jackson stared at the old woman.

"That was the purpose that drove the *Ha'taalii* Henio." Her gaze softened on Jackson.

In the depths of Margie's eyes, Jackson saw the same patient understanding of Ainii's gaze.

"You said *Hastiin* Henio found the child?" He had to force the words past an unexplained tightness in his throat.

Margie nodded. "The evil that came to him in the ceremony led him to where *Yenaldlooshi* had killed. He found the magic wolf standing over the boy, guarding him, as if the child were a treasure he had won. At that moment, *Hastiin* Henio knew *Yenaldlooshi* planned to keep the child. He challenged *Yenaldlooshi*—yelling his name, waving a stick. *No one* yells the name of the magic wolf." Margie grew silent for a moment.

"The wolf stood tall, higher than *Hastiin* Henio, and he roared. Adobe crumbled from the walls of the hogan. Then the wolf turned to the boy. *Hastiin* Henio let the evil fill him, fill the air in his lungs, the thoughts in his head." Margie stood, her arms lifted to the sky. "When *Hastiin* Henio yelled, the power of all the witchcraft echoed. *Yenaldlooshi* lunged, his bared claws still bloody. He took *Hastiin* Henio to the ground and stood over him. But *Yenaldlooshi* saw the mastery of the evil in the great *Hastiin* Henio's eyes. He could not attack. He ran from the powerful *Ha'taalii*. In a *whoosh*"—Margie swept her arm through the air—"the wolf was gone." Margie looked down at Jackson, her eyes glistening.

Jackson cleared his throat. "Margie, what does this story have to do with Arland?"

Margie shook her head, as if Jackson were simple. "From that moment on, *Hastiin* Henio and *Yenaldlooshi* were locked in battle, each baiting the other. The magic wolf wanted the *Ha' taalii's* magic; he stalked *Hastiin* Henio and the children. Years went by, and soon Arland was old enough to train. But the son did not have the strength of his father and *Hastiin* Henio sent Arland away, fearful that *Yenaldlooshi* would find the boy's weakness." Margie looked at Jackson, her gaze expectant.

Jackson thought of Arland, shipped away. The hollow pit in his gut twisted. With rapid, routine dispassion, he fisted down his own irrational emotions. Jackson rose. "So his father sent Arland away." His voice sounded detached. "What was Arland's reaction? Did anyone think to ask him?"

Margie faced Jackson; her penetrating gaze locked his eyes with hers. "He reacted as any son would who was sent away. He cut off all communication with his home, with his people. That was for the best." She nodded slightly. "For some, their weakness of heart can only be strengthened when they are alone. For others . . ." Her gaze reached straight to Jackson's core. "For others, their heart can only live when they find their other half."

She spoke to him as if imparting some old medicine woman wisdom, but Jackson didn't need to hear what was best for his heart. "So you were angry at Arland for returning because he is better off by himself away from Navajoland?" Jackson shook his head at the meddlesome ways of the Navajo.

Margie's eyes filled with sadness. "If you have to ask that question, then you have not understood."

Jackson didn't care what Margie thought. He paced in front of the loom. "And Ainii? How did she feel about her brother being sent away?"

"You would have to ask her that question," Margie replied matter-of-factly.

"Why wasn't she sent away with Arland?"

"Ainii was a girl-child." Margie glanced away from Jackson to the distant mountains, their tops golden in the rising sun. "He did not expect his daughter to be a medicine woman."

Jackson looked at the proud medicine woman and, in her straight back and stoic countenance, he saw the determination necessary to be a medicine woman in a culture that expected male chanters. She had had to work against hundreds of years of tradition. Suddenly Jackson had the strangling sensation of being bound in the fabric of a thousand threads of legends and superstitions.

Maybe Arland had been the lucky one. He'd broken

free of the bonds. Ainii, on the other hand, had had to live within the confining expectations.

But that picture didn't match the Ainii he knew. It had been his experience that, once Ainii set her mind to something, nothing would stop her. She would have the determination to be a medicine woman. She was certainly stubborn enough. The mere admonition from her father would not have stopped her. "But she did get some training."

Margie smiled. "Ainii followed her father everywhere. She would not give up. I told *Hastiin* Henio that she had the strength that Arland did not have. But—" With an abrupt shake of her head, Margie stopped talking.

Jackson thought he glimpsed the trace of an old argument between Margie and the father. "But you didn't win that discussion."

"No," she said simply.

"Did it ever occur to you how manipulative you and *Hastiin* Henio were?"

Margie glanced at Jackson, her gaze unapologetic. "Of course. Only with constant adjustments do you keep your balance."

Jackson shook his head at her circular logic. "You have an answer for everything."

"I am *Dineh*, Jackson Walker. Answers for the Navajo are written everywhere—in the rocks, the stars, the wind. You only have to listen and you know what to do."

More Navajo wisdom that Jackson didn't know what to do with. "Well, you didn't have to be angry at Arland, Margie. He didn't come back on his own."

"What do you mean?" Now Margie looked surprised.

"The Bureau brought him here because of the murders he was investigating in New Mexico."

Margie stared at Jackson, concern in her eyes. "The same kind of murders?" she asked quietly.

"Similar. We asked for his cooperation. But he's gone now. He's back in his place, as you would put it."

Margie walked up close to Jackson. She stretched her

arms up and clasped his shoulders. Her eyes glistened. Jackson thought he saw pride there. "You have so much anger in you, and also so much love. You have a great moment facing you, Jackson Walker. I will watch to see what you do." With that, the old medicine woman walked away.

Jackson stared after her. The place where she'd grasped him was still warm; his skin still felt the impression of her small fingers. The churn in his gut of frustration mixing with anger was gone.

His thoughts went to Ainii. Her touch brought him the same calmness, and something else—as if she reached within his depths with some unqualified understanding. Jackson severed the growing tenderness.

Jackson got in his Jeep and pulled out of Margie's yard. He pondered the hapless Arland. Jackson now understood why the detective had been reluctant to help on the cases. Arland had even more reason than Jackson not to want to be here. This place, and its people, were seductive, drawing you in with quiet enchantment that no one could resist—including himself, he realized. It was good he was leaving.

Not until he was miles away did it occur to Jackson he hadn't learned what had happened to the child *Hastiin* Henio had rescued.

Midafternoon, Jackson strode into the Phoenix office. Some of the agents looked up as he walked to his desk, their glances hurried and sideways. Jackson figured his reputation as the "hotshot" had suffered, his impermeable armor dinged and dented. He told himself it would have happened someday, sooner or later. That his fallibility should catch up with him here—a place where so much seemed beyond his understanding—was appropriate. He'd been sent away from here once; the second time was no big deal—poetic justice.

"Where's Agent Nez?" he asked an agent who wasn't quick enough with his furtive glance.

"Back in interrogation," the agent said.

"With who?"

"An Albert Johnny. Brought in this morning on a Re-patriation charge. Caught him with the goods in a store in Gallup."

"Thanks," Jackson called, already heading down the hallway to the interrogation rooms. He peered in the window of the first door and saw Nez across the table from a young Navajo male.

Jackson rapped a knuckle on the window. Nez looked up and nodded, then, after a word with Johnny, pushed back from the table and joined Jackson in the hallway.

"I tried to reach you on the radio," he said after closing the door.

"I was out of range, up by the Chuskas, talking with Margie Torreon."

Nez gave a quick glance of surprise. "I thought you went to talk to Ainii Henio."

"Did. But she wasn't there. What's going on?"

Nez gazed to the man in the room. "He tried to sell a mask to a store owner in Gallup. The trader recognized it as ceremonial and called us. Lucky for us. It's one of the masks missing from Newcomb's post."

"What's his story?"

Nez faced Jackson. "He says he got it from Clah."

Jackson stared at the young man, his head resting in his hands. Irene Johnny's face came to him—nervous at Ainii's place, drawn tight in fear the first time he'd met her. "What do you think?"

Nez turned to Jackson and lowered his voice. "Instincts tell me he couldn't have done Newcomb. I don't even think he could have stolen the mask from him. I mean, this kid couldn't break into a cookie jar."

"So, he's telling the truth. He got it from Clah."

"Except he won't tell us how or when. The only words out of him in the last twenty minutes have been to ask for his wife. I sent someone out to her place."

"She's not there. Call your man and have him go to

Ainii Henio's. Irene's taking care of her animals."

Nez went to one of the agents and relayed the information. Jackson stared through the glass window at Albert Johnny and tried to picture him wielding a club with nails, tearing Clah's body apart, striking the lethal blows. He looked at his slender shoulders, his thin arms with barely a muscle. Albert moved his hand from his face and Jackson could see tears streaming down the young man's cheeks.

Jackson had to agree with Nez. This kid couldn't have killed either Newcomb or Clah; Jackson would stake what was left of his reputation on that. Then when did he get the mask?

Nez returned and reached for the doorknob. Jackson laid a hand on Nez's arm. "I saw Irene today and she was nervous. Back when I first went to see her, she was frightened. Let me question Albert."

Nez nodded and opened the door, then followed Jackson in. "Albert Johnny, this is Special Agent Walker. He'd like to ask you a few questions."

Albert looked up, his eyes imploring Jackson. "I already told Agent Nez everything I know."

"Well, Albert, you know that's not quite true, because you haven't explained how you got the mask."

"I got it from Clah."

Jackson took the seat across from Albert and leaned close across the table. "When?"

Albert looked away. "I don't remember."

"I see," Jackson said with understanding. "Then tell me, Albert, *why* would Clah give you the mask? He would need it for his ceremonies."

"Not for *his* ceremonies." Albert's voice was harsh. His face twisted in hatred.

"Why not, Albert?"

"He was not a medicine man." In Albert's half-turned face, Jackson could see a glisten in the corner of Albert's eyes and the clench of his jaw.

"But the people of Cottonwood say that he was."

"Clah used people," Albert said with disgust.

"He doesn't sound like someone you would want to know," Jackson said quietly.

"I didn't," Albert agreed.

"You didn't know him, Albert?"

"I mean, I didn't want to know him," Albert said quickly.

"But still you took a gift from him?"

Albert stared at Jackson. "He owed it to me." Albert's eyes carried the conviction of his words. Jackson pondered the strong purpose he saw in the eyes of this young Navajo.

"He owed it to you," Jackson repeated. "You mean you had done something for Clah and then he owed you?"

Albert's brows furrowed. Jackson didn't give him time to think of an answer. "Or maybe someone in your family did something for him?"

"No!"

Jackson had found the trigger point. He felt the familiar satisfaction inside. "Maybe it was Irene who did something for Clah?"

"No!" Albert came out of his chair. Nez held him down with a hand to his shoulder.

Albert's reaction sent a chill through Jackson. He recognized the utter hatred in the man's eyes and he knew where this was leading. But he had to get Albert to say it.

Jackson thought carefully about his next words. "You know, Albert, you seem like a good man." Jackson held the Navajo's gaze. "A good man who got involved in a terrible thing." Jackson shook his head in sympathy. "No one will blame you when they learn the truth."

Albert's eyes filled.

Jackson took an inward breath, going straight on his instincts. "They're bringing in Irene now, Albert. Then everyone will know who was to blame."

"She didn't do anything! It was Clah!"

Jackson's hunch worked, but a chill froze out his satisfaction. "What did Clah do to Irene, Albert?"

Albert sighed deeply. "I told her not to go to Clah. Ainii even told her."

Jackson's heart jumped. "Ainii Henio?"

"Ainii said she would get some poultice for Irene. But Irene couldn't wait."

The chill crawled through Jackson's gut. "Why did you forbid Irene to see Clah?"

"I didn't trust him," Albert said simply. "No one knows his training."

"What do you mean?"

"No one knows who trained him," Albert said again, his tone implying that Jackson should understand this significance.

"But still Irene went to Clah."

"Irene thought she had been bewitched and might die."

"Why did she think this, Albert?"

"Because of my mother. She . . ." Albert looked up. He had the face of a beaten and hurt man—his eyes wet, red, and swollen. "She has been hard on Irene." He reached across the table to Jackson. "Please don't make Irene say what happened. Please."

"If you tell us, Albert, it will be easier on Irene." Jackson kept his voice calm, though his insides twisted.

Albert stared at Jackson. "He touched her." He choked the words out past a stream of tears.

Jackson understood, at gut level, how torn up Albert was inside. "Where, Albert? Where did Clah touch Irene?"

"Where he shouldn't!"

Jackson leaned closer, trying to gain eye contact with Albert, but the husband was sobbing. "Did he molest her?"

"He tried to. Irene got away."

Suddenly Jackson saw Wynema Begay, murdered, raped, and dumped on the mesa. Had she been with Clah? And maybe hadn't been as lucky as Irene? His thoughts leaped to the girl found in New Mexico. "Albert, what else can you tell me about Clah?"

Albert looked up. "What do you mean?"

"You said you didn't really know him, but what had you heard?"

Albert looked past Jackson, as if trying to remember. "First time was years ago. During the Hanta Virus," he said. "Clah had powerful words about the witches causing all the deaths. People believed he *knew*. Later, I heard rumors about him in Chinle."

"What did you hear?"

Albert rubbed a hand across his forehead, as if trying to remember. "He made mistakes in some ceremonies. I don't know. You just hear about bad medicine men. A few years ago, the stories stopped. Maybe he quit for a while." Tears welled in Albert's eyes. "But then I heard Irene talking about him."

Jackson stared at the blank wall behind Albert. He saw the connection between Clah, the girl in New Mexico, and Wynema Begay. Coldness crept all the way through him. He pushed away from the table.

"What about the mask?" Nez's voice came as a surprise to both Albert and Jackson. "How did you get the mask, Albert?"

"I went to Clah. To tell him never to touch Irene again. But"—his eyes widened in horror—"he was dead." His voice came out pitiful.

"Why did you take the mask, Albert?" Jackson pressed.

"I don't know. He had no right to it." He stared at Jackson, his gaze begging to be believed.

"Albert . . ." Jackson touched the man's arm. "Did you see anyone or anything?"

A shudder ran through Albert. "I saw an evil painting in the sand."

Jackson stared, baffled. "What?"

"A closed painting. They're not supposed to be closed."

Suddenly Jackson saw clearly, in his mind's eye, the blue flakes in the sand outside Clah's hogan. "You mean you saw something blue in the sand?"

Albert shook his head. "No. It was a painting. Filled with the things that crawl. I scattered the sand." He looked up at Jackson, a flash of bravery in his eyes. "Then I ran. I called the police from Cottonwood." His face lit a little. "You can check that, can't you?"

Jackson walked to the door. Nez followed him out. "What do you think?"

"What did he mean when he said the painting was closed, that it was evil?"

"Drypaintings are used to heal," Nez explained. "The chanter always leaves an opening in the painting to let out the evil."

"What the hell . . ." Jackson said to himself. He looked at Nez. "I think you need to reexamine the evidence from Newcomb. We know Albert got the mask from Clah. But how did Clah get it from Newcomb?" Jackson let out a long sigh. "And you need to look for a connection between Clah and Wynema Begay."

Nez nodded.

"And call Detective Henio. See if he can place Clah in New Mexico at the time of that other girl's murder."

Nez eyed Jackson. "Do you think he took a sabbatical from Arizona and struck in New Mex?"

"It's worth checking out," Jackson said.

Nez shook his head. "What a coincidence that a wolf picked Clah."

"Yeah, what a coincidence." Jackson started down the hallway, trying to leave behind the aching coldness.

Nez followed. "If we're right about everything, that leaves only the Harrison murder unexplained."

"And the judge in Albuquerque," Jackson said absently, as he walked to his desk.

"That was a good interrogation, Walker." Nez stood across from Jackson. "A good way to end. I mean—"

Jackson held his hand up. "I'll be finished here soon. Then you can have the files."

Jackson pushed the mess to one side and sorted: Books went to one pile, folders pertinent to the cases to another. After a moment, Nez walked away.

Jackson's hand stopped at the file of interviews taken from the medicine men. It didn't include the one he'd just had with Margie. He sank into his chair and stared at the folder. He could debate the usefulness of what she'd said and how the information on Arland would be viewed, but he couldn't ignore his responsibility to report it. Jackson turned on his computer. He typed in everything she had said, until he got to the story of the child and the murder. That was hearsay without any corroboration.

Jackson exited his report and punched in the numbers for homicide cases, then realized he didn't have the year of the murder. Margie had said Arland was a baby at the time of the murder. If Arland was around twenty-six now, then 1972 would be a logical place to start.

He scanned the homicides of that year with the facts he had: murdered woman, orphaned child, and, he could presume, an unsolved crime. He came up empty for 1972 and tried 1973.

He stopped the cursor at August 1973. A woman in Chinle was found dead, her body torn up. The M.E. had concluded the woman was mauled by an animal. There wasn't a mention of a boy. Any more information would be in the woman's file.

Jackson went to the file room and pulled her folder. The few papers included the initial police report, the M.E.'s protocol, and the witness statement from *Hastiin* Henio. Jackson found a chair as he read. The story Margie had told him came alive—the mother's horror, the child's terror, the beast a great shadow at the door.

Sweat broke out on Jackson's brow. His heart pounded. He told himself he was reacting strongly only because of the session with Albert. He hadn't conquered his emotions, yet. Abruptly, he stood from the chair, sending it rolling across the floor. He dropped the file and the papers fell out, except for two attached at the back with a paper clip. The top one had the official emblem of the Navajo tribe at the top. He scanned down and saw the word "adoption." Had Henio adopted the boy?

Jackson read further. The letter said that Henio had permission from the tribe to put the child up for adoption and that the Navajo tribe would relinquish all claims to Julian Teller, also known as *Baa naha zhdool nih*.

Jackson's heart clenched at the cold words. They were so matter-of-fact and ordinary, and final. With this letter, the tribe had given away one of its own. He flipped up the letter to see the paper behind—the official adoption papers.

On this date of December 1, 1973, The Navajo Tribe waives any tribal birthrights to Julian Teller, born June 3, 1968 to Sylvia and Harlan Teller, and officially consents to the adoption of Julian Teller, by Warren and Mary Walker.

Jackson's heart stopped. He couldn't catch a breath. He sank to the floor, still holding the file, still staring at the words . . . the names of his parents.

Seventeen

The nightmare owned him. Jackson succumbed readily, without a fight. He would watch it, take in every detail, and relive it—this time, for his mother.

The shadow of something huge filled the doorway, blocking out almost all light from the hallway. *His* hallway, *his* doorway—he knew now. The shadow truly *was* a monster. Jackson told himself these things, as the images stole over him, changing the tile he sat on to a wood floor and the white walls of the file room to dark adobe.

The beast stepped into the room, walking upright on hind legs. A scream caught in Jackson's throat. The beast snapped its head to where Jackson huddled. Its eyes gleamed—huge brown eyes that held Jackson's gaze, though every part of him cried out to close his eyes, hide. Where was his mother? He could yell for her, but something stopped him. She would die here.

The beast dropped to all fours and moved in. Its gaze never wavered from Jackson. Its white teeth gleamed. Its massive head loomed above Jackson. Jackson's heart beat in his chest like a fist pounding on a locked door, desperate to escape.

"Julian," his mother's voice sang out. "Is that you?"

The beast snarled. Jackson opened his mouth to shout, but he couldn't make a sound.

The slender shape of his mother appeared at the door. "Julian?"

Those were her last words.

The monster spun and lunged, all in one lethal motion. His mother's screams tore through Jackson. He heard the snaps of the beast's jaws. He wanted to run to her, to save her. The beast's wild growls sawed through Jackson, split open his heart. He couldn't move.

Suddenly it was over. In one instant, all was deathly silent. Jackson saw the beast, its black hairs spiky sharp in the light, standing over his mother.

A mortal wound opened in his gut. All his pain, his tears, the screams of terror he hadn't voiced, flowed into the hole. Everything he had ever felt drained away.

A sharp jab at Jackson's shoulder pulled him from the memory. He didn't want to leave. He stared hard at the past, a man awakened from the midst of a dream, still clinging to it.

". . . all right?"

Jackson tried to focus, but he couldn't bring the energy to bear.

". . . doing on the floor?" It was Nez.

". . . All right." The words croaked in Jackson's throat. He swallowed. "I'm fine," he managed. He braced a hand to the floor to push himself up. His body weighed a ton, yet at the same time felt empty. It took Nez to help Jackson stand.

"What happened?" the agent asked.

"Nothing. Just looking through some old homicide files." Jackson tried for normalcy—straightening the papers back into the folder—but the file trembled. He slapped it against his thigh and strode to the door.

"You sure you're all right?"

"Fine." The violence from the memory filled the hole in him. The terror, the cramping helplessness that had paralyzed him, mutated into anger and flowed through him to the pit, where new life formed.

"Where are you going?" Nez called out.

Jackson was already two strides out the front door. "To

find Ainii,'' he said, though he hadn't known that was his goal until he spoke the words.

"Walker, what about Dallas?" Nez yelled.

Jackson winced at the sound of his name. "To hell with Dallas," he muttered.

Jackson roared up Highway 191. He didn't have a plan. He didn't have a destination. All he had was a drive pounding through him to find Ainii.

The black cauldron churned in him. A hot mix of anger and loss bubbled, steaming out his pores, cleansing him from any residue of control. There had been too much goddamned control!

All his life he had controlled the nightmare, only to discover it controlled him! The violence raced through his veins as if freed through a floodgate, freed from a place where it boiled within him.

The thought struck him cold. Had his whole professional life been built on a trembling reservoir of terror and violence?

He thought of the victims he had touched, reaching into them to understand their pain, their last moments. What he had been doing was tapping into his own violence, channeling it.

He had thought he owned his life, but now he felt the fibers of this place winding around him, through him, tying his thoughts, his emotions . . . and his logic in a knot.

How did he understand that a wolf could stand upright? How could he accept his own mother killed by a rampant wolf? A myth! Was he now supposed to believe in supernatural powers, in paranormal beasts?

Jackson's foot laid heavy on the gas.

This place had turned his life inside out. He'd known who he was before he came here . . . Jackson Walker.

Now he had a name for the mother who had died. And a name for the child he had been: Julian Teller. The words throbbed at his temple.

He also had a name for the person who gave him away: *Hastiin* Henio. Why?

Why not? answered an angry voice. The man had been capable of sending away his only son. What hardship would there be to give away someone else's child?

He shouldn't care, Jackson told himself. He had known he was born here and given away for adoption. It shouldn't matter who did it or why.

He should get on a plane and fly out of here—leave this place, his past, these incomprehensible people far behind.

What remained of his logical mind told him to do just that. But he couldn't move his foot to the brake. He couldn't take the pressure off the accelerator. A need pounded through him, forcing his foot down.

The need was simple. Jackson didn't know what was real any longer. In his heart, the place he had always found the truth, he had thought Ainii might be the real thing. He had fought the attraction, cast doubt on every one of his perceptions of her. But he could not exorcise her hold on him.

Ainii's face floated before him—calm, collected, full of silent purpose. She had been in command since he first met her, clouding his own mind, tangling up his emotions.

But what did she feel?

Yes, he had felt her passion when they made love, yet she had ridden away from him without an explanation. Maybe her passion served her own agenda—a part of her own plan, just as her father operated according to his own plan.

Her father had manipulated Jackson's future. Had Ainii manipulated his feelings?

Suddenly he realized that his blind race down the highway was for an answer. She would have to tell him to go. Ainii would have to look him in the eyes and tell him she didn't care.

He was weak with the need for just those words. And the weakness ate away at him, gnawing at the last of his control. If he was any kind of man, he would turn back now, save what was left of his dignity.

The labor of wrangling with his emotions tied his guts in a knot. Helplessness owned him—owned his hands on the wheel and his foot on the gas. It owned his heart and mind and soul.

The Jeep ate up the highway. The landscape flashed by in a blur of pink and brown. He would find Ainii. He would see the truth in her eyes and be able to walk away.

Then he could have his life back.

North of Chinle, he left Highway 191 and took one of the hundreds of unmarked roads. He didn't care where the road led—in the distance he could see the foothills of the Chuska Mountains and, after a few miles, he simply left the dirt road and drove off into the desert toward the mountains.

Sagebrush scraped the underside of the Jeep. Gnarly cedar branches reached out and snagged the side mirrors. Jackson kept his sight on the mountain range and the canyons hiding there. The Jeep jounced and bounced and Jackson navigated. Every hard crunch of the Jeep's belly on bedrock drove home the single goal with a clearness of purpose he hadn't felt in weeks.

With little effort, he maneuvered the Jeep past sudden boulders, picking the surest path with some inner instinct. The sun set, turning the cliffs golden, and Jackson found himself, without knowing how he got there, at the mouth of the canyon he and Ainii had explored.

He drove up the canyon, past the abandoned sweat lodge, to where the trail finally narrowed and disappeared in the cliff face. No Ainii.

He sat there, the Jeep's rumble tossed back and forth between the canyon walls. He was sure he'd find her here.

He jammed the Jeep into gear and turned around. He took the dry wash out of the canyon, down into the arroyo, then into another wash to the next canyon.

He drove deep into the second canyon, to where the cliff walls curved and met—a dead end. No Ainii.

The towering walls shut out the last of the sunset. The certainty that had brought him here, that he would find Ainii, now slipped through his fingers as easily as the day slipped to night.

Jackson turned off the Jeep and sat in darkness. What the hell was he doing here? The reason eluded him. What had he thought would happen? He'd driven here like a wild man intent on . . . what? Some words from Ainii?

He choked out a laugh, shaky in the night's chill. Jackson stepped from the Jeep and stood there, at the end of a canyon in the middle of nowhere. Total quiet surrounded him; such utter silence it hummed in his ears like a ghostly wind. He shook his head, but the hum increased to a roar and reverberated through him, as if the ground he stood on were quaking.

Suddenly the air whipped around him. A deafening screech pierced his ears and great wings flapped right before him, fanning the air. He stared at the massive hawk as if it were an apparition, hovering only feet away.

The hawk stared back, its bright yellow eyes studying him in perfect concentration. Jackson could see every detail of the hawk's face: the dark ring of pupil flecked with gold; the shiny black feathers on its head so smooth they looked combed. He thought he had never seen anything so beautiful.

Then, with an imperceptible shift of its powerful wings, the hawk lifted and, before Jackson could take his next breath, it soared effortlessly up the sheer canyon. Jackson could hear the rush of air beneath the hawk. For a harrowing moment, he could even feel it, as if he were gliding up and over the canyon, the sheer walls fleeing beneath him.

He sank to his knees, to the solid ground. The hawk disappeared, leaving Jackson with only the incredible sensation of a suspended moment, weightless, unencumbered. It was the same sense he had had in the past with victims—that second of panic when he stepped off the abyss, focusing himself ahead of the fear, ahead of his own doubts—ultimately trusting himself.

He climbed back in the Jeep and drove out of the canyon, then turned across the foothills to the shadow of a smaller canyon. He parked the Jeep at the entrance and walked, letting his instincts lead him.

He rounded a corner in the canyon and stopped. He could never have prepared himself for the sight before him.

There, in the curve of the canyon wall, was the silhouette of someone dancing. The elongated shape drifted over the crevices and craggs—a disembodied form stretching down the cliff and across the ground to a fire.

Jackson walked closer, drawn in silent awe to the sight of Ainii swirling across the desert floor. Amber firelight outlined her naked body: the subtle curve of her back, the merest width of a waist. Her arms hung suspended, splayed like supple wings from her side. She danced with a grace reserved for birds, not humans—a soundless symphony of motion and light. She moved in one area, her bare toes tossing the sand. Her arms swept through the air in giant circles, her face lifted to the sky.

Jackson watched from the periphery, a voyeur in the shrubby sagebrush, his gaze claimed by the wonder of Ainii's body. Then he noticed the vibrant colors painting her. Blue smeared her legs and arms, across her flat belly and over her breasts. Her face was bright yellow, with streaks of red around her eyes and mouth and down her cheeks. Dots of black speckled her whole body, from her face to her toes. She looked like some exotic bird—beautiful and unique.

Jackson caught the strains of a melody, low and rhythmic. He inched closer, staying hidden in the brush, but still couldn't hear what she sang. She held the song close within her, letting an occasional note glide out—only to have it swirl from reach on the fire's plumes.

The slow, lithe movements gradually gained momentum. Her arms rose higher and higher, and finally they reached straight up. The sand at her feet flew in bursts of energy. The song increased, the notes building and building as if she had endless air and the melody could expand forever like the shadow stretching up the cliff wall.

The chant echoed through the canyon and circled Jackson, sending a wave of aliveness over his skin. He couldn't understand the words, but he heard the power in each haunting note. No living thing could ignore this song.

As he watched, overtaken with this extraordinary vision, it struck him how little he really knew about Ainii. Where was the quiet, reserved weaver he knew? Where was the woman whose fathomless dark eyes slowed all time to the moment?

Suddenly Ainii stopped, her body rigid. She held one arm straight up, her hand fisted at the sky, and Jackson thought he saw sprinkles of something trail from her hand. Her chest rose and fell with each breath, then stopped on a rise and she yelled, "*Yenaldlooshi!*"

Her voice, wild and powerful, raised the hairs on his arms. *No one yells the name of the magic wolf.* Margie's words came to him and his heart leaped. Ainii stood out there, alone, under the stars, challenging *Yenaldlooshi* to a battle. In that instant, it struck Jackson that Ainii truly believed in the shapeshifter, believed in the powers of evil, and believed in her own death if she should make a mistake.

He was seeing the child of the medicine man—the daughter *Hastiin* Henio had forbidden to train. Yet here she was, naked to the sky and stars, dancing alone with the fire.

And here Jackson sat, watching her, with the thoughts of a poet.

Ainii stood like a statue until the yell finished circling the canyon and slowly died. Then she started with the dance, once again.

She repeated the ritual over and over, every movement the same. He didn't know how many times, but enough

that he could anticipate what came next. He could feel
the rhythm inside him, hear the notes in his head. So he
noticed immediately when one arm fell a little too low
and when a couple of her steps came down a little too
hard.

How long had she been dancing? How long had he
been watching? Jackson glanced at his watch and lost a
breath. He'd been here three hours. He looked up at Ainii
and saw the lines of exhaustion on her face. How much
longer could she go on?

She kept dancing and the number of falters increased.
Her breath was shallow and her lips drawn back. Jackson
couldn't stand to watch her in such pain. He stood awkwardly, his muscles tight and one foot asleep. But as
clumsy as he was pushing through the sagebrush, Ainii
didn't notice.

As he neared, Jackson saw Ainii was dancing on a huge
drypainting. She had trampled the center, but Jackson
could see hundreds of shapes sprawling over the sand like
shadow creatures crawling away from the firelight. He
stared dumbfounded at the magnitude of what she had
created. Jackson had never known anyone, man or
woman, with such an indomitable heart.

He looked over at Ainii, his emotions clogged in his
throat. He saw the agony the paint had obscured on her
body. Every muscle was frozen tight and the arteries at
her neck stood out stiff and blue. When he looked in her
eyes, his heart cracked. They had the desperate look of
failure—a failure she wouldn't accept. She didn't even
see him, she was so focused on whatever kept her going.

Gently, Jackson touched her shoulder, but she didn't
stop moving. She was lost in the dance. For a moment
before he applied more of a grip, he worried about startling her. The next instant, she crumbled beneath his
hands. He caught her as she fell and slid to the ground
with her in his arms. Her fist opened and corn pollen
dusted the sand and left a residue of yellow on her palm.

She lay limp across his lap. Jackson pushed the hair

back from her face and trailed a finger down her cheek. Dry yellow and red paint flaked off at his touch. He ran a hand down her arm, the rough texture of the blue paint catching and rubbing against his palm. He turned his hand over to see glistening chips of blue. On her arm, he saw the sheen of bare skin.

Jackson moved his hand to her leg, kneaded her muscles, rubbing off more paint. His gaze took in all of her. He caressed. The paint fell away. His hand glided over her—her slender legs, her shallow stomach, her round breasts—until his touch ached with the preciousness of what he held.

Desire flooded Jackson—a tidal wave that built deep within him and crashed over his head. Blood drained from his veins and pooled deep inside—leaving him with only the purest sense of touch at every one of his nerve endings.

He cradled her face in his hands. His fingers pressed against her temples and he felt the thrum of her heart beneath his fingertips. Her pulse beat with his in a drumbeat that echoed in his head and reverberated down to his core, driving home a need.

He kissed her and his heart leaped—the mere touch of their lips sent a jolt through him. His body tensed with the ache of wanting her. His gentle kiss slanted, deepened, his thoughts lost except for where his mouth pressed to hers. She tasted of earthen sweetness, like the fresh root of slender grass.

She sighed, her air slipping from her mouth to his. Jackson started to ease away, stricken for a second with how he had taken advantage. Then she shifted toward him— he felt her hand at his shoulder and her lips moved against his. Her fingers slipped through his hair and she curled toward him in his lap, pulling him closer. Her response weakened him down to his toes and any thought he'd had of control vaporized.

He slid his arms around her back. His hands braced her head, her thick hair a wave of cool pleasure between his fingers. He had the sensation of clutching a cloud, riding it high into the night—and if he let go, she would slip through his hands. He couldn't let that happen.

"You found me," she murmured.

"Yes. I found you," Jackson said on a tight breath as his mouth captured hers.

Ainii sank deep into the kiss, letting it claim her. She forgot her exhaustion and the ache in every limb. The taste of him in her mouth brought her to life—his strong arms brought her strength. If he would only hold her tighter, closer, she could believe this was true—that he would want her . . . now . . . at the moment of her greatest failure. Sadness slipped behind her eyes and pricked tears.

Jackson eased back, separating their lips, and Ainii's eyes filled with the certainty he had come to his senses.

"Do you know how I found you tonight?" he said, his breath warm at her temple.

His heart thumped at hers. Ainii shook her head, unable to manage any words.

"A hawk came to me." He pressed his lips to her ear, kissing and nibbling.

Shivers ran through Ainii—from his words, from his kisses. "A hawk?" Her voice trembled.

Jackson's tongue circled the rim of her ear. The shivers exploded to waves of pleasure.

"I had given up." His tongue probed deeper.

The pleasure within Ainii drew tight as a cord. She fought to keep her mind focused on the oddity of the hawk coming to Jackson. She had to know more. Jackson's tongue found the core of her ear and Ainii's thoughts disintegrated.

She turned his head, sought his mouth, his lips. She was vaguely aware that his hands left her and of some movement to the side. A flutter of air grazed her and she saw Jackson's shirt settle on the ground. Then he braced her back and took her down to the ground, to something soft, she noticed, but she didn't care. It wouldn't have mattered if she lay on rocks and cactus. All she felt was the heat flowing between her and Jackson. His lips on hers, a hand framing her face, his thumb gently limning her jaw, a hand trailing down her arm, fingers sliding next to the curve of her breast . . . all the details mounted, every touch overlapping the one before, until she couldn't distinguish the touch from the pleasure.

She gave herself over to him. Her hands trailed up his back, over the deep molds of his muscles. A shiver ran through Jackson under her fingers and she opened her eyes to see him staring at her. His black eyes reflected streaks of firelight and Ainii thought he had the eyes of night, able to see over miles, from great heights, and into the depths of her soul.

With those eyes he looked beyond the moment to the past, searched the most terrible thoughts of people—strangers—to find the answers they couldn't give. And now he looked on her. Ainii's chest tightened with the thought of what he saw: someone who thought she could be more, who dared think she could defy the rules set down, a silly, willful woman who had told herself she could do anything. She looked into the eyes of the man who truly *could* do what she only dreamed of. She saw the power swirling there, felt it beneath her hands.

She turned her head into the crook of Jackson's elbow, hiding her eyes from his gaze. She kissed the soft underskin of his arm.

"I saw something extraordinary tonight," he said. His voice, deeply textured as a distant mountain, rubbed over her, puckering her skin.

She didn't want to ask him what he'd seen. She captured some of his skin with her teeth, desperate to distract him from his thoughts. Jackson expelled a hiss of air.

"Something unique and wonderful," he muttered.

Ainii's thoughts fled to the hawk. A hawk had appeared for Jackson. No animal had better sight or more perfect control. Jackson *was* a hawk. His instincts were his vision. Ainii buried her head in the crook of his arm. She felt

Jackson's lips at the corner of her mouth, down her jaw and neck. He settled between her breasts.

"I have never known anyone with such a powerful heart, Ainii."

His breath skimmed over her breast to where that very heart shuddered. A tear slipped from the corner of her eye.

Jackson slipped a hand along her cheek and turned her to face him. Ainii choked back the tears, tried desperately to bury her despair deep, out of Jackson's reach.

His hands framed her face—the hands he placed on victims and their blood, the hands he used to find the truth. Ainii's shame escaped her grasp and rose swiftly. She stared back at Jackson, helpless to hide her emotions.

"Do you know how beautiful you are? Not just . . ." His gaze scanned from her face and down her body. When he looked back, his eyes were intense. "I watched you tonight. For hours." His voice had the tone of a confession. "When I came here, I needed—" He broke off. His brow furrowed, as if fighting against the next words.

The sight of the struggle on Jackson's face to control his words, his emotions, had the power of a strong wind, lifting her out of her own despair, drying her tears. Her own frantic thoughts calmed and in the strength of Jackson's gaze, she stared at her fears. She chased them down with her inner gaze and they fled. In their wake, she saw the truth: She needed Jackson.

She needed him because she couldn't do this alone . . . Margie had been right. But the need went deeper—to the place in her that recognized when something was *right*.

She saw in Jackson's eyes that he needed her, too, though he couldn't say the words. She laid a hand on his cheek. "I'm glad you're here, Jackson."

His brow furrowed deeper as he stared into her eyes. Then he brushed his lips against her palm and the rush of wanting surged through Ainii and fell from her lips on a moan.

Jackson captured her moan in his mouth. He had never

wanted someone so totally. Her tongue slid over his lips and Jackson felt his need down to his toes. His mind, the voice of reason, of self-preservation, told him to slow down, back off, leave, before she owned a part of him he could never reclaim.

One thought ruled: It came from his heart and commanded his body. It was a thought that should have struck terror, yet instead brought fulfillment, as if he'd found a missing puzzle piece and made the final connection.

He felt Ainii's hands at his sides, his hips, then reaching beneath the buckle at his waist. His hands joined hers, unfastening, slipping the cloth over his hips and off. His fingers trailed up her legs, to between them, to where he pressed against her, then slipped within her.

Her body took him, arched toward him. Jackson felt, at his fingers, the strength within Ainii, the power of her body, and the pooling of her own need. He needed to feel himself inside her, have that power surround him. He shifted, spread her legs, and eased within.

As she took him willingly, deeper inside her, waves of passion engulfed him. The thought pounded—a litany of truth that pulsed from his core to his heart. He suddenly remembered Ainii's words when they'd first met: Thoughts were powerful. And the word circling his heart claimed his soul.

Eighteen

⁓

Ainii rolled over within the clothes Jackson had wrapped around her and watched him tend the fire. His silhouette loomed like a huge humpedback *Yei* on the canyon wall—as if the ancient rock symbol had stepped to life. Ainii smiled at the comparison because, for all his estrangement from his people, Jackson carried the bedrock character of a Navajo man within him. She watched him poke twigs and arrange large sticks just so—his attention, as always, focused on his immediate task. He was nothing if not thorough.

That thought produced a swell of pleasure in Ainii as her body remembered the effect of his competent hands. He had explored every inch of her, leaving no part of her untouched. Along the path, he had tapped into wellsprings of arousal Ainii hadn't known existed.

It was as if his hands already possessed intimate knowledge of her—and he knew best what she needed . . . what she wanted.

Ainii had never felt so loved.

Her thoughts stopped on the word. She turned it around and around in her mind. Yes, she had been loved last night, though Jackson hadn't put it in words. In fact, he hadn't said much of anything. But Ainii had felt the love within his hands and she had seen it in the depth of his eyes as if he held the thought just beyond what he himself could put a name to.

In truth, he might try to resist ever recognizing the word or uttering it aloud. But that made no difference. Thoughts embedded themselves with the tenacity of a splinter. You might not know where it came from; you might try to ignore it, avoid it, tread lightly upon it, but eventually any splinter worth worrying about was a splinter worth doing something about.

Ainii only had to wait.

She could do that right here. She snuggled within the clothes, hugely content to lay here forever, her gaze set on Jackson, savoring every inch of his body. Amazing that she could feel so utterly satisfied despite her colossal failure last night to bait *Yenaldlooshi*.

She searched for a trace of the despair, but it had disappeared, as if vanquished in the night under the strong stare of keen eyes. Jackson had given her that strength. It lasted even now, pumping through her with renewed confidence.

Ainii pulled her eyes from Jackson to the trampled dry-painting. It would take her the day to repair it. Luckily, she had reserves of the piñon gum and juniper berry dyes for the colors. The error could be within the painting—she had only the memories of her father's painting to go on—or the error could be within her words, even within the dance.

Sluggish doubt crawled through her like a sightless snail, imperceptibly slow and destructive, chewing away at her confidence. She stared at it, her mind poking the timid snail back in its shell. She remembered, then. She had *felt* the power of the ceremony for a time during the night. Whatever her mistake, she was close—as close as reaching for the right thing from a pile of possibilities on a table. She only had to concentrate. Her mind narrowed on the thought, analyzing it.

"Good morning."

Jackson's gravelly voice raised another wave of awareness in Ainii, prickling her skin. She looked over with a smile, but his brow was furrowed, his gaze troubled.

"Is it?"

Jackson glanced at his bare wrist. "I seem to have misplaced my watch."

She hadn't questioned whether it was morning, but rather his opinion. She got her answer nonetheless when he turned back to the fire—a fire which Ainii now saw he had nearly smothered with attention. He had stacked stick upon stick, some with roots and green leaves dangling—a pile she could only describe as haphazard, a mindless effort of his hands while his thoughts were elsewhere.

Ainii smiled inwardly. The splinter was already working its way through Jackson.

"I don't really care what time it is," she said.

"You should sleep more. You were exhausted last night." Jackson's gaze went to the scattered sand, blue, white, and black tossed in so many directions. "You will do this again tonight?"

"Yes."

He nodded, giving Ainii the impression that he had expected that answer. "You'll go through it all over again." He made it sound so pointless.

"Yes. I have to."

He looked at her, a myriad of questions creased in his brow. Ainii wondered which question he would use next to distract himself from what really bothered him. He cocked his head to her and Ainii saw he had decided.

"Why didn't you tell me your father was a medicine man?"

She answered honestly. "I didn't think about telling you or not telling you. I don't talk about him."

"You don't think it would have been helpful for me to know?"

"Was it?"

His mouth dropped slightly. He turned away and Ainii saw his jaw clench. "It did help me understand some things," he said finally.

"Then I'm glad you know."

Jackson raised his gaze skyward and shook his head. "For you to know and me to find out, right?"

"You make it sound like a game. For me, it was my only choice. It's how I've lived ever since he died." The truth fell from her lips to be judged by Jackson. "I kept my father and his work a secret because I was afraid."

"And now you're not afraid?" he asked, as if it were as simple as that.

Ainii thought of the enormous task ahead of her. She drew Jackson's leather jacket closer to her. "Now I can't be."

"And now you're not afraid of me." He spoke the words almost like an accusation.

"I was never—"

"Then why did you pull away from me in the canyon?"

Ainii knew what he meant. "I thought it was for the best. I could see you were vulnerable—"

"So that seemed a good time to put distance between us?"

"Yes," she answered.

"Why?"

"Because of how you reacted to the fur."

"The fur," Jackson repeated. He rose and walked to her with such presence he seemed to move the scenery with him. Ainii's breath caught. "You mean the nightmare, don't you?" he asked, his gaze holding hers. "The nightmare I couldn't control?"

He knelt beside her and Ainii saw the beat of his pulse at his temple. "Yes. I saw that the evil in *Yenaldlooshi* affected you. But you wouldn't admit it."

Pain flickered in his eyes—and a hint of distrust. Ainii's heart clenched around the truth. She *hadn't* trusted him to believe; she hadn't trusted in his strength to face *Yenaldlooshi*; she had made a decision and acted on it, without giving Jackson so much as an explanation.

It occurred to her she had treated Jackson exactly the way her father had treated her.

She framed his face with her hands. "I'm sorry."

The turbulence calmed in Jackson and he stared back, his emotions stripped to the bone. The love she felt for him welled so swiftly from her heart, Ainii's eyes pricked. "I couldn't stand to see you hurt."

As the words fell from her lips, Ainii thought of her father. She saw his loving face smiling at her. A thought skipped just out of reach, something she should understand. A warm touch at her face, tangling through her hair, brought her focus back to Jackson. He looked down at her, a sad smile in his eyes. "You come by it honestly." He rubbed a thumb over her cheek.

"What?" Ainii's thoughts scattered at his touch, his look.

"Making decisions for the good of others."

She tried to follow the train of his thoughts, but Ainii had the sense she'd missed an important connection—like an intricate pattern she saw with her heart that her mind couldn't yet perceive.

"It doesn't matter," he whispered, his tone so sad, Ainii could hardly breathe. "But some things we have to decide for ourselves." He let his hand glide down her cheek and across her shoulder.

Ainii's skin ached beneath his touch—his callused hand rubbing across her emotions. An unreasonable urgency gripped her—along with a panicked doubt: What if Jackson could never admit he loved her?

She tilted her head up, looking to his eyes for an answer. His lips captured hers, taking her breath. His arm went around her back, pulling her close—all with too much need, too much desperation . . . as if he were reluctant to let her go. Ainii's heart beat furiously.

Suddenly he sat back, his gaze over her head and beyond, and Ainii saw him looking back to where he had come from, as if he thought he had merely made a bad turn and could retrace to find the right direction. Ainii's heart gave a little jump. He still didn't understand that life was not a highway with side roads, but a ribbon that looped back on itself, eventually taking you to the beginning.

"I'm leaving today. Back to Dallas." He looked at her, his features drawn tight.

"Why?"

"I've been taken off the cases."

Ainii sat up to look him in the eye. The jacket slipped to her lap. "What about the murders? How can you just quit?"

"I didn't quit, Ainii. I was asked to hand everything over to Agent Nez," he said quietly.

She saw Jackson's eyes drift to her chest. She could *feel* his gaze on her, but the tingling heat he evoked in her succumbed to a chill racing over her skin. "I thought—" But Ainii couldn't finish the sentence, because now, as daylight claimed the canyon, her emotions scrambled for cover.

Jackson's gaze softened. "Don't look so worried." He ran his hand up and down her arm. "I would have been finished, anyway."

Ainii's mind raced, trying to pull the pieces of her thoughts together. She stared at him, at his deep eyes now veiled from her, and Ainii realized that his decision to leave had been made long ago.

"What . . . ?" The question stalled. She knew she meant to ask what had made him come here to begin with, but the words stuck in her heart.

"What happened was that Albert Johnny tried to sell a ceremonial mask in Gallup." Jackson's hand slid to Ainii's shoulder and rested. "You should have told me about Irene, Ainii."

"I . . ." Ainii shook her head to settle her thoughts. "I made a promise. I couldn't tell you. You don't believe Albert—"

"No, we don't believe he killed anybody. Though Clah deserved it." Jackson's voice drifted off, along with his gaze. "You were right about Clah," he said, his voice a final, cold judgment.

"I know I was right about Clah, Jackson. I don't understand how this ends everything."

"I'm betting the M.E. will find pieces of him under Wynema Begay's fingernails. And we know the mask Albert Johnny stole from Clah came from Newcomb. We'll never be able to prove Clah killed Newcomb, but it doesn't matter. Clah got what he deserved."

"Nobody deserves to die like he did."

Jackson's gaze riveted on Ainii. "You're right. No one deserves that death."

Ainii lost a breath at the look in his eyes. His eyes erupted with pain, searing her with the force. His face twisted from inner agony. Unbidden, her hand reached to his face. She felt the clench of his jaw, the turmoil pounding at his temples.

He grabbed her wrist, his fingers encircling, his grip so hard Ainii's pulse leaped. Without a word, he drew her hand from his face, then stood. He stepped into his jeans and walked away.

It took minutes for Ainii to find her voice. She stood, letting all the clothes drop to the ground. "If you feel so strongly about it, Jackson . . . why . . . How can you walk away?"

He turned on her, glaring. He stared at her for a second; the glare died, leaving only a furrowed, questioning brow. He shook his head, as if to right his thoughts, and ran a hand through his hair. He walked a few paces, then turned, his features composed. He held his distance.

"I know so little about you," he said. The quiet sadness in his voice quickened Ainii's heart.

"But you know enough."

The certainty in her voice circled Jackson's heart and squeezed. She was right. He knew he loved her and that *should* be enough. But when he asked himself why—what did he love about her—the answers ran against everything he knew about himself. Even the way she looked, standing there, all golden brown, her black hair falling free—as if she had sprung from the land, shaped by its prevailing beauty and endless endurance. Her full, deep eyes were forever patient and nonjudgmental and full of belief.

His eyes were a window to violence. And all his beliefs sprang from that violence—from one night of terror of his short life as a Navajo on the reservation.

He had lain awake all night, trying to remember something else of his life as that small boy, Julian Teller. But there was nothing—none of the small things that built, gradually, integrating themselves into a life. All he had was the nightmare.

If that one night had made him what he was, so be it— at least now he understood. It didn't change who he was: Jackson Walker, FBI agent, profiler of serial killers. Navajo was no more a part of his psyche than being impatient or callous was part of Ainii's.

In the end, all he knew was that he would leave because he couldn't stay. He didn't belong here.

"Yes, I know enough," he finally said. He tried to plaster a matter-of-fact look on his face. "It's not complicated, is it, Ainii?"

He looked down the canyon, away from her, as if already on his way. Ainii managed to ask, "What's not complicated, Jackson?"

"Who we are. What we are. We don't have to look so very far for the answer. It's all very straightforward, really."

He walked to her, put his hands on her shoulders. He looked as if he might apologize for something, then he drew her close, slowly, tentatively, awaiting her resistance. Ainii could never resist him. She sank against him, wanting to feel, one more time, the beat of his powerful heart.

"Consider yourself, Ainii," he said, his breath tangling in her hair. "You came here, alone, determined to do what you'd been told you couldn't. You left the past behind you and you made your own path."

A terrible shudder ran through Ainii. He spoke so calmly, so logically of something that came straight from her heart.

"Despite tradition," he continued. "Despite what your father told you, in spite of your own doubts, you went ahead. And you'll go through it all over again tonight because you believe in the shapeshifter."

Ainii finally understood. He could not bring himself to believe the unbelievable. Which meant he also had no faith in her. He loved her, but at his heart that love was only passion. Ainii placed a hand on his chest and pressed; inside, she felt the retreat of her own heart. "Yes. But you don't believe, do you, Jackson?"

She stood there naked, forthright, unashamed . . . and fearless. Jackson wanted to pull her to him, hold her close, protect her, cherish her as she deserved. What he wanted was a piece of her inside him, giving him the strength he lacked, the courage he needed. He only had to say yes, tell her he believed in men who could turn into wolves, and he could have what he wanted, what he needed . . . Ainii.

They were only words, words with meanings he could rationalize; he certainly knew hundreds of criminals who qualified as beasts.

Ainii didn't want his words. She wanted his thoughts. The thoughts that drove him and gave meaning to him. But the thoughts she wanted were part of *her* history, *her* culture, nourished by countless ancient stories she heard at her father's knee—stories Jackson had never heard, the whole history from which he'd been excluded.

The truth was that he was not man enough for her or for this place.

His heart ached with the promise of a lifetime. He knew he would forever remember this moment, when he had let go of her. He summoned all his courage to seal his fate. "No, Ainii. I don't believe in shapeshifters, or in magic wolves. I also don't believe in ghosts, goblins, witches, or warlocks." He heard his flippant, sarcastic tone, but couldn't stop himself. "I'm democratic about my beliefs—multicultural, you might say. I—"

"Stop it, Jackson." Her eyes glistened, but the tears never fell and the struggle he saw within her to control her emotions dealt Jackson the lethal blow.

Jackson started to reach for her, but stopped himself. He didn't deserve to feel any better about this.

Instead, it was Ainii who tried to make it easy for him by taking a step back. "I have a lot of work to do. You should go."

Jackson hesitated. His mind raced for the words to make everything all right. But those words didn't exist. The words never *had* existed. Ainii's father had been right. Jackson didn't belong here.

He let his gaze take her in, from head to toe, then turned to leave. That the daughter of the man who sent Jackson away was now telling him to leave wasn't lost on Jackson. He had forced history to repeat itself.

Jackson walked out of the canyon, his senses assaulted with smells and colors. The canyon seemed deeper, the cliffs higher than he remembered. He hadn't noticed before the long streaks of brown on the pink canyon walls—as if God's hand had slipped with the paint, letting it drip from the brown desert on the mesa top. He strode through a small thicket of cedar and could practically taste its pungent smell at the back of his throat.

As he drove the Jeep across the foothills, he looked down at the awesome sprawling vista. He had never seen so many shades of green—the colors more vibrant for the marked difference with the rest of the sandy brown landscape. Clumps of green pushed through the porous skin of the land; from pale to deep green, yellow green to true forest green, it covered the distant mountains, trailed down the foothills, and lined the deep-cut arroyos—like green arteries pumping life from the heart to all the extremities of Navajoland—an endless drama.

A land of harsh contrasts, yes. And possibilities.

He drank it all in, letting the scenery fill him, until he

found himself parked at the motel with no memory of actually driving the Jeep there, as if he had been a passenger along for the ride.

He cut off the Jeep, slammed the door, and walked to the motel, his stride on one purpose: to pack up and leave this place before his thoughts were as paralyzed with enchantment as his heart.

He walked the desert barefoot. He thought of the long distances he could cover if he weren't a man and the hot sand and unforgiving rocks wouldn't affect him.

Spikes of pain drove through his feet, up his legs, and pounded in his brain. But he welcomed the misery, just as an insomniac would welcome a nightmare in place of sleeplessness—for him, this agony was an escape from *his* nightmare.

He focused on finding her. He had felt the imbalance, the result of someone provoking the Holy Ones, gathering their wrath to one place. There was only one person who would dare call forth all the evil powers. And it could be for only one purpose: his destruction.

Even as his mind grappled to comprehend how she had commanded the powers, he accepted this moment as inevitable. He had always known this day would come.

In his bleakest moments, he had hoped for it sooner than now—even by his own hand. But, as a man, he was too cowardly—and the beast was never bothered with human frailties . . . like a conscience.

But now the beast in him was afraid. It gnawed at him from the inside, eating out of the hole in his mind where he buried the monster. It sensed, with acute animal instinct, a threat to its survival. In this, the beast was wise.

If only his message with the dead sheep had been understood or taken seriously. He had chosen the sheep carefully and made the obvious marks.

At the thought, his human mind and body rebelled at the memory of the act. His stomach lurched with nausea and he forced his parched throat to begin the hum, his

song, the one he'd been given so long ago for protection
He had sung into the morning, night after night, his heart
pleading with the stars to change his fate. The song had
failed to protect him, and he had learned nothing could
save him from himself. But the song always calmed him.

And when he was calm—at dusk—in the presence of
both day and night, he could consider his life and find
some peace. Because he was a part of the balance. He
kept the balance between good and evil. His own human
capacity to care was the only barrier to the beast's ultimate power.

The beast inside snapped his unmerciful jaws.

He had kept his sanity, finding his purpose within the
eyes of the victims whose own atrocities demanded re-
tribution. And he had survived with an inner struggle no
man would ever know: a creature both man and beast,
both good and evil, justice meted out without mercy.

He had become what was in all men's hearts.

It made him weep . . . in fear for his own redemption.

Could he be forgiven? Could he even be understood?

Who, in the end, would care about him?

*The beast in him growled, angry at the weakness. It
clawed at the barrier, tearing at the fabric of his own
humanity.*

He realized with horror that, this time, he might not
have the strength to control the beast. Just as he had no
strength to resist the inexorable pull to the one who called.
And, in the face of the person who called him, he might
not have the will to care anymore.

If so, he knew what he would have to do.

*The beast snarled and snapped his teeth, impatient for
his next victim.*

Nineteen

~~

Ainii sat in the center of the trampled drypainting, in the midst of the hundreds of impressions her own feet had made last night. In her lap, she held her father's box, all the tools that he had made—and blessed—to lure *Yenaldlooshi*: the bladder of the blue lizard; the witch bag, filled with the powdered remains of things that crawled; and the corpse poison, the most dangerous of all the contents, and the most irresistible to witches and were-animals.

The box also contained the protections for the singer during battle with *Yenaldlooshi*: charcoal from a lightning-struck tree; rock shavings from Echo Cave for the talking rock medicine; white sage and eagle feathers; the gall medicine used as antidote to the corpse poison; and finally, her father's ceremonial necklace of turquoise and coral—a union of the healing blue stone and the blood-red of a mortal wound. She slid the necklace over her head to rest on the bare skin between her breasts. Ainii removed the protections from the box and set them in a pile.

Last night, she had used bits of almost everything, praying to her father to release his power over the sacred objects. One item, however, she had left alone. Ainii lifted the unscarred deerskin sack. Inside were locks of black hair.

Almost certainly, this was the hair from a witch—probably collected by her father to reverse a curse. But was it from a were-animal witch? To use something so personal, yet so unknown, was tempting horrible dangers. She could unwittingly call forth the power of another witch.

Ainii set the box and the sack beside her. She dug in the sand beneath her, feeling for her own deerskin bag— the one she had buried with the fur from *Yenaldlooshi*. Her fingers closed on the soft leather and she set it alongside her father's bag.

She stared at them both, hesitating to take the next step. A chasm opened in Ainii. Hot breath of fear rose from the dizzying depths, carrying her own doubtful voice. *I can't do this.* Ainii teetered, balancing on the edge of the black emptiness. Pure stubbornness, a ramrod of steel up her back, kept her from bending, falling in, giving up. Her fingers trembling slightly, she loosened the leather drawstrings on each of the bags.

She turned over her father's bag and let the strands of hair drift into her hand. Black tendrils snaked between her fingers and across her outstretched palm.

Instantly, her palm itched, but not with the repulsiveness she had expected. Instead, each nerve in her sensitive hand seemed to twitch with a life of its own. Energy pulsed through each tiny vein, bringing a sense of new life. Whoever's head this hair came from had commanded—maybe still commanded—great power for the hair to cause such a reaction.

Her nervousness calmed, as if strong hands held her steady, infusing her with strength and purpose—the same feeling of empowerment she'd had when wrapped in Jackson's arms.

She closed her eyes and let the memory surround her. Her thoughts conjured his face. The planes and angles made him appear hard, aloof—until you looked into his eyes. Then all hope of distance from him was lost, because his eyes promised a place of uncompromised truth. There was safety in those eyes . . . and bravery.

He went beyond what the rest of the world could see every time he placed his hands on victims' blood, every time he let the remnants of their life tell him about their death. He could let his mind walk through their thoughts, *see* past the obvious and be guided to an answer ... yet he couldn't believe in *Yenaldlooshi*.

He could see only so far.

The irony was that, between the two of them—her and Jackson—Jackson possessed the most innate ability.

Maybe if she had not simply left him after the sweat lodge, maybe if she had not let *him* walk away this time ... maybe if she had pushed him harder ... But you didn't push a man like Jackson Walker. He stood fast to his beliefs at any cost.

That was one of the things she loved about him. Her heart smiled with bittersweet pride.

A twitch at her hand reminded her she had a job to do ... without Jackson.

Slowly, she turned over her own bag. The fur dropped into her palm on top of the hair.

Instant terror seized her—not fear of a *thing*, not the terror of facing a monster. But the heart-stopping dread of facing something *inside* herself. Her heart slammed against her chest. A scream stuck in her throat, cut off from any air. Slowly, she closed her fingers into a fist around the hair and fur, fighting the instant urge to swipe them away. She stared inside at her fear, chasing it through her and out.

As her hand tightened, she started her song, letting the hum grow from her belly and up her throat. *She* now claimed this power.

Ainii rose and whistled for Shoogii. Her horse came trotting from where she'd sent him, far back in the canyon. A cloth bag she used for gathering plants swung against his side. Ainii placed the box into the herb bag and climbed onto Shoogii's back, never loosening her grip on the hair and fur, though they almost felt alive, squirming with life against her palm. Shoogii snorted when she brushed him with her hand.

"Have courage, Shoogii," she murmured.

He flattened his ears in protest, but kept walking.

Ainii gave a last glance to the remains of the drypainting. In the center sat the protections she had emptied from the box.

She hoped she was doing the right thing. If not, she would find out only when it was too late.

Jackson pulled shut the door to his motel room and heard the final click of the lock. He bent to shoulder his bag and blood rushed to his head, throbbed at his temples. He rose slowly and stood there, weaving slightly, fighting a wave of dizziness. Finally, he gave in and leaned his forehead against the door, the cool metal a relief on his clammy skin.

He'd felt sick for the last half an hour, the symptoms building gradually from a general unease. At first, as his stomach clenched and churned, he had thought it was hunger—he couldn't remember the last time he'd eaten. Then the gut cramps had progressed to rolling waves of chills.

Through it all he'd packed, told himself what he needed was a meal and then some sleep—for about three days. He had convinced himself he would be fine once he got on the plane. Then his skull had erupted in a mind-splitting headache as if someone were yanking out chunks of his scalp.

Jackson eased himself from the door and, after several deep breaths to gain his equilibrium, took a step down the hallway. The muffled ring of a phone stopped him. Yes, it was his phone. But whoever it was, was too late. Jackson strode out of the motel to his Jeep.

He dumped the bags in the back and slid one hip into the seat, one leg stretched to the ground outside. He sat for a while like that, without starting the Jeep, without adding its rumble to the other midafternoon noises: the arrivals of other guests parking, unloading their cars; kids falling out and running to the pool or to the cottonwood-lined arroyo to look at the passing shepherdess and her sheep.

One youngster, with goggles, squirt gun, and towel, stopped on the sidewalk right in front of Jackson and stared with curiosity at the man just sitting there in his Jeep.

Jackson smiled. "Hello."

"Hi," the boy answered and glanced at his parents, who were two rooms over, still unpacking their car. His mom cast a look at Jackson, then smiled at the boy.

"Going to the pool?" Jackson asked.

The boy nodded.

"Do you like frogs?"

The boy's eyes lit and he nodded aggressively.

"Well," Jackson said, "if you go swimming at night, you will see *lots* of frogs. They like the swimming pool."

"Frogs in the pool? Cool!" He ran to his mom. "Mom, there's frogs in the pool!" The mother made a face—an opinion Jackson had agreed with not so long ago.

He nodded at the excited boy. *Yeah, cool.*

Jackson started the Jeep and pressed the gas, drowning out the rest of the boy's exclamations. He drove slowly from the motel, with a last look at the shepherdess—the same old woman from yesterday, and countless other yesterdays. Her crinkled velveteen skirt echoed the deep lines in her leathery face. She would be here tomorrow and the next day, ushering her wards along a path that happened to skirt a modern motel, as if no obstacle could distract her from her responsibility.

He stepped on the gas and left the shepherdess, her flock, and the inimitable frogs.

With each mile, his head burned hotter, the incessant pounding more profound, until it settled behind his eyes with such acute pain he could barely see. He tried to force himself past the pain by relaxing his thoughts and letting them drift down the highway. But familiar landmarks snagged him, jolting him with memories.

He passed the highway leading to Black Mountain. Farther along, he passed the turnoff to Ainii's. He turned east on State Highway 3 and passed the road leading to Sanders Trading. Each one called up memories that unfolded along the highway miles until he reached the next landmark.

When he drove past the place where he had almost hit

the cow, his heart even gave a small jump and he looked quickly toward both sides of the road.

He didn't need a map anymore to navigate these roads.

He could see himself as if from above, bounded by the Chuskas to the northeast, Black Mountain to the west, Sanders Trading to the south. He was a speck heading east—to Window Rock, to Dallas. With nothing to stop him—like the opening at one end of a sandpainting letting out all the evil.

The radio squawked. Jackson ignored it. But the incessant noise threatened to explode his head.

"Walker," he answered.

"Walker, glad I caught you." It was Nez. "Where are you?"

"Between Ganado and Window Rock."

"So you're leaving."

Jackson heard a touch of concern in Nez's voice. "You have my number in Dallas. I'm sure you won't need it," Jackson added, with as much flat distance as he could muster in his tone.

Nez paused. Then, "I'm sure you're right."

Jackson winced at the cool tone he had provoked from Nez.

"One last thing, Walker. Do you know where Ainii Henio is?"

The coldness in Nez's voice didn't mask the still-present concern. Jackson's pulse skipped. "Why?"

"I need to talk to her."

"Is this about Irene Johnny?"

"We haven't found Irene yet. But the agent who went to Ainii's place . . ." Nez hesitated. "I just need to talk to her."

"About what, Nez? What's going on?"

"Look, Walker, it's only a warning. When I find her, we can keep her here for a while until we figure it out."

Jackson parked the Jeep at the side of the road. "What the hell are you talking about? A warning about what?"

For a moment, only cold air answered him. Jackson's skin pricked with anxiety.

"The agent I sent to get Irene found a dead sheep at Ainii's place," Nez said.

"Dead from what?"

"It was slaughtered, Walker. Whorls of skin were sliced from its nose and from the skin at its rump."

An uncontrolled shudder fled over Jackson.

"It was placed at the center of the Great Black Star drypainting. There was no opening," Nez said.

Jackson cut off the rumble of the Jeep. "No opening in the painting?"

"Right. Someone went to a lot of trouble to get a message across to Ainii."

Pain streaked across Jackson's head and straight through the sockets of his eyes. For a second, all he saw were white sparks. Jackson laid his head on the steering wheel. "Spell it out for me, Nez. What's the message when all four sides of the painting are closed?"

"It's a warning to Ainii that someone else has more power—power enough to dare contain all the evil summoned by the painting."

Jackson was already on the highway, heading back the way he'd come.

"I don't understand it, Walker," Nez said. "Times like this, when there are unexplained murders, medicine men are the target. Not weavers."

Jackson's mind leaped to Ainii, alone in the canyon, doing the very ceremony that had drawn suspicion to her father. If anyone heard about it, what would they think of her, this child of the medicine man killed for witchcraft?

"Hold on, Walker."

Jackson could hear Nez talking aside to someone else.

"I'll be damned," Nez hissed into the radio.

"What?"

"Just heard from APD regarding our inquiry on Clah. They found an old complaint filed against him by someone in Canoncito." Nez paused. "There's our connection to Wynema Begay and the girl in Canoncito."

Cold satisfaction spread through Jackson's gut. "That son of a bitch," he muttered.

"There's more, Walker. The district judge in Albuquerque? The M.E. report is practically a carbon copy of Clah's. He was beaten savagely, his body shredded almost beyond recognition."

Suddenly Jackson could barely breathe. "The marks, Nez. Does the report mention the marks on the judge's body?"

Jackson's body tensed and he listened impatiently to the sound of Nez ruffling papers.

"Five marks. Just like Clah," Nez muttered. "Walker, this doesn't make any sense. No wolf, mutant or not, could travel that distance—"

"Henio said he didn't know about any marks." The thought fell spontaneously from Jackson's lips, as quiet and terrible as stepping blindly on a scorpion.

"What are you mumbling about?"

"Henio," Jackson repeated. He thought of the day he had taken Henio to Clah's hogan.

"That was something else I was going to tell you," Nez said.

A sense of foreboding drove the adrenaline through Jackson. "What?"

"No one seems to know where Detective Henio is. He hasn't called in to Albuquerque or here."

"Dammit!" He slammed his hand on the steering wheel. "Get someone over to Sanders Trading and to Margie's."

"If you're worried about Ainii Henio, don't." Nez said with confidence. "We'll find her, Walker. "I'll keep you posted."

"I know where she is," Jackson said.

"Tell me and we'll get her," Nez offered.

"She's in a canyon north of Chinle."

"Then she's probably safe enough that far from home."

"She's performing a ceremony, Nez, to bait the wolf."

Now Nez cussed. "She's doing what?"

"The ceremony her father did, to catch shapeshifters." Jackson cursed under his breath for leaving her there. "Nez, as far as I know, there are only three people who would know this about Ainii."

"Who?"

"Sanders, Margie Torreon . . ." Jackson paused, "and Arland."

"What are you getting at?"

"According to Sanders, Ainii never got any training with her father, but her brother did."

"Detective Henio trained to catch shapeshifters?"

"There's more," Jackson continued. "When I took Detective Henio to Clah's hogan, I asked him if there was a particular number of claw marks on the judge. He never answered."

"So?"

"You don't find it curious that *Detective* Henio, a man trained in details, the son of a medicine man, doesn't make a connection between the number of claw marks and the signature of a supposedly legendary shapeshifter?"

"What are you saying, Walker?"

Jackson heard the edge in Nez's voice—the warning tone to tred carefully when discussing another officer of the law. He ran a hand over his forehead. "Ask yourself this, Nez: Where is Henio now?"

Nez cussed. "Are you accusing Detective Henio, Walker?"

"I'm not drawing any conclusions, Nez, just observations."

"You know what my observation is? You're the one who didn't want to be here and nothing's worked right for you since you came. Now Dallas wants you back and Henio and I get your files."

"What's your point, Nez?"

"Like you said, just some observations."

"You're the one who called it a warning, Nez." Jackson hung up.

His thoughts flew at him with the same blurring speed as the passing landscape. How could he have been so blind? In hindsight, he now saw what he should have detected earlier: Arland's reluctance to be near the site of the last crime; Arland's concern about Ainii's involvement, almost demanding that Jackson get her under control; the disparity in the level of brutality on the victims, with Clah's wounds the most savage . . . the most personal, but Harrison—and, evidently, the judge—not far behind.

It was all just a string of coincidences, he told himself.

Except he didn't believe in coincidences. He didn't believe in randomness, or unexplained phenomenon. Everything had a reason, a cause and effect, a connection.

Jackson tried to build a case against him. Henio was the investigating detective of two unsolved murders in New Mexico—murders that carried the same signature of shredded victims. As the son of a medicine man, Henio would have recognized the claw marks as similar to what a supposed shapeshifter would inflict. Yet he had kept this important information to himself. Henio also had a reason for vengeance against Clah, but Jackson had no reason to think Henio was anywhere in Arizona when Clah died, let alone when Newcomb and Wynema were killed. The only murder that had happened since Henio came on the cases in Arizona was Harrison's.

Jackson thought back to when he'd first heard Harrison's name. He was at the Bureau and Nez had complained that Harrison escaped a double murder because of shoddy police work. Henio was there, too, and he hadn't given any sign of recognizing Harrison. His only comment had been that Harrison shouldn't get away with murder. Jackson had agreed.

Jackson remembered looking in Henio's eyes and seeing the volatile mix of frustrated anger. Every law enforcement officer knew the feeling behind that look—the overwhelming level of exasperation every time a sicko slimed out of their fingers. It was the look one step away from doing something about it.

Jackson's thoughts stopped cold. What if Henio *had* done something about it? Jackson's mind leaped to the judge, a real sleaze, according to Nez, with a long, questionable history of dismissing cases.

Two victims—Harrison and the judge—who, one might argue, deserved to die. One could argue the same about Clah. And that one person who could make the argument for all three murders was Arland.

Was the detective a one-man vigilante, targeting people who had escaped justice? Had he used the myth of the magic wolf to cover his crime?

Jackson's heart pumped on the scent of blood.

Henio could have set up the perfect ruse: a detective whose investigations led him to the most heinous criminals, medicine man training that gave him secret ritual knowledge to confuse any investigation, and the final coup de gras: Henio *himself* was the investigator.

The truth drummed through Jackson: there was no rampant wolf on the reservation, killing randomly. Instead, there was a calculated, trained killer, personally selecting his victims according to his own code of justice.

A cop with a vendetta—the nightmare of any agency.

But then why, asked Jackson's voice of reason, would Henio threaten or warn Ainii, his own sister? Whatever she was doing was of no consequence to him. There was no ceremony she could perform, no spell she could conjure that would bait him, let alone trap him.

It didn't make any sense.

A sharp pain at the nape of Jackson's neck shot with laser accuracy straight through his skull to the back of his eyes. Jackson swerved onto the shoulder of the highway and back again. He pressed a hand hard against his temple, desperately trying to ease the agony.

He drove that way—one hand on the steering wheel, one at his head, kneading his scalp. With each passing mile, his head pounded more violently, as if some demonic hand were tightening a vice. The pain flowed like acid through his veins, eating through him, dripping into his gut. Twice he pulled over to the side to throw the door open and wretch.

By the time he got across the desert to the canyon, he could barely see past the searing pain. He caught every sagebrush, boulder, and dead limb in his erratic path up the canyon—to where he had left Ainii just this morning. Except she wasn't there.

Jackson let the Jeep die at the edge of the open, empty area. All that remained as proof she had been here were some objects neatly piled at the center of the ruined dry-painting. He stared, as if she would materialize before his wavering vision.

He could picture her standing there—naked, fearless—her eyes challenging him to believe, her words telling him to go. Sanders was right: She was too much for him, more woman than he could ever comprehend . . . more woman than he would ever have again.

The truth circled his heart and squeezed.

Silence flowed over him. No life stirred in the unnatural, deadly quiet. The only movement was a mellow wind, lightly ruffling through his hair. The breeze cooled the sweat on his skin. His breathing slowed.

He listened intently for any noise drifting to him, but only empty air brushed softly against his cheek.

The wind reached around him with calm, relaxing arms that eased the clenching pain in his gut. Jackson settled back in the seat and closed his eyes. His thoughts—weightless, empty—carried him off on a cloud.

He drifted within an infinite landscape of billowy white, his mind floating free beyond him. A murmur, like a distant hum, parted the angel-hair mist. It didn't seem unusual to Jackson to hear the low, reassuring tone.

The hum went into his ear, spiraled through him. The murmur had words, but he couldn't understand them, as if he were hearing another language. He would just listen.

The sound was not as patient. The hum increased to a moan resonating against his ribs. Its pitch went higher, grew more urgent and demanding, chilling his insides with each breath, as it blew, in and out.

It was as if the wind were alive and now breathed through him.

Baa naha zhdool nih. It was his Navajo name! He heard the words as clearly as if someone had whispered in his ear.

He who will tell the story. How had he known the meaning?

Jackson's eyes flew open, expecting to see ... who? Ainii? He was alone, but he couldn't shake the sensation of a presence. He could almost feel the shimmering weight of something leaning close. Yet only the wind pressed against him.

Stare at your fear.

Jackson shook his head to restore his own thoughts, his own mind.

Baa n'diildeeh! Do it!

The translation came simultaneously as if with intuitive understanding. How could he understand Navajo? It had to be this headache, his mind playing tricks.

Yet the words still pounded through him like a father's command. *Do it! Stare at your fear,* the voice demanded urgently.

Jackson stumbled from the Jeep and staggered toward the drypainting, as if he could walk away from the insanity of hearing voices. Wave upon wave of adrenaline surged through him, prickling his skin, catching his breath in a lump at his throat. It was the instinct of fight or flight.

He whirled around, his reflexes ready for a battle. But there was no one there.

Baa naha zhdool nih. Baa naha zhdool nih. His Navajo name—a name no one would know—a name *he* had only just learned—resounded off the canyon walls, as if every rock now joined in the chant.

He was going crazy. Right here, in this godforsaken canyon in the middle of nowhere, he was losing his mind.

He looked down and found himself standing over the

pile of things Ainii had left behind. On top was a sprig of sagebrush unlike any he had ever seen: pure white, without a trace of green. He squatted, picked up the sage, and twirled it between his first two fingers.

The motion released a sweet, pungent scent. It filled his head with a smell he knew. Before the memory could take hold, an enormous pressure built at the base of Jackson's throat, pushing up his windpipe, tickling his neck with the sensation of hundreds of bubbles of gas. He opened his mouth to release the air and words tumbled out on the bubbles—Navajo words that his brain instantly translated.

Hear me White Shell Woman! Awake from your sleep at Mount Hesperus! Let loose the darkness, the black colors, and the ghosts from the safety of the underworld!

This is my mother, White Sage. She knows me in four ways and she comes to me from the four directions: the white east, the turquoise south, the yellow west, and the black north. She will guide me. She will protect me. She brings the power to protect. I bring the power of the harsh male thunderclouds to battle.

Tell this to Yenaldlooshi!

The rush of words died on a gasp of air. Jackson collapsed to the sand, clutching the sage. His last conscious thought was of the sage—its scent surrounding him, lifting him, and carrying him.

The beast covered the last miles in a lope. He could taste the promise of vulnerable prey just ahead, alone, unaware of its mortality. He ran with labored breath, as if lugging something. Each step was harder and many times he stopped, brought to a halt by a sudden clenching in his legs. But he could not be stopped for long. He could not be deterred from the prize awaiting just ahead. Small animals fled from his path. He noticed, but had little interest. He kept his sights set on the nearing mountains and licked back the saliva pooling at his mouth.

Twenty

Ainii smeared the last of the blue down her leg. Her pores itched beneath the quickly drying wet paint. But it was a welcome distraction from the constant prickling sensation within her palm—an ever-present reminder of what she still gripped in her hand.

She set herself to the next task: applying the bait. At Ainii's whistle, Shoogii ambled over and Ainii unhooked the herb bag holding her father's box. Shoogii snorted, obviously eager to be rid of the box containing witch objects.

"Go now," Ainii said, though Shoogii hardly needed any encouragement to trot well away.

Ainii sat in the warm sand facing the sweat lodge and the three drypaintings she had already completed. She had made them small, only about two feet square, with pictures of black power concentrated in the small areas. One depicted the Black Star, with the added imbalance of a comet. The second crawled with Blue Lizards. The third drypainting held the jagged lines of lightning. None had an opening.

From the box, Ainii pulled out the witch bag. Her fingers stilled at the drawstring. With a deep breath, Ainii loosened the bag containing the powder of things that crawled. A rush of anxiety fled down her spine. She could *feel* the power of the black dust.

With forced care—for her hands urged her to dump the

whole bag quickly—she sprinkled the powder over the
black lines of lightning, and gave a silent prayer. She
prayed to the hard winds and the harsh rain—to the power
of the male thunderstorm. She drew on the strength of
those things male, let them fill her, join with her, just as
Father Sky and Mother Earth mated in the falling rain.

The wind's breath circled through her, whispering a
chant as old as the sound of creation. As the small grains
accumulated, she swore she felt a quiver in the ground
beneath her, a tremble within Mother Earth—not unlike
the shudder Ainii felt at Jackson's touch.

In that instant, she was caught in his embrace, wrapped
in his arms of steel, held fast by passion in his dark eyes.
For a moment, she forgot where she was, what she was
doing, enveloped in the strength of Jackson's touch.

He's not here, because you sent him away, her mind
scolded.

Ainii sank to her knees, laid a gentle hand on the sand
beside her, and whispered a comforting prayer to Mother
Earth. *I will do this,* she said.

Then she stood and faced the lodge, a wooden match
and flint she had taken from the box now resting in her
hand. She would set fire to the lair of *Yenaldlooshi,* draw
him to the flames, to her. She struck the match and approached the dry tinder, but what she saw in her mind
was Jackson, laying beside her, his hands holding her, his
body moving in rhythm with hers.

She lost a breath at the image, the perfect unison. The
flame of the match died in her trembling fingers.

Ainii shook the image from her mind, though she
couldn't lose the feelings flooding her body: a wave of
achingly wonderful passion her body couldn't contain, her
mind couldn't comprehend. It was beyond her, more than
her—the sense of being greater than herself. He was her
other half.

Margie's words came to her: *You cannot do this alone.
You need your other half.*

The words trembled through Ainii. She forced her

thoughts away from Jackson, away from their lovemaking and from the power she felt in his arms and saw in his eyes.

With shaking hands, she struck another match to the den of *Yenaldlooshi,* the place of evil.

The fur squirmed within her hand as if pushing to get out. Ainii smiled. It was good that *Yenaldlooshi* should feel threatened.

She held the match to the dead branches. The fire encircled the wood, embraced it, climbed the limbs. Hot pain circled Ainii's fist.

The flames crawled up the sticks, turning the wood black. The fire climbed the lodge; blue tendrils snaked within and without, consuming in a hungry rage. Live embers landed at Ainii's feet. The flames prevailed, reaching skyward from the top of the lodge as if searching for more.

Intense heat seared Ainii's body, as if she were licked by the fiery tongues. Agony fled up Ainii's arm—her flesh was the branches, her tendons and muscles the meat of the wood. Sticks snapped and cracked in defeat.

Ainii's knees buckled. She fell to the ground, her bones useless.

The lodge gasped and moaned. The air squeezed from Ainii's lungs. The dying wood gave a last hiss, and overwhelming sorrow consumed Ainii, squeezing her heart. A sob lodged at her throat. As she watched the lodge collapse on itself, Ainii stared, paralyzed by loss—a loss she had caused, as if she were a murderer.

She suddenly had the sense of teetering on a revelation—of standing on an edge, desperate to keep her balance. The sensation triggered the memory of her first Night Way—a night of deliberate disorder and contradictions, when she had learned the first lesson of balance.

A dozen *Yei bi chais,* led by Talking God—his crown of feathers surrounding a ghostly white face—had descended on the ceremony. She had watched the dancing gods in fearful awe. Slowly, insidiously, the drumbeat, the rattles, the rhythmic chant had claimed the pulse of her own heart, and she was one with the supernatural beings. At the very moment she understood their great powers, they removed their masks. The *Yeis*, the powerful gods, were human!

Hasttse baad, the female *Yei*, then slipped her mask on Ainii's face and Ainii had viewed the world through the eyes of the god. And she had learned the basic truth of two parts to every whole: that everything, even gods, have two sides.

Confusion swept through her. There weren't two sides to *Yenaldlooshi*. He sprang from the First World, the black underworld—a place before emergence, *before* harmony. A place of disruption and utter chaos.

Ainii stared at her hand. It was the fur causing the turbulence. *Yenaldlooshi* was throwing everything at her, trying to confuse her, stop her. She knew it in the same way she would know by touch the color of a ball of her yarn in the darkness. The knowledge was in her fingertips.

So much power concentrated within this small ball of fur—she shuddered to think of the confrontation ahead with the whole beast. Determined, she squeezed her fist tighter and reached her other hand for the final item. Her fingers hovered over the deerskin bag decorated with an owl's feather. Inside was the corpse poison, the ground remains of witch victims. Waves of tremors washed over her from her scalp to her toes. She dropped the bag. Fear consumed her, rushing on her blood to every part of her, rippling her skin.

Stare at your fear, shi yaazhi.

But even her father's voice, strong in her head, couldn't stop her quaking.

Ainii closed her eyes, slowed her breathing, commanded her heart to still. Still trembling, she reached for the bag, her eyes closed, her right hand guided by her heart. Her left hand, numb from clenching the fur and hair, lay as useless in her lap as a lead ball.

She opened the bag and dipped her hand inside. Her

fingers touched the dust. It was cold and dry as air from a black hole. The cold chilled her fingers, then her hand, and crept up her arm with the deadly stealth of a ghost. Her insides screamed against the consuming evil.

Ainii steeled herself, dug her fingers into the bag, and grabbed a handful of the witchly powder. With the last remnant of her courage, she held the dust over her head and let the corpse poison fall in a stream over her head.

Terror snapped at her ears. She heard the gnashing of fierce teeth, the growl of an evil so immense she felt no bigger than a speck of worthless sand. And Ainii saw, in her mind's eye, the evil worth fearing: a wolf bigger than a man; his enormous head framed in spiky black fur. In the image, he moved straight for her, his great paws eating up the ground, his eyes focused . . . on her.

A sound fell from Ainii's lips—not a scream; more like a helpless cry. A nudge at her arm brought the scream from her throat full force. Ainii's eyes flew open, her hands raised in defense. A soft muzzle pushed past her arms. Shoogii snorted, the air through his nose brushing Ainii's cheek.

"Ah, Shoogii. *Doo anisht ehi da.* I'm okay. Don't worry."

But Shoogii only pressed harder against Ainii, until she had to scoot back along the ground.

"*Shoo hei! Do tah!* " Ainii pushed back against the horse's massive body, but Shoogii wouldn't budge. He placed his front hooves on each side of her, effectively blocking Ainii from rolling away.

Ainii slid herself out from under him and stood. "*No woh di naa nina!* " Ainii pointed down the canyon, but Shoogii ignored her command. He lowered his head to her chest and pushed. Ainii staggered back. Shoogii followed and pushed again.

"Shoogii! Stop!" Her words were useless.

Shoogii forced Ainii to retreat several feet down the canyon. Ainii gave up talking sense to her horse. She sidestepped him and headed back to the site.

Shoogii let loose with a long, high-pitched neigh. It raised the fine hairs at the base of Ainii's scalp. She turned and faced her frustrated companion.

"*T'aa doo bina nilzidii,* Shoogii," she said in a soothing, reassuring voice. "Do not be afraid. Go now, my friend."

Shoogii stood his ground and Ainii realized he could be a problem. She couldn't let him stay and interrupt the ceremony. He might even try to defend her from *Yenaldlooshi.* Ainii couldn't bear to see him injured. She stared at her determined guardian.

Her eyes locked with his and she slowly raised the hand holding the fur and hair. "*No woh di naa nina!* Go!" She punched the air with her fist and glared at Shoogii—a look he had never received from her.

Shoogii backed up a few paces, gave her a last look, then turned and headed to the mouth of the canyon. Ainii watched until the night closed around his white rump and he disappeared from sight.

Now she was truly alone.

She lifted the bag of corpse poison and, before she could reconsider, she loosened her grip on the fur and hair and poured what remained of the powder into her palm.

Before her eyes, the fur doubled in size, and what had been long tendrils of black hair mutated to short, bristly hairs. She quickly closed her fist, her fingers barely able to contain the increased mass of both the fur and hair. They pushed between her fingers and climbed over her hand. Ainii stared with alarm, her mind on one thought: This was a mistake.

A throbbing headache forced Jackson's eyes open to a black, grainy world. *What the hell had happened?*

He tried to remember, forcing his thoughts to focus, but they slammed against an invisible wall. A blinding pain shot from his eyes to the base of his neck. He braced a hand to his side and felt the ground. With effort, he pushed himself up and found himself sprawled on the canyon floor.

Where was he? *Who was he?* Frantically, he searched his mind for an answer.

He scanned his surroundings and saw a Jeep. He remembered driving here, looking for . . . Ainii.

His mind settled on her. He saw her eyes—the deep, reassuring pools of brown—and he relaxed. His name came to him as if on a whisper. *Baa naha zhdool nih.*

No! That wasn't it! He focused again on the Jeep, gritting his teeth in determination. The image of Ainii dissolved. He felt the wind and he remembered . . . words drifting through him . . . the sage. He looked at his hand to see he still gripped the plant. He let it fall to the sand.

Screams of a hawk echoed off the canyon walls and added to the pounding in his head. The shrieks grew louder, more insistent.

He reached for the sage, ignoring logic—just a desperate gesture by his body for some relief.

The shrill cries ceased.

He sat there, questioning his own sanity, but unwilling to test it by releasing the sage.

To hell with the reason, he thought viciously.

He staggered to his feet, fighting a wave of dizziness and nausea. *What was he doing here?*

To find Ainii. She was in danger and he had come to warn her. . . .

But you don't believe, do you, Jackson?

It was Ainii's voice. His name was Jackson. Jackson Walker. But the relief he should feel was drowned in an overwhelming sense of futility—as if he were damned to hell regardless of who he was or what he did.

He thought of Ainii, of her eyes, her lips. He felt her mouth on his, the passion . . . her love. He held fast to that memory and his desperation abated.

He stared beyond the canyon, to the distant band of light blue on the horizon. Soon it would be night. Ainii was out here somewhere and his chance to find her was sinking with the setting sun.

He climbed into the Jeep and brought it to life. At the mouth of the canyon, he turned right to take the Jeep over the foothills. The headlights caught the sudden movement of something white and very large. He aimed the Jeep toward it. A horse emerged from a crop of sagebrush. It was Shoogii . . . riderless. No Ainii.

Shoogii faced the Jeep. The horse was obviously disturbed—his ears flat back, his eyes wide. And the look in those eyes sent a frisson of anxiety through Jackson.

Jackson cut the lights so Shoogii could see him.

''It's okay, Shoogii,'' he said as he stepped from the Jeep and held his hand to the horse. ''What are you doing out here alone?''

He stroked the horse's neck and let his hand trail over the bridle and reins, checking for soundness. He moved slowly to the side, his hand gliding over Shoogii to his back. He couldn't find anything remiss—nothing to hint at a fall, for instance.

So where was she?

Jackson looked back over his shoulder to the canyon and saw the faint trail of smoke. It rose high up over the top of the canyon, as if wafting from a great bonfire. He knew he had found her.

Jackson walked to the Jeep. A hard push at his back sent him stumbling past the door. He turned to find Shoogii just inches away, lowering his head for another shove.

''It's okay, Shoogii.''

He tried to ease between Shoogii and the Jeep to turn it off, but Shoogii wouldn't move. In fact, the horse advanced on him, forcing Jackson to step backward. For a second, he swore he saw fear in the horse's eyes. An icy breath of foreboding raced over Jackson's skin.

''Don't worry, Shoogii, I'm not leaving without her.''

He left the Jeep, its engine still running, and turned to the canyon. With a glance over his shoulder, Jackson saw Shoogii standing his ground, watching. Jackson walked on, alone, the searing pain in his head overshadowed by a haunting sense of dread. With some irrational relief, he realized he still gripped the white sage in his hand.

Jackson entered the canyon and saw in the distance the glow of a huge fire. As he neared, he recognized the location as where the sweat lodge had once stood.

A sudden rush of adrenaline raced over his skin, prickling his hairs, taking his breath. He had the acute sense of facing a horrible battle, a battle he couldn't possibly win.

The thought terrified him. Just as swiftly, he quashed the feeling. He was accustomed to facing the unknown, to staring down fear, to pursuing his prey.

A lonely melody drifted over him. Ainii's voice, pure and wonderful, filled his head, flowed on his blood to every part of him.

He stared at the fire—his goal—and he drew on his last resource: the power he held in his mind to go beyond the worst memories, to reach past any terror.

He walked to the fire, to Ainii. He didn't see her right away, then movement just beyond the firelight's glow drew his attention. She stood at the edge of the shadows, staring into the darkness.

"Ainii?"

She jerked around to him. "Stay there," she ordered and turned back. Her firm command brought him up short. Then he registered the look in her eyes.

Slowly, Jackson pulled out his gun and stepped outside the globe of firelight. Gnarly branches of cedar stabbed his side. He stifled a grunt and stared ahead to where he'd seen Ainii. But she had walked farther into the night, her darkly painted body camouflaged in the shadows. He wrestled through a clawing bush of sagebrush and found himself in a small clear area.

"Ainii, where are you?"

"No!"

He swiveled to her cry and thought he saw the outline of her slender body. Then he heard her song, her voice

halting as if nervous . . . or afraid. He crouched, moved
closer, staring hard into the darkness just past Ainii. He
thought he saw something black facing her. It was too big
. . . too big.

Jackson wanted to yell to her: *Back up, come to me.*
But he couldn't make a sound. His heart beat at his throat.
He braced the gun. Took aim.

The black form moved, turned his head, and looked
straight at Jackson. Ainji jerked her head around to Jackson.

''Get the hell down, Ainii!''

The wolf leaped at Jackson, clearing Ainii. In the instant that Jackson hesitated, the wolf was on top of him.
The animal's solid weight—like that of two men—
knocked the air out of him. He dropped the gun.

Jackson couldn't maneuver. He couldn't push the wolf
off or to the side. The wolf snapped at his neck, his lethal
fangs just inches away, his hot breath on Jackson's face.

This time, he would die.

Jackson's mind stilled. He saw the child in the corner.
He felt the fear clenching his heart, stealing his breath.
He had known then that the beast would find him because
he was what the beast sought.

He had known it all his life.

He had known it in the recesses of his mind, where
violence dwelt; he had known it in his heart, in the place
where every man hides his evil side. The beast was not
fooled by any veneer of goodness . . . or any feigned bravery.

And now he understood the fear he had lived with. It
wasn't the fear of any unknown, but of himself. He *was*
the beast inside.

The knowledge pounded through him with deadly truth.
The scent of blood settled at the back of Jackson's tongue
with a familiar coppery taste. His heart pumped. The hot
coals of violence, burning in his gut, sprang to life in an
arc of sparks between him and the beast. Rage ripped
through him—ready, willing.

He heard a cry. It was Ainii. Jackson understood the final truth: He would be whatever it took to protect her.

Jackson surrendered himself to his last place of strength: where instincts ruled.

He lunged for the beast, his fingers sinking through thick fur to find the beast's neck. He squeezed, intent on strangling out the last bit of life.

Jackson gagged, fighting for breath. His hands trembled at the wolf's neck as his own life choked from him. His whole body struggled, desperate for air, screaming against the death-hold grip.

A shudder ran through the wolf, beneath Jackson's fingers, through his own hand, and down his back.

Do it, Baa naha zhdool nih. The deep voice came at his ear. Sure that his mind was slipping, Jackson stared in horror at the wolf. Their eyes met. The wolf stared back, his brown eyes wide, as if with fear.

Brown eyes, Jackson realized, not the yellow eyes of a wolf. And in those eyes, he saw something he recognized. He couldn't find the words. He didn't *want* to find the words. But he couldn't tear his gaze away.

In disbelief, Jackson swore he saw a flicker of confusion. A moment where reason collided with madness. A realization lanced through Jackson's mind, slicing through his sanity.

Jackson *knew* those eyes. In the same instant, he saw a glint of acknowledgment in the wolf's eyes. His hands loosened at the wolf's neck.

In that unnatural, still moment, Jackson heard the cylinder rotation of his gun.

"No!" he screamed.

The wolf leaped off him and faced Ainii.

Ainii aimed the gun. She meant to fire. She could stop the terror of *Yenaldlooshi* right here, right now.

The wolf just stood there, staring, as if awaiting the inevitable. His eyes seemed to plead with her. Then he opened his mouth to the sky and screamed, the bone-chilling shriek of a human in agony.

"Ainii, *t'aa doo bina nilzidii. Shika'anilyeed!*" *Do not be afraid. Help me!*

The cry shattered through Ainii in ever-widening circlets of heartbreaking despair. Her eyes locked with the gaze of the wolf. She looked deep into his eyes—brown eyes, eyes full of pain and longing and infinite sorrow . . . the eyes of a human.

"Ainii, *shika'anilyeed.*"

The low, pleading voice rippled through her in ever-widening circlets.

Suddenly Ainii understood. She fell to her knees at the foot of *Yenaldlooshi* . . . her brother.

A sob clenched her heart and fell from her lips. "Why?" she cried.

She stared into Arland's eyes and saw the answer etched in a fathomless soul. Sorrow welled within their dark depths and tears flowed free down Ainii's face.

"*Nika iishyeed,*" she whispered. *I will help you.*

Arland's eyes filled, deep pools of love. Then they flashed with wildness. Ainii's heart jumped. She saw a maelstrom of emotion, a battle within him that she couldn't reach.

Just as suddenly, his eyes grew steely and hard. His lips pulled back and, with a flash of great white teeth, he tore the sacred necklace free from Ainii's neck. With a last look at her, he leapt into the air, over Jackson, and ran to the clearing. Before Ainii could scream out, he hurled himself into the fire.

Ainii ran to him. Arms of steel wrapped around her, held her back from the fire. "No!" she screamed, struggling against Jackson.

"You can't do anything," he said, his low voice caught on each word.

Ainii knew the truth before he had even said it. Before her eyes, the body of the wolf changed to a man. The fire she had built to lure *Yenaldlooshi* now consumed her brother. Waves of mortal grief swept through Ainii, buckled her knees. Only the strength of Jackson's arms kept her from falling unhindered to the ground.

How could she not have realized the truth about her brother? How could she have been so blind, so self-consumed? The reality of his existence racked her body in shivering waves. She felt Jackson's arms lift her legs and settle her in his lap on the ground.

"I'm sorry," he whispered.

Ainii heard the pain in Jackson's voice, but she couldn't concentrate on it. All she could think about was her brother and the horror of his life. How could he have become the very thing they were raised to fear and despise?

"I don't understand." The words fell from her heart. "How could he . . ." She couldn't finish the question. Her mind rebelled against the terrible truth.

"I don't think he had a choice," he said, his tone flat, distant.

Ainii realized his arms were stiff around her. She felt Jackson's jaw clench against her cheek. Anger rose swift in her at his cold judgment.

She pulled away from him, appalled. "What gives you the right—"

The look in his eyes stopped her: a chilling mix of pain and fear—the same dark emotions she had seen in Arland's eyes the moment before he leaped to his death.

"What is it, Jackson?" She laid a hand on his face. His torment erupted through her with more power than she had the will to defeat.

"He had no choice," he said again, grinding the words out.

This time she heard the despair. He wasn't judging Arland, he was mourning with her.

"We always have a choice." The words escaped from her heart.

Jackson stared at her in disbelief. "He wanted none of it! No more than I do."

"What are you talking about?"

Jackson didn't seem to hear her. He stared beyond her, to the fire. "He had more courage than I would ever have. He faced his destiny."

His monotone scared her, as if he were already walking away, into the night. Ainii grabbed his shoulders. "Jackson, you're—"

He trampled her words. "He couldn't change what he was. He couldn't defeat the beast within. But he *could* make a difference." He smiled at her sadly. "I understand why he killed the ones he did."

"What do you mean?"

"The judge in New Mexico, Harrison, Clah . . . and probably more that we don't know about." His gaze held Ainii's. "He forced the beast to kill the ones who had preyed on others all their lives. He focused the evil on the people who deserved it."

Ainii's love for Arland welled from the crack in her heart, pricked her eyes. "He *used* the beast," she murmured.

She thought of the elders, using the masks of the *Yei bi chais* to teach balance, to drive home the lesson of the integral presence of good and evil, the dual nature of all things. Arland—her brother, a man—had lived his life on that razor's edge.

She realized that same edge existed in Jackson. The torment she'd felt in him was the pain he harbored, slicing him in two pieces. The power he was so close to commanding held him hostage with fear. She looked at him, her vision blurry with love. "What are you afraid of, Jackson Walker?"

"Myself."

She framed his face in her hands. "I'm not," she said. Ainii drew him to her and kissed him. All the raging darkness within him rose to her lips. Ainii tasted the myriad of his emotions—a tapestry of colors more rich than she could ever imagine, the solid weave of a man she could fold herself into.

She slid her fingers to his temple, to the place of his

thoughts, and heard what he wouldn't let himself say. The thought circled her own, becoming one.

"I'm not afraid," she said again.

Ainii's words flowed into Jackson, a flood of passion and love so deep, he had a panicked moment of drowning. No one could love him like this. No one could accept all of him!

The logic screamed at him, told him to fight the impulse of surrender, just as he would fight to get air back into his lungs.

He tried to pull away, before she saw all of him—the dark place where the beast in him dwelled. The same beast that had conquered Arland.

God, so little separated him from Arland—a slight twist of fate, the small decision made by a man Jackson had never met, a simple action that had set Jackson's life on a different course. He had come *so close* to being the same as Arland.

Could he have lived with it?

Ainii was right, Arland had used the beast. He had taken his destiny and used it, choosing a path that gave his life meaning. In the end, when the beast had threatened to prevail, Arland had found the strength to make his choice in the power of his love for Ainii.

Jackson stared at the woman who held him fast. She really *wasn't* afraid. The depth of her love claimed him completely and as magically as the whisper of home.

"Your thoughts are powerful, Ainii. Will you say them aloud?"

"My thoughts—"

Jackson smiled at her surprise. "Will you make me ask you four times?"

Ainii lost a breath at the passion in his eyes. "Will you stay with me, Jackson Walker?"

He circled her with his arms and held her so tight Ainii could feel his heart beat against her chest. "I could never leave," he said finally. "I don't know how I thought I ever could."

He bent her down to the ground. His hands tangled within her hair—the hands that held his power . . and his courage.

Ainii slid her hands over his. ''Your thoughts will al ways be safe with me.''

He brushed his lips against hers, up her cheek to her ear, and Ainii heard the jagged edge of his control in his short breaths as he whispered in her ear, ''And tell me Ainii, what am I thinking now?''

Ainii turned her head and saw the love flare in his eyes. ''You are wondering how it is your heart is doing the thinking and not your head.''

Jackson caught her lips with his and Ainii felt his whole body strain with the kiss as if he held the most precious thing in his hands. And she smiled, because that was what she felt about *him*—as if she touched the heart of a leg end.

He was exactly the right one

Epilogue

Ainii paused at the threshold of the trading post and nodded to the women gathered at the woodstove. They stopped their chatter long enough to return her greeting.

Ainii approached the high wood counter, but stopped a few feet away to wait her turn with Bill. She shifted the heavy rug and the stack of papers to her other arm.

Curly Joe stood at the far end, devouring a can of peaches. His chin jutted out with each bite as if to catch all drops. He was so fully occupied with the peaches, Ainii wondered if he even saw her standing there.

"Let me take that, Ainii." Bill was beside her relieving her of the burden.

"*Ahehee*," she thanked Bill in Navajo for the benefit of the tourist looking on in interest from the counter.

"And where is Jackson? He should be carrying this load. You have your own." Bill gave a pointed glance to Ainii's swollen belly.

Ainii rubbed a loving hand over her tummy. "He has his own burden," she said with a wicked smile. "Big Shorty and Gray Whiskers have cornered him outside. Some talk about allowing medicine men to get past the fence surrounding Window Rock."

"Aiee! He'll be there for hours," Bill commented as he finished the sale of postcards to the tourist. "They think he is their personal officer on the Tribal Police."

Ainii chuckled with Bill. "I thought I would give him ten minutes to suffer before rescuing him."

A form filled the doorway, casting a shadow across the wood planks to Ainii's toes. "And what if I don't need to be rescued?"

His deep voice flowed over her with the comfort of a favorite song. Ainii turned and smiled at her husband. "But it gives me so much pleasure," she teased.

He quirked a smile and a flutter erupted through Ainii's middle. "Well, you'll just have to wait for the next opportunity," he said, walking to her. "Which shouldn't be long." He nodded to the stack of fliers she held.

"This *won't* be a disaster, Jackson," she said firmly.

"What won't?" Bill took one of the papers from Ainii. "A storytelling hour at the chapter house," he read aloud and looked up. "This is a great idea."

"Jackson thought of it." Ainii couldn't help the pride in her voice. "He decided there should be a place where all Navajo children could hear the legends."

Next to her, Jackson shifted his feet in embarrassment. Ainii put a comforting arm around his waist. "He could tell many himself, after all the reading he's been doing."

Bill gazed at Jackson. "Yes, I know he could," Bill said quietly.

The moment extended, finally broken by a nearby cough. The three of them turned to see Bitter Water Woman hoist a flour bag of yarn onto the counter. "You will weigh this," she commanded, staring straight ahead.

Jackson chuckled. "Just another busy day at the trading post, right, Bill?" he said amiably. Then his gaze slid to the lean Navajo at the end of the counter.

Curly Joe looked up at Jackson and tilted his head slightly in acknowledgment, then looked back at his can.

"*Daa sha'nit'e?*" Jackson asked him.

Curly Joe grunted. His answer could mean he was doing fine, or to leave him alone, or maybe he just had a mouthful of peaches.

Jackson strolled to him, then stopped the respectful

three feet away and leaned an elbow on the counter. He waited in comfortable silence until Curly Joe was ready to speak.

"Those people bought ten bracelets from me," he said finally.

Jackson smiled at the solemn statement. "Watch out, Curly Joe, they'll make a name for you in Dallas and you'll have more orders than you can fill."

"That is what worries me."

Jackson laughed aloud. "I'm sure it doesn't worry Mouse."

Curly Joe smiled, the unlikely expression such a surprise to his face that the wrinkles extended into his hairline. "Yes," he said almost wistfully, "she is not worried."

Jackson had to restrain himself not to pat the stoic Navajo on his back. He knew Curly Joe probably still waged a battle every day not to gamble.

Curly Joe glanced to Jackson and his eyes said a silent *Thank you* with more meaning than spoken words.

"I'm glad to see you," Jackson said and nodded goodbye. "Just apply the rug to our credit, Bill," Jackson offered as he neared the trader.

"And can we leave these on the counter?" Ainii handed him some fliers.

"Of course," Bill said. "This is a good thing." He smiled at Jackson. The look in his eyes was one Ainii remembered from years before, when she had stood next to her father. She marveled at the sense of old friendship. "It's never too soon for children to learn the stories," he said to Jackson.

Jackson gripped Ainii's hand. "And it's never too late."

Dear Reader,

The Navajo beliefs of witches, curses, and shapeshifters may seem medieval and unsophisticated. In fact, most Navajo will not discuss these beliefs with outsiders—they have heard the derogatory remarks labeling them primitive. But these aspects of the darker side of humanity, the evil part of man, are integral to the Navajo precept of duality: every living thing is comprised of both good and evil, female and male. The Navajo know that life is precarious, a perilous journey from birth to death. Their environment guarantees even more hazards of flash floods, droughts, harsh winters and merciless summers. The Navajo Way, then, is to continually seek to put *yourself* in balance with the world around you. In bad times, medicine men look to the patient for answers—and sometimes that answer lies within the evil machinations of others.

The genesis of LEGEND began with a story told to me by a Christian Navajo. She was leaving a church service and saw a shapeshifter in the parking lot. She described the wolf, his tail hanging straight down, his size as large as a man, but he didn't threaten her and she felt no fear. Her first thought was that the man/wolf had come to remind her of her Navajo roots and traditions. I then wondered if the shapeshifter—the Navajo witch capable of so much terror and evil—might not also have its own unique agenda, a purpose beyond explaining evil. What if he were not evil incarnate, but instead the ultimate struggle for balance?

I would love to hear from my readers. You can write to me at P.O. Box 23203, Albuquerque, New Mexico, 87192 or at my email address of **lbaker10@aol.com**.

Enjoy this latest journey into Navajoland, where anything is possible!

All My Best,
Laura

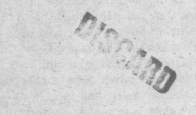